TELL ME NO LIES

NOLON KING

STERLING & STONE

TELL ME NO LIES

Chapter One

Sunday Night ...

NATALIE

THE LAST TIME I'd seen Olivia, our sorority sisters were holding her back as she sobbed and screamed that I was a treacherous whore who'd slept with her soulmate.

Not exactly true. Ryan had made his choice, and he chose me. He married me. In spite of the fact that his friends, his family, and even his graduate advisor suggested that he make up with the much prettier and much better-connected Olivia. He gave up a lifetime of opportunity to be with me instead.

Can you blame me for believing that he was *my* soulmate?

After two kids and a mortgage, our marriage felt less like a fairy tale and more like a cautionary tale. But no way was I admitting that to Olivia.

Ryan didn't know that she'd contacted me yesterday,

asking if we could get together for drinks, like we were old friends who'd lost touch and she could hardly wait to catch up with me. No recriminations, no insinuations, no explanation for why she'd suddenly reached out now.

I said yes, because wouldn't you? Or am I the only one whose curiosity outweighs my common sense?

It had been twelve years, for Christ's sake. And before Ryan, Olivia had dated a different guy every day of the week. I figured it had probably taken a week for her to stop missing him, and eleven years, eleven months, and three weeks to get over the fact that she'd come in second for once in her life.

Maybe she wanted to make sure I knew she'd moved on.

Maybe she wanted to find out how it had all worked out, to reassure herself that she'd gotten off lucky, that she was better off without Ryan.

Maybe she wanted to know if my life was as boring as my Livelyfe profile suggested, or to rub it in my face that she was successful enough to wear designer everything.

Or maybe she wanted to make amends. She'd been a heavy drinker in college, and Daddy's money could buy an awful lot of rehab.

As I watched her slip between tables, I couldn't help think that she belonged here at Drink, a swanky LA bar where I never would fit in, even if I ditched the soccer mom chic, lost my two-pregnancy pudge, and upgraded my Smart Snips haircut.

Olivia looked as perfect as the last time I'd seen her – nipped and tucked in all the right places, from her head to her Louboutin-wrapped toes.

"Natalie." She smiled her pageant smile as she sat down opposite me. "You look exactly like your Livelyfe picture."

You look like a million bucks, or whatever it costs to keep a plastic surgeon on retainer, I didn't say as I smiled back. "I was so surprised to hear from you."

A waitress approached our table, and Olivia ordered without asking me: two vodka sodas, no fruit – our usual, back in the day. I guess since she hadn't changed, she was assuming that I hadn't either.

Once we were alone again, she pulled a manila envelope out of her Prada purse and laid it on the table between us.

This time, it wasn't the pageant smile she flashed. This was her *time for your punishment, Pledge* smile.

Shit.

I ignored the envelope. "How've you been?"

She ignored my attempt to put us back on equal terms. "I thought about sending them to you on LiveLyfe, but that felt too ... impersonal."

Meaning, she wanted to see my face when I got my first glimpse of whatever was in that envelope.

The waitress brought our drinks. I took a sip to delay the inevitable.

"Just rip off the Band-Aid," Olivia said. "Every second you spend not opening it only makes this harder."

"You could just tell me, you know."

"You're right. I could."

But she wouldn't, because she'd always been the alpha female whose periods the rest of us synched up with.

I took another sip of the vodka soda and forced myself to swallow. I was sure I'd felt this nauseous before, but I couldn't remember when. I'd been imagining forgiveness, or an apology, or maybe even a scene.

Who waits twelve years for revenge? Besides the Count of Monte Cristo, which we both read in the same Survey of the Modern Novel course, sophomore year.

And which I was sure she wasn't thinking about right now because she didn't have a nerdy bone in her body. Unlike me, who'd only made it into Yardley by studying my ass off hard enough to land a full scholarship.

No point in procrastinating. Whatever was in that envelope, there wasn't enough vodka soda in the world to make it okay.

I ripped it open and spilled a small stack of photos onto the table. Of Ryan, with other women.

Eating in fancy restaurants, the kind he no longer had the time or inclination to take me to.

Sneaking into swanky hotels, like we hadn't done since before the kids.

Kissing in public, the way he used to kiss me.

Olivia beamed. That bitch.

You're probably thinking I deserved it. Maybe I did. Should I hate him or myself? Both maybe?

"I know this must be a shock—" Olivia clearly didn't see that as a down side.

I cleared my throat and tapped on the woman in the photograph closest to me, because no way was I giving her the satisfaction of seeing me fall apart. "Is this the girl from that show, *Adulting*?"

She nodded. "Jess Lindley."

While I'd been wiping the kids' noses and helping them with their homework, Ryan had been fucking a starlet. Perfect.

I forced myself to keep a neutral expression as I flipped through the pictures. Blonde, redhead, brunette. These women had nothing in common except they were all drop-dead gorgeous, in a way that I'd never been.

Fuck you, Ryan.

Olivia took a long and lingering sip of her drink, then licked her lips before setting it down.

"You know what they say," she said, without an ounce of sympathy in her voice. "Once a cheater, always a cheater."

What was the point in arguing?

"Okay, you win."

"Of course I do." She took another sip of her drink and smiled like it was ambrosia. "But what I want to know is, what are you going to do about it?"

What was I going to *do* about it?

Fuck me, what could I do about it? "Nothing."

She raised her perfectly threaded eyebrows. "You can't be serious."

"What do you want me to do?"

"Leave him, for a start."

"I can't." She opened her mouth to say some other snotty, entitled thing, but I interrupted. "I can't afford to leave. *I* don't have a rich daddy. *I* have no job and two kids."

She looked at me like she was seriously disappointed with who I'd turned out to be.

That made two of us.

I downed the rest of my drink, then signaled for the waitress. "Margarita, don't be stingy with the tequila."

Olivia held up two fingers. I guess she was staying.

"You know he's cheating and you're staying with him anyway?"

"Jesus, I found out two seconds ago. I don't have a plan for this."

I should've, though.

I should've known that if Ryan had cheated with me, he'd cheat on me.

I should've known that if rich, beautiful Olivia couldn't hold his interest, I wouldn't be able to either.

I should've known when he stopped having sex with me and started working late.

That motherfucker.

"You can't let him get away with it," Olivia said.

Of course I couldn't. But … "Why do you care?"

"I'm here because know what it's like."

Yeah, right. "You came here to gloat."

The margaritas arrived, and I gulped half of mine.

"If you think about it, you already knew." Olivia tapped the pile of photos that showed my husband had been banging six different women behind my back.

"I did, even though it took me a while to put my finger on it."

That uneasy feeling when he was working late, the artificial buoyancy when he came home after being out all night, the way he deflected when I inquired about work.

Yeah, I knew, goddammit.

But it was easier to fight about money. He was always talking about the big bonuses that would be coming his way — *BIG! he always said, spreading his hands to show me* — but then he'd get mad at me for indulging in a little bit of retail therapy. He'd tell me he was about to land a gig that would bring in 30,000 dollars then he'd yell at me for spending 300 dollars on new shoes for the kids.

Last night, I grabbed his laptop while he was in the shower and logged into his bank account.

And we are fucked.

He's been making payments to credit cards I didn't even know we had. And payments on loans he never told me he'd taken out — high-interest loans from the kind of companies that cater to people with terrible credit. All of them taken out in both our names. In the eyes of the law, I was just as responsible for paying it off as he was.

I checked our retirement account. He closed it a year ago.

Our mortgage company confirmed the worst of my fears — not only did my husband take out a second mortgage on our house, we couldn't even pay them off by selling it because the market had dropped off shortly after the second was signed. We owed more than our house was worth.

It wasn't even an option to clean out our accounts and move out. Our checking account had less than a grand in it, just enough to get us through with groceries and miscellaneous expenses until the end of the month. The 15,000 from the job he'd just finished hadn't been deposited yet.

As long as he didn't get suspicious and change his password, I could wait until that cleared and withdraw it all. But then what? As soon as he started missing payment on all that debt, the bill collectors would be after me too. And even if they only held me responsible for half of it — which of course, they wouldn't — 15,000 dollars plus whatever I could make at an entry-level job wouldn't even come close to getting me free.

I stuffed the photos back into the envelope and handed it back to Olivia. Ryan was an asshole, but I was stuck with him for now.

None of that was Olivia's business.

"Nat, you can't let him get away with this."

"Why do you care?"

She hesitated, then drained her margarita glass and gestured at the waitress to bring us another round.

"You taught me some things."

This ought to be good. "What things?"

"Look." She leaned forward, lacing her fingers under her chin. "I can help you."

Seriously? "You've helped way too much already, thank you very much."

"You need money, right?"

"Fuck you." Where was the waitress with that new round of margaritas?

"As far as I can tell, you haven't had a job since Alec was born."

"You've been *spying* on me?"

"If I'm going to hire a private investigator, I want her to be thorough."

Je-sus. "We are done."

I tried to stand, but the floor tilted and I tilted with it. Olivia grabbed my wrist, which kept me from falling on my ass, but also humiliated me. I straightened and yanked it back, then flopped back into my chair.

I usually have a glass of white wine with dinner. I'm a lightweight when it comes to vodka and tequila and finding out my husband is a cheating asshole, all in the span of twenty minutes.

The waitress finally replaced our empty glasses with full ones. I licked the salt from the rim of mine, but that just made me want to take another sip.

Ryan was watching the kids, so what the hell? Let him wait up and wonder, for a change.

Olivia nursed her own drink as she watched me slurp mine.

I didn't care what she thought of me.

I didn't care if she stayed or left.

I didn't care about anything right now, and it felt good.

Except that Olivia had to go and open her mouth again.

"If you won't accept help for yourself, do it for your children."

"Fuck. You."

But now I was thinking about Lena and Alec. I couldn't let them suffer because their father was a liar who'd spent all our money without telling me. What was I going to do? I'd spent the last twelve years being a stay-at-home mom who'd never used her degree. My last job had been working the grill at Sloppy's in college, to make money for the little things my scholarship didn't cover. And I was pretty sure I'd forgotten everything I knew about that job.

I'd intended to start a side business after we married, something that I could build slowly while Lena and Alec were small, and scale up once they didn't need me so much. But Ryan argued that it didn't make sense to deprive them of a full-time mom when his career was going so well.

Mo-ther-fuck-er.

How was I going to pay private school tuition — by going back to flipping burgers?

I hadn't just ruined my life, I'd ruined my kids' lives too.

Swallowing my pride, I asked, "What do you mean, you can help me?"

"I can hook you up with a great opportuni—"

"Oh my god, was this all a trick to get me into some kind of pyramid scheme? What is it, vitamins? Makeup? Superfood smoothies?"

Olivia laughed.

Then I laughed.

Because it was fucking ridiculous, no matter what she was trying to do.

By the time I managed to breathe again, my face was streaked with tears and the muscles in my stomach ached. But I felt better.

Olivia wiped her own eyes and started her sales pitch

again. "I know a way that you can make enough money to leave your husband, no pyramid scheme, no selling at all, just an honest night's work."

"A night shift job?" That was actually a good idea, I could sleep while the kids were at school and still be there for them in the mornings and at dinnertime. "But I don't have any employable skills."

"Trust me, anything you don't already know, you'll learn on the job."

"What *is* the job?"

"You'd be an escort. The expensive kind."

"You couldn't pay me enough."

Olivia quoted me a number that would easily allow me to support myself and the kids for a week.

"That's for one night," she added.

"Shut the fucking door," I slurred.

Olivia giggled. "Front door."

"What?"

I reached for my fourth — or fifth? — margarita, but she moved it before my hand got there. Everything was moving in slow motion, including my brain.

"Shut the front door," she said. "Or shut the fuck up."

"What the hell are you talking about?"

"Money. Lots of it. If you pass the audition."

I shook my head, trying to think.

I was screwed because Ryan had spent all our money and cheated on me. I could leave him only if I was willing to make money by cheating on him.

I wouldn't have to do it long, just enough to pay the bills until I could start that business I'd been dreaming about before the kids came along. A few months, maybe half a year at most. I could work for a week to earn enough for the month, then I'd have plenty of time to rebuild our lives before I had to do it again.

It made so much sense when I thought about it that way.

But I was worried it might be a trap. Olivia was mad at me for sleeping with Ryan. She had told me about his other women because she'd wanted to hurt me.

The same Olivia who wanted to give me a way to fix my life. It didn't make sense.

"Why?" I demanded, hating that I sounded stupidly petulant, but too drunk to pull myself together. "Why would you help me, after what I did to you?"

She stared at me for a long, thoughtful moment, as if she was trying to decide whether I would believe her.

Then she said, "Because Ryan deserves to be punished."

I couldn't argue with that.

"I'm in."

I DON'T how many drinks I'd had before we left Drink. Enough that I didn't remember getting in the car, or Olivia driving us here. 'Here' was an office suite that had been converted to a dressing room in Victor's place of establishment, stuffed to bursting with racks of lingerie I would've considered too rich for my budget even before I found out we were destitute. It was on the second floor of a building that Victor owned, mixed use with office space and luxury apartments. Apparently a lot of his "girls" lived on the upper floors.

Aside from the TV on the far wall, displaying the news silently with captions, the room was nothing but full-length mirrors and racks of leather, Lycra, and spandex. I could've been backstage at the world's naughtiest fashion show.

Olivia held a sheer red teddy up to my extra ten

pounds for two pregnant seconds before shaking her head and diving back into the rack of baby dolls, negligees, and various undergarments fluent in the universal language of *fuck me.*

I was feeling that phrase in one more ways than one.

Olivia shook her head for us both, disappointed in the choices, or at least how they were looking on me. She had already told me twice that even if I looked good, it wasn't exactly "recruitment bonus-worthy."

I had no idea that the escort business was so ... corporate, but apparently business is business.

Don't think I didn't see the irony of all this — twelve years ago, Olivia calling me a whore, and today, trying to turn me into one.

Would this be my revenge on Ryan, or Olivia's revenge on me?

There was another way to look at it — twelve years ago, Ryan made me look like a whore by being too cowardly to break up with Olivia before he'd seduced me. And thanks to his treachery since, I now had no other way out of this mess than to become one.

I was too drunk to tell which was the truth. Or maybe not drunk enough.

Would it matter when I was living in a homeless shelter with Alec and Lena? Not one little bit.

I looked over without meaning to and saw the thing that I'd been trying not to see for the third time in two minutes. A girl changing with zero inhibitions. But why would she have any? She had the same perfect, round little ass I used to shake in front of Ryan's face; the same full tits — not too big or small — he used to knead by the handful; and the same nubile body I would rub against his for thirty to forty minutes at a time, two or three times every night, back when we were first getting started.

Before two rounds of childbirth turned me into … this … and Ryan started cheating on me.

But I couldn't leave him until I was sure I could support myself and the kids.

Step one: Find something that would make me look "recruitment bonus-worthy."

"There's gotta be something that you think will look good on me."

Olivia looked from the simple black slip in her hand back to me. "The lingerie isn't the problem."

"Then what's the problem?" I said, trying not to sound irritated. If she didn't think I could do this, why was she bothering? Was this her revenge, to dangle the hope of economic freedom in front of my nose before explaining to me how I wasn't good enough to be a whore?

"You. You have zero confidence." Olivia looked at me the way that drill sergeants look at fresh draft recruits in movies. "This is an interview for an escort agency. You can't just dress sexy, you have to believe you're sexy. If you're not a 100 percent in on that, then we should leave now. Are you in?"

"I'm here, aren't I? Just tell me what to do."

Just tell me what to do.

Would I be saying the same thing in a different voice if this interview went well? And did I even want it to? Wasn't I hoping that it would go absolutely nowhere?

"I need you to focus. Either you're serious or you're not. I don't want you making me look bad."

How could I know whether I was serious when I was so holy shit drunk?

The hazy reality of my situation was settling in. Sure, my husband was apparently some sort of serial cheater who had been living a double life, but was my only option to audition for Victor, a guy who sounded like the opposite of charming, so that — hopefully, only if everything went well — I could trade access to my most intimate affections for money?

No, absolutely not. It was thoroughly batshit.

But as hard as I racked my brains, I couldn't think of a single other option. My parents were both dead, grandparents too. I was a single child, no other family I could turn to. I was in my early thirties and my resume consisted of part-time shifts at Sloppy's. Welfare wouldn't even come close to paying for the life I'd grown accustomed to — or that my kids had grown accustomed to. I could file for divorce, but giving Ryan warning would also give him time to move things around in his business and make it look like there wasn't anything for the courts to give me; he'd helped his best friend do just that a couple years ago, to get out of paying alimony.

Even if I waited for him to land another big gig and withdrew the money from his account before he could spend it, I'd only be delaying the inevitable for a few months.

I could stand to be broke and homeless, but I couldn't ruin my children's lives.

I owed it to them to take the audition and let it be my stopgap, until I could come up with a better plan. Or at least until I'd made enough money to hire a lawyer good enough to find me another option.

The nubile twenty-something finished changing, and she looked stunning in something that shouldn't have worked, or at least never could have on me. Black panties and a lavender halter, barely there and sort of see-through. As she strutted in front of the mirror, seeming aroused by her own reflection, I felt myself involuntarily responding to her sensuality.

I tried to imagine what it would feel like to be so

comfortable in my own skin that being nearly naked in front of other people would be an erotic act instead of a shameful one.

And I realized that I *wanted* to experience that.

I wanted to look in the mirror and see a goddess instead of a tired, frustrated housewife.

I wanted to be admired the way I was admiring her lithe body right now.

I wanted to feel sexy.

I turned to the rack and picked out something sheer and black. Beautiful but not obnoxious. The matching panties had enough fabric to hug my ass, and the baby doll itself would throw the best sort of shadows across my tummy. I loved the scallops, on the straps and looped along the bottom, because they invited the eye to rest on places where I still looked mostly my best.

I could look hot in this. Maybe not nubile waif-hot, but MILF-hot.

I stripped, ignoring Olivia's look of surprise, and wiggled into the outfit, which probably cost as much as the cheap engagement ring Ryan had bought for me after I'd told him I was pregnant. The drape of the sheer, silky fabric made my curves seem even more voluptuous while obscuring my baby belly just enough that I could barely notice the little pooch that daily yoga and power-walking at the mall hadn't been able to get rid of.

I stalked toward the mirror, turned around to examine my ass. Not bounce-a-quarter-off-it tight but not as bad as I'd worried. In this outfit, I did look MILF-hot.

To Ryan, I was a mom he didn't want to fuck, and I'd started to think of myself that way too. Unsexy. Undesirable. Unwanted.

No more. I was good enough for him to sneak around

with behind Olivia's back. I was definitely good for what-ever I needed to do to get free of him.

I raised my chin, put one hand on my hip, and pivoted on the balls of my feet, like I'd seen beauty contestants do. I wobbled a little at the end of the spin, thanks to all those margaritas, but I pretended not to notice.

"How do I look?"

Olivia eyed me up and down, smiling for the first time. "Much better. Are you ready?"

I gave Olivia jazz hands.

"Be serious."

"I am serious. This is literally the most serious I've ever been. If I can't give you jazz hands, I'm probably going to punch a wall. How do I look?"

"You look great." Olivia smiled. "But I want you to try on one more."

I was about to object that she risked messing with my MILF-y vibe by making me change just as I'd found some-thing I could rock, but the thing she pulled off the rack and held out to me …

It wasn't just beautiful, it was *me*. Lingerie of the lightest blush, mesh in the middle, almost like a mist, edged by the softest pink everywhere else. The tiny bows looked like they belonged on a doll. I would look like the world's most fuckable angel in it.

I nodded, taking the lingerie, surprised to suddenly feel like the next moment might be okay.

The last time I'd worn lingerie was nine years ago, when Alec was three and I was trying to prove I still had it. Ryan had barely glanced at me before he turned out the light without a single word, so *fuck him*.

I only bought the stupid thing because it was the first thing I'd tried on in nearly four years that didn't make me feel fat, and I only tried it on because Victoria's Secret sent me an email with a promise that the teddy would make me feel better about myself.

If I'd been wearing this, Ryan wouldn't have been able to help himself.

Or maybe he would've, because the pictures Olivia had shown me proved that he'd already been cheating on me then.

"Not to rush you, but we've taken way too long and Victor is waiting." Olivia looked from the lingerie to me. "Let's get going, 'kay?"

I changed, trying not to be self-conscious about the extra ten pounds of pudge around my middle as I peeled off the baby doll.

It was hard maintaining my post-childbirth figure. I could eat better, but snacking while shopping was fun, terrible as it is for you. I could do more than yoga, but that's a great time to breathe and think. It's not like I'm going to give that up, and adding any exercise on top of that would totally suck.

She raised an accusatory finger and stabbed it at me. "Jesus Christ, what the hell is that?"

"Give me a break! I'm sorry I had kids."

"It's not baby weight after a decade, honey. And that's not what I'm talking about." She pointed again, this time right at my crotch. "Your Barbara Bush looks like a bird's nest made of Brillo pads."

I guess she'd been busy going through the racks when I'd changed the first time.

"Sorry, I forgot to put *wax my snatch before I have drinks with Olivia* on my calendar."

She shook her head, then grabbed a pair of thick black panties, almost like boxer briefs. They were probably supposed to go with matching thigh highs or something.

"Here," she handed them over. "Maybe you can shove all your short and curlies up in here."

"No," I said. "We're late, and this is perfect."

Olivia sighed. "I'll give you the number for my esthetician. You need to take care of that, because ohmygod you're giving new meaning to *going through a rough patch.*"

And the nerves were back again. "Seriously, can you please say something nice? I'm about to go out of my fucking mind."

Olivia appraised me again. "Sorry. You're right. Except for the bounty of pubes, you look terrific. I'd pay to fuck you for sure."

She smiled like she actually meant it.

For all I knew, she did. "Thanks."

She took me by the hand, the gentlest she'd been with me since our reunion, and led me out of the dressing room and into a sort of reception area where she explained that I'd have to sign some paperwork before the audition. A short profile, an even shorter NDA, and an initial contract, just in case I got the job I didn't really want.

The contract stated that I agreed to take ten clients if I passed the audition. After finishing the first ten, I would have the chance to re-up, or walk. If I didn't make my quota, I would have to buy myself out.

That would be enough for the kids and I to live for ten months, if I sneaked into Ryan's bank account to make sure the next deposit paid the rest of their school tuition for the year and if I was frugal in every other aspect of our lives.

Olivia waited with me while I filled everything out, then glanced down at my hand as I handed the tablet back to her. "Your wedding ring. You need to take that off."

A slap to the face, a punch to the gut, a tempest set loose inside me.

Taking off my wedding ring would make all this real. I would be agreeing to cheat on my husband, for money. I would be lowering myself to his level, for the sake of protecting our children. There was still time to change my mind, put my own clothes back on, and find another way out of this mess.

But Ryan would still be Ryan, the faithless and financially fucked husband. And I would still be me, the unqualified stay-at-home-mom with no way to support her family.

If I took off my wedding ring, there would be no turning back.

I took it off.

I KNEW Victor was a prick the second I met him. The guy was eyeing me like a slab of alcatra at a Brazilian steakhouse.

I stood in the doorway, working to stay steady as he raked my body with misplaced appreciation from his spot on the sitting room couch. He actually smirked. Pure Snidely Whiplash.

It was hard to tell how tall he was since he was sitting down, but I could still see just about everything else. His close cropped hair, almost fuzzy, matching the scruff on his face. He would have been handsome, if he didn't look mean; his emerald eyes might have been bright with life if they weren't so obviously cruel. He was younger than I had expected, probably not thirty.

He made a come-here gesture, so I slinked across the room, stopping in front of him.

He motioned for me to twirl around.

Dizziness surged, the room whirling even faster than I was. Too many margaritas. I swallowed hard, not wanting to blow the job interview by barfing in his lap.

Still smirking, he patted the spot on the sofa beside him and said, "Have a seat."

For the first time, it occurred to me that this audition might involve more than taking off my clothes and being inspected like a cow at auction. Shit. Could I go through with this?

"You seem nervous," he said.

"Not at all."

"Maybe you should be."

I sat down, as far away from him as I could get on the couch without seeming like I was retreating.

"Why would you want one of your potential girls to be nervous?" I asked. "Isn't confidence part of the crack that you're selling?"

That seemed to surprise him. "Exactly. But confidence and arrogance aren't the same. And I'd expect caution from someone like you. Maybe anxiety."

"Is that what you want?"

"I want to see the real you, and I want to decide if that's something worth paying for."

Something sour seeped deep into my stomach. I wanted to move over, but I refused to budge an inch.

"Are you ready?"

"I'd still be in my LuluLemon if I wasn't."

Victor eyed me with something that might have been respect, if I wasn't delusional.

But look where I was, so who really knew?

"Let's start simple. Why don't you tell me about your education."

"I graduated from Yardley with an anthropology degree."

Victor raised his eyebrows, but I think he already knew. "Yardley. Impressive. You come from money?"

"Not at all. But I'm a hard worker. I got a lot of scholarships and kept my nose down."

"That's where you met Olivia?"

"We were sorority sisters there."

"Hot. How about now, are you still close?"

No way was I going to dig into my feelings for Olivia in front of this man. I shrugged like that was an irrelevant question. "Close enough."

"Did it always bother you that she was the hotter one?"

"No, because she never was." His eyebrows went up. So did Olivia's, but she didn't interrupt. "Some people like Betty, and others like Veronica."

He smiled, but this time it was appreciative more than leering. "Hobbies?"

"I love shopping, and hanging out with my—" I coughed and laughed a little, gently reset myself.

You're not a mother right now, you're a high-class escort. Besides, he didn't really want to know what I enjoyed doing, he wanted to know what I was good at that might serve him.

"I guess I love cooking the most, probably because it's one of the things I'm best at." I did my best to sound like Miss Ohio doing her best to become Miss America. "I love it when someone slurps their soup or makes a quiet *mmmm* while they're eating something I've cooked."

Victor acted like he didn't give a shit about my answer, but I could tell that he liked it.

He scooted closer. I forced myself to keep smiling, instead of planting my hand on his chest and suggesting that he back the hell up, like I would if this were a party and one of Ryan's friends was hitting on me.

"How many sexual partners have you had?"

Did he have to lick his lips when he said it?

"Ten."

"Ten in the last year?"

I laughed. "I was married this last year."

"You married now?"

"For the time being."

"So you're not very experienced?"

The siren in the dressing room looked like she was barely twenty-one. If he were hiring based solely on experience, she'd have been a well-preserved forty-something, so that was a bullshit question.

"Are you looking for quantity or quality?"

He actually laughed, and it seemed genuine. "Tell me, how would you get a guy off?"

I laughed like Victor was silly.

"The first thing I'd do is not think about it as *getting him off.* I'd think about giving him an experience."

Victor looked at Olivia and nodded. She looked relieved — I guess she'd been sweating whether or not I'd pass the audition more than she let on. I wondered if there was more to her finder's fee than the percentage she'd mentioned.

I was relieved too. Ryan usually tapped me on the shoulder when he was in the mood, then he'd roll me over, lift my nightgown — his perennial preference for easy access — pump for under a minute before I started slamming my ass back to hurry it up. I wore shorts to bed to let him know that I wasn't in the mood.

So, if I wanted the job, I needed to avoid giving an accurate description of my sex life with Ryan at all costs.

"You let your husband fuck your ass?"

I'd never wanted to slap someone more. Well, except maybe Olivia, for showing me the picture of Ryan and his bimbos.

But instead, I answered, "No, I never have."

"Why not?"

"He never asked."

"You don't think your husband's ever wanted to?"

"Probably." But if he wasn't interested enough to at least have a conversation with me about it, then I wasn't interested in finding out if it hurt.

"What you have let him if he had asked?"

"I don't know. Probably not."

"What if you're asked that question on the job?"

"Then I will say no and be submissive to them in some other way, because that's all anal sex is about, the crudest form of domination. I'll tell him that he can eat my ass like a cupcake, and then I will fuck him to Venus, but no anal penetration."

Fuck him to Venus? Where did that come from?

"Fair enough. You ever been with a girl?"

"A few drunken makeout sessions in college." I shrugged. "Because sometimes it's fun to live the cliché."

"Any objection?"

I was surprised by my immediate, genuine response. "No objection."

"What's your favorite sexual position?"

"I like them all."

"Everyone has a favorite position."

Of all the things he'd asked, this was the first one that made me feel dirty to answer. Probably because I was sure that as soon as I named a position, he'd be imagining screwing me in it.

He cleared his throat.

"Doggy," I admitted, having to make an effort not to squirm as his smirk turned into a leer.

"Much better. Congratulations, you've earned another question." He petted my knee. My skin crawled, but I didn't pull away.

"Do you regularly orgasm from sex, or are you the kinda girl who fakes it?"

"No faking." Although I supposed I might need to start. Did clients care if their escort had an orgasm? I'd kind of thought it was all about making the client come.

"Why not?"

"Haven't needed to." Which sounded better than, *My husband doesn't care.*

Victor squeezed my knee, then began to slide it up my thigh.

I shook him off and inched away, smiling. "I'm having a hard time concentrating while you're doing that, and I'd like to give you my best possible answers."

"You're doing great, and believe me, this is exactly the sort of stuff you'll have to navigate on the job."

"True." I moved even farther away. "But then I'll be earning two thousand dollars an hour, minus your commission. I'll be focusing on that."

He actually backed off. I couldn't believe it worked.

"How often do you masturbate?"

"I don't," I lied, because I didn't want to say *every day,* and because he didn't need to know to decide whether or not to hire me.

"You don't masturbate, but you come whenever you fuck?" He laughed. "Which of those fantasies do you want me to believe?"

"Do you want to hear that I'm horny all the time?"

Victor laughed. "Something like that."

He turned toward me and brushed my shoulder with the tips of his fingers, sliding one strap down off my shoulders, then the other.

My breasts were dangerously close to breaching the thin barrier of fabric still holding them up.

His fingers drifted down, stopping at my nipples, where Victor made slow, teasing circles around them.

I hated my own arousal, forced myself to arch into his touch and bite my lip and let my breathing get heavier, like I was enjoying all this. Because if I couldn't tolerate a little groping from Victor, how was I going to spend an entire night with a stranger?

I was about to find out if I was the kind of woman who could fuck men for money. Maybe women, too. I don't know why, but right now, that actually sounded easier.

I wasn't sure what would be worse: if I got the job, or if I let Victor fondle me and then I didn't.

Because I'd already crossed a line I couldn't uncross. Even if Victor said no and Ryan never found out what I'd done. I would know, for the rest of my life.

Suddenly, Victor stood, took me by the hand, and led me over to a splendid floor-length mirror on the other side of the room, with gleaming glass and a platinum frame.

I barely recognized myself -- the lingerie barely covering the rise and fall of my breasts, the flush in my cheeks, the strange light in my eyes. I felt more like one of the women in those erotica novels I like to read on my Juke than a loving housewife with two adoring children.

Something collapsed inside me as I realized that I was more aroused than I had been with Ryan for years. Not because I was attracted to Victor, I wasn't. Not because the situation was hot, it definitely wasn't.

But because I was doing something I hadn't done in the twelve years since I'd married Ryan.

Taking a risk.

Sleeping with Ryan had been exciting, because of the risk that Olivia would find out. Then she did, and he proposed, and he became safe.

And I'd been playing it safe ever since.

"Show me," Victor said, startling me out of my trance.

"I'm sorry?"

"I'm a client." He sounded slightly irritated. "Demonstrate how you'd service me."

I froze. What did he want me to do? Kiss him? Do a striptease? Drop to my knees and undo his fly?

Everything I'd tried to rekindle Ryan's interest after Alec was born had failed, because he'd already started screwing someone else. When we did have sex, it was as perfunctory as it could be and still involve one of us coming. I was seriously out of practice.

I was going to flunk the test, and it was all Ryan's fault. I didn't want to screw Victor. I wanted to punch him in the nose for being a prick, just like my husband.

Somehow, the anger made it easier. I turned around and grabbed Victor by his collar. "You want to fuck me?"

He smiled and gave me an encouraging nod.

I let go of him and stepped back.

"I'm not going to fuck you until you're nice and hard for me." I glanced back at the sofa. "Maybe I should go over there and play with my pussy instead ..."

That did it.

Victor grabbed me by the arm and spun me around, then bent me forward. I barely managed to catch myself on the ottoman as he ground his erection against my ass. I turned back to look in the mirror. Mistake.

I started to get wet.

"You're a mom, right?"

Was that a trick question? Olivia must've told him. Did he want to know if I'd lie? Or were MILFs his thing?

"Yes."

"Never had a mom in the lineup," he said, still grinding, and now he was looking in the mirror too. I couldn't tell if he was staring at me, or himself.

Victor stopped talking, but the grinding continued. It had tumbled past sexual right into awkward. He seemed to be ... thinking? The grinding became thrusting and I seriously had no idea what I was supposed to do. Grind back? Turn around and take him to the couch? Was I supposed to give him a blow job? While Olivia watched?

This was a massive, mammoth, monstrous mistake.

I was about to pull away, tell him that I'd changed my mind, but I never had to make that choice.

Victor slapped me hard on the ass, took two steps back, then dug into his pocket to retrieve a burner phone.

"I'll be in touch," he said, handing it over.

I felt like I'd just won first place in a loser contest.

Chapter Two

Monday Morning …

I SCRAPED SCRAMBLED EGGS – I'd gotten up too late to make anything more complicated — onto three plates, one for each child and one for my cheating husband.

I swallowed hard as a surge of nausea flooded my throat with hot bile. I'd drunk more alcohol last night than I usually had in a month, but the hangover seemed a suitable punishment when I replayed the memory of what I had done.

Last night, it had seemed like poetic justice: Ryan had made me out to be a whore, so I would be one long enough to get back on my feet. But now that I was sober (mostly), it was time to forget it ever happened and get back to my regularly scheduled life. Figure out what to do about Ryan. Do the math. Make a plan. Maybe get a job.

I had to be qualified for something better than Sloppy's.

I dropped the plates on the table and shouted, "Breakfast!"

I wouldn't have had to call them if I'd started earlier. No one came running for scrambled eggs. If I'd made my lemon crepe pancakes, or my chicken sausage breakfast hash, or that bacon thing that made Ryan drool, they'd have been standing in the kitchen with plates in hand, begging for me to fill them.

Alec and Lena came running into the room, taking their usual spots on their sides of the table.

Thank goodness they'd never know what I'd done last night.

I kissed Lena on the forehead, then gave her a hug that lasted so long she giggled and squirmed.

I leaned over to kiss Alec, but he leaned back and squinted at me. "You okay, Mom?"

Twelve-year-old boys. Gotta love 'em.

"Of course, sweetie." I swooped in for a kiss on the top of his head before returning to the kitchen.

Where I wondered if I was ever going to be all right again.

Of course I had to tell Olivia I'd changed my mind.

Of course I wasn't going to become a ridiculously expensive escort in the name of supporting my kids.

Of course I was going to find another way to get the money to leave Ryan.

How would they ever respect their mother if they found out she'd supported them by prostituting herself?

I was doing what was best for them by saying no.

I jumped and yelped as arms closed around my waist. Ryan. Why wasn't he eating his damn scrambled eggs?

"Hey ..." he tried to sooth me. "Why so tense? Is it Lynette? Is she stressing you out again?"

Lynette Wilder, supermom who seemed determined to

make every weekend a playdate for her kids and mine, was the least of my concerns today.

Although maybe she shouldn't have been. Maybe Ryan was secretly screwing her too.

"No. Not Lynette. I just have a lot on my mind."

"Anything you want to talk about?"

Yes. No. Fuck you.

I turned around to face him. He dared to kiss me, right on the mouth, the bastard.

How did he do that? Act so normal when his every breath was a lie?

I would have to learn, and judging by the shadow of a migraine lurking at my temples, it wasn't going to be nearly as easy for me as it apparently was for him.

"What time did you get home from dinner with the girls last night?" He sat at the breakfast bar. "I didn't even hear you come in."

"We lost track of time." The lie felt easier on my tongue than I expected.

"Oh." He didn't question it. Part of me wished that he would, the part that felt hurt that he didn't care enough to ask. But why would he?

Ryan headed to the dining room, finally. I bonded with the kids all day, but when he was in town, he made a point to have breakfast with them no matter what.

I needed to figure out the job thing, but I was afraid Ryan would try to sneak up on me from behind again and ask what I was doing.

So I did what I usually did during this time, leaned against the counter, sipped my coffee, and scrolled through LiveLyfe. It was a stupid, empty habit, and I wasn't sure why I kept doing it to myself. I should never log on again. Maybe not all of the time, but *most* of the time it makes me feel worse about myself, and pretty much every choice that

I've made, from the color of my curtains to the timeline of my life.

I was most addicted to checking — okay, maybe stalking — all of my old sorority sisters from Yardley. It was hard not to, seeing as most of them had it all. Perfect lives. Living in giant McMansions, driving perfect cars, killing it with high-powered careers and perfectly fuckable husbands. And yes, most of them were managing to do the mom thing in between it all by now, much better than I had ever come even remotely close to doing.

I wasn't sure what I felt more, the envy of wanting all the things I didn't have, or shame for not appreciating the abundance I already did have. If only they could—

"Hey, honey, when is that thing with the Wilders again?" Ryan dropped his dishes in the sink. "That's coming up, right? Maybe we're not synced because I seem to remember you telling me about it, but I didn't see anything when I looked."

Fuck. I still can't believe I even agreed to "Family Day" with the Wilders.

Ryan didn't care for Lynette's husband all that much, but he was willing to pretend for the sake of an afternoon out on their yacht on the open sea.

I should've realized that if Ryan was pretending with everyone else, he was probably pretending with me too.

"I'll double check and let you know."

"Great." Ryan seemed like he wanted to give me a kiss on the cheek or something, but instead he gave me an awkward sideways hug. "So I guess I'll see you next week?"

"I guess so." Could he tell that I'd been thinking, *Not if I see you first?* "Looking forward to New York?"

"I guess. I really hate how busy it always is. It's not like I'll get to see a show or anything."

He laughed, because that might convince me that he

wasn't a dog who had been sticking his dick into things he wasn't married to.

"Right," I agreed, because fuck him and the horse he rode in on. And double fuck him for making me ask. "Did you remember that I need the next tuition payment for Constellation?"

He looked at me, shaking his head. "I'm really sorry. I'll go take care of that right now, and I'll leave it on the kitchen counter."

"I'd rather wait, so I can take it when I drop the kids off." Last week, the principal had been waiting out by the drop-off area to ambush me with a "quick reminder" that we were already past the deadline and that she was giving us an extra few days as a courtesy, for Lena's sake. "It's overdue, remember?"

I studied Ryan's reaction, chastising myself for not seeing it sooner. Now that I'm paying attention, he's an easy read. The clenched jaw, the suddenly shallow breath, the narrowing of his eyes. And I know the floor isn't that interesting to him. The bastard hasn't touched a broom in years.

Ryan gave me his best smile and pulled me into his arms. It took all my willpower not to stiffen with disgust.

He kissed me tenderly, like he meant it, then leaned into me, nibbled on my ear, and whispered, "I'll miss you."

I resisted the urge to push him away as I lied, "I'll miss you, too."

I could hardly wait to never see him again.

LYNETTE

I HAD BEEN TALKING to Susan Foley for fifteen minutes, but already it felt like an hour.

"And it's not like I *do* his homework for him," Susan said. "But I'd rather sit there until he finishes than have him tell Mr. Herrera that he doesn't have it done. Are you listening, Lynette?"

"Of course I'm listening."

But I didn't have to be upset about it because Susan was upset enough for both of us.

She cared more than any of the other moms, always first in line to volunteer for whatever the school needed. The poor woman had even been willing to supervise the halls during standardized testing. In exchange, we all pretended not to notice that her twelve-year-old son was still on the nipple. All of us except for Natalie, who always found the most diplomatic way to say what she meant. But she was a saint. It took a lot of skill to call someone out with elegance, and Natalie definitely knew how to do that.

Someone needed to say it -- Susan wasn't doing her son any favors. It wasn't just the double-checking his lunch to make sure he has his snacks, asking him if he's filled in his learning log, or his permission slips, or whatever other overprotective robot question she had at the ready. Poor kid was constantly humiliated in front of the other kids.

"And really, it's too much homework for their age."

Do you really think you can meet with every teacher and grade grub all the way to college? It doesn't work that way, and in the meantime, you're turning Owen into an idiot.

"It is a lot," I said. Then, "Hey Betty!"

Betty turned and gave me a wave and a smile. I could tell that she barely meant the first and I doubted she meant the second at all. She wasn't nearly as bad as Susan, but she was another helicopter parent who monitored all of her children's Internet activity, including her nineteen-year-old son, who, by the way, is soiling the family name by skipping city college. I've seen him at Perfect Burgers three times this month, just sitting there swiping on his iPad with nothing to do. You would think the kid would've gone to a school out of state, just to get the hell away from his mother.

I was about to go home when the reason I was sticking around swung her silver Volvo Hybrid into the parking lot.

Alec and Lena scrambled out of the back. Natalie stayed in the driver's seat, though I couldn't see her through either the tint or the glare. Making a phone call? Or avoiding the rest of us?

She must've finished whatever she was doing because she got out of the car, stunning as always. I wanted to think of her as a skinny bitch, even though I didn't really like that word, because that would make all the times when she didn't want to hang out with me feel better. She wasn't a B-word, like so many of the other moms. Smart, assertive, and the kind of friend you really want to have? *Absolutely.*

We all pretend we're not comparing, but when it comes to Natalie, I think we all are. We all looked up to our Natalies. Beautiful without showing too much. Strong yet soft. Demure as she was brazen, depending on either her mood or her need.

Everything about her was natural, easy, and enviable.

MILF.

Mom I'd like to fuck.

A mom all of us want to fuck. I mean, not really. Once in high school, twice in college, drunk at a party all three times, and just because. Why wouldn't I be curious?

Our sons were best friends, so really, it would make sense that we would become best friends too. It was only a matter of time. Except that the boys were growing up fast, so if something was going to happen with Natalie, sooner was better than later.

I watched as she kissed both kids and sent them on their way, but she wasn't getting back in the car and—

Yes!

I wondered if Natalie was coming over to talk, or if she had business in the office. Maybe she'd like to grab a cup of coffee. Except ... Susan. Like Natalie would stop if she also had to chew the cud with that cow. Not that Susan was fat. In fact, it looked as if she might be back to bingeing and purging again.

"Natalie!" I called out, when it became obvious that she was walking fast and about to pass us.

She stopped, but somehow still managed to appear like she was in motion, saying — *Sorry ladies, I'm in a rush this morning* — without being mean about it.

Natalie gave us a wave that was probably meant mostly for me. "Hey girls."

"Hey Natalie," Susan said. "Don't you think the kids are getting too much homework? Especially math?"

Screw you, Susan.

Natalie was obviously in a hurry, and Susan wanted to have the same conversation that every other dumbass mom had been having on that same patch of lawn since the school was laying its foundation.

"What are you up to?" I asked Natalie, turning ever so subtly away from Susan.

She held up a check and waved in the air. "I have to take our tuition check into the office. Like an idiot I didn't realize that it was due today, and Ryan is going to New York, so the house was a little chaotic."

She turned and was about to say goodbye.

I touched her lightly on the arm. "You know Constellation has autopay now, right? We announced it at the CPA meeting at the beginning of the year. You might want to come to the next one. There's going to be a lot to cover and …"

Oh, fudge.

"Thanks for the reminder," Natalie said.

Then she followed my eyes to see why I stopped talking.

Theresa Akers: *Slut Mom.*

I supposed every school had one, so why would ours be any different? Sure, Constellation charges a hefty tuition, but like every other school worth its caps and gowns, it also offered scholarships and financial aid. More than its share, actually. I don't like to brag about it, although I did tell Natalie once, and Susan several times just to shut her up, that Frank and I sponsor two students in addition to our own.

I'm glad Slut Mom's daughter isn't one of them.

Susan scowled at Theresa, but Natalie gave her a wave.

Slut Mom had made her first unfortunate appearance at the beginning of the year, showing up in her wretched Ale Mary's uniform every weekday since. Her daughter Emily had perfect attendance. Of course she did — how could a divorced waitress at a bar earn enough to take her daughter on vacation?

The woman's uniform is obscene, especially so early in the morning. Short shorts. A top cut so low that her barely there boobies are practically falling right out of it. I don't have a problem with the scholarships, really I don't. Like I said, Frank and I pay for two ourselves (so, that's three tuitions total). It's that Theresa Akers is the kind of trash that I — and all the other moms at Constellation who can afford to — pay good money to keep our husbands away from.

"She's single you know," I told the girls, though I was pretty sure I had told them before.

Susan leaned in, which is why I suddenly smelled frozen waffles. "What's with women disrespecting themselves? Have you seen any of that story about that escort service? The one that had the leak?"

"You mean Rosebud, right?"

Of course I'd heard. I'd spent hours reading all about it. Frank liked the trades, but I liked to follow what he was doing without being bored, so I always read *Hollywood Hunted*. And last night I read it for hours.

"Right," Susan said. "So many of those men involved had families. How can women be okay with being home wreckers? It's—"

"I'm sorry," Natalie interrupted, "but I really gotta go.

My hand was back on her arm, gentle like before. She gave me a smile.

"Are we still on for tonight?" I asked.

That look on her face said that she forgot.

"Girls Night?" I prompted.

"Right! Every time Ryan leaves I get stupid. I'm really sorry.

"Don't mention it at all. Can you still make it?"

It was sad how much I wanted her to say yes.

And how happy I was when I saw her reassuring smile.

"Of course," she said.

Natalie scampered off with her check, leaving me alone again with Susan.

As I listened to the woman bitch about how the civics teacher was poisoning Owen's mind by saying positive things about Jimmy Carter's presidency, I made a mental list of everything I'd need to make sure tonight was perfect.

Chapter Three

Monday Night …

NATALIE

FUCK.

I would seriously rather go without toilet paper for a week, or work retail, than waste any more of my life at one of these stupid Girls Nights. I was dying for a drink, but to get it, I'd have to walk past a swarm of Constellation Parent Association moms, all cackling and gossiping with Lynette. Somehow, that seemed even more dangerous.

My burner phone buzzed with another text from Victor.

Why didn't I throw it away after I sobered up this morning?

I already decided that I'm not doing it. Didn't I?

The thing has been buzzing all day, but for some reason I couldn't make myself get rid of it. Maybe because I haven't found a single job opening I'm qualified for — I spent half the day searching through JobMart and other similar sites. But it seems as though a college degree is the baseline, on a par with "must be alive." Even some of the entry-level positions said I would need experience in the form of an internship.

I can't even afford to live on an entry-level salary, let alone spend months in an unpaid internship just to qualify to get paid peanuts.

And my degree is more than a decade old. I'm going to be competing with the latest batch of college kids, who can afford to get paid shit because they're still living in their parents' basements or they're sharing a two-bedroom apartment with half a dozen other recent graduates.

What if Victor is my only choice?

Even if it's a terrible option, it's better than being homeless with kids. Or worse, being homeless and losing the kids to Ryan.

Who am I kidding? He'd be better off financially if he wasn't paying private school tuition. Maybe he'd even be able to get ahead on all the debt he's racked up.

Holy shit, what if he's already planning to leave me so he can do just that?

I've been thinking in terms of divorce, but he could shut down the company, move to another part of the country, and start over again with one of his mistresses. If all that debt is in both our names — and it totally could be, he's that kind of rat bastard, I'm realizing — he could change his name and disappear, leaving me holding the bag of IOUs.

If that happened, Victor would be my only way out.

My phone buzzed again. I ignored it again. The last text had definitely been impatient, demanding that I confirm my acceptance of the job he'd offered ten texts ago.

Of course I wasn't going to confirm my acceptance of anything. I was going to find a legitimate way to support myself and my kids.

I didn't mind volunteering at the school as I minded all of this. Ever since Alec went into kindergarten, I had fundraised and baked and chaired committees. It was part of being a good parent, and it made me happy to know that I was doing something that made a difference not just for my kids, but for others too.

But I did mind that my children were with a sitter while I was stuck here at Lynette's.

It's not that Lynette is desperate, exactly, but she has this way of looking at me that makes me want to go fetal. I can usually come up with a conflicting appointment when she tries to corner me into lunch or a mani-pedi or whatever other new time-waster she was in the mood for.

But every so often she has me clenched so tight that I agree with her just to get out of the moment.

"More wine?" Susan asked, approaching me with a bottle of Chardonnay.

"Sure," I said, holding out my glass. Third one's a charm.

At least everyone was talking about school. Half of the time these Girls Nights turned into impromptu infomercials for essential oils, handbags, candles, soaps, anything weight loss, and twice now — the only two meetings that were any fun — sex toys.

Tonight's topic: over-involved versus absentee parents. I still can't believe there's an argument. As annoying as helicopter moms are, that's way better than not being there at all. I get the feeling that Lynette is trying to prove a point with Susan, not like that's any surprise. She's just so awkward about it.

I added my two cents to the conversation so that no

one would think I was rude, then drifted to the other side of the room as quietly as I could while Lynette repeated the same argument she'd been making for the past half hour, but with slightly different words.

Her place is obnoxiously large, thanks to her husband Frank. He's a successful entertainment lawyer, and according to Lynette, "always in such high demand."

The only thing she liked to do more than show off her wealth was to talk about her perfect husband. But she had to be wearing beer goggles, or dollar goggles, I guess, because the guy was revolting. Their home was littered with pictures, but they were like exhibits in some monstrous museum. The guy triggered my gag reflex. Involuntary, but true. He's that gross. Enough to make me sympathetic toward Lynette. I sure as hell couldn't imagine having to fuck that bowl of jelly.

At least he's not cheating on her.

My phone buzzed again. I took a large swig of wine.

"Do you need to get that?" Roberta asked.

"It's been ringing a lot," Susan added.

Then Lynette said, "Sometimes us girls have to screen our calls, isn't that right, Natalie?"

"Uh, right," I agreed. "I guess I got on some list because I keep getting all of these spam phone calls. I just changed my settings so that the phone buzzes instead of rings when it's someone I don't know."

By the time Victor had buzzed me another couple of times, I was pretty buzzed myself. Maybe a little more than buzzed. I would've given anything to be home alone with a blender full of margaritas, packing Ryan's shit into boxes and throwing it out of our bedroom window onto the lawn.

But since that wasn't an option, I let myself get sucked

into the conversation. Until it turned into a competition for who had the best husband.

Susan said, "Marty is a gift that God has given me to cherish and nurture forever."

Roberta said, "We're still best friends, even if it's a rollercoaster. I still like that feeling in my stomach, both on the rise and after the fall. Damon still does it for me."

Gabrielle said, "We grow and mature because of consistent change, and that helps us to renew our bond."

I have no idea what that meant, but it sounded like bullshit.

Lynette went next. "Frank and I still have date night twice a week, but the days are always different because of his schedule. And sometimes he's so busy that we'll go without date nights for almost a month. But then he'll make it up to me with something special. We went to Greece the last time."

"We still fuck every day that Ryan's home," I lied. "Sometimes twice."

The room froze. Susan went all bug-eyed and choked on her Chardonnay.

"What?" I smiled at the crowd and took another sip. "It's like Maslow's Hierarchy of Needs with our relationship. After twelve years, we've reached the tip of that triangle." Another sip, and then I whispered like it was a secret, barely managing to keep a straight face. "That's all self-actualization is. The realization that you can have too much stuff, but you can't have too much sex."

"I think it's wonderful that you and Ryan have such a great sex life," Lynette said. "And that you're so open about it. What do you say ladies, anyone else want to share?"

Ha. Choke on that, Susan.

But before the storytelling could start, Theresa walked

in. Or waddled in, I should say. Poor girl was *so* pregnant it made my belly ache just to look at her.

"You told me to just come right in," Theresa said, looking at Lynette.

"Of course. Girls, you all know Theresa." Lynette looked like she was handing them each a gift card for Nordstrom.

The gaggle tittered, all except me. Maybe because I was suddenly feeling very pissed off, because I could see where this was going, and I didn't want any part of it.

"It's great that you could make it to Girls Night," Lynette said, grabbing a glass and a bottle then walking over to Theresa. "And to see you outside of school, and out of that uniform!"

Lynette laughed, and the girls laughed with her.

I bit my bottom lip.

Roberta whispered to Gabrielle, even though everyone in the room could obviously hear, "Too bad her closet doesn't have anything larger."

"Probably because tight clothes turn you into a tight ass," I said, loud enough to prove that I wasn't a coward.

The tittering stopped.

I didn't. "At least Theresa has the body and self-confidence to dress how she wants to. And she isn't ashamed to be who she is."

Theresa shot me a look: *Thank you.*

I gave her one back: *Of course.*

Even though I've never stuck up for her before. I guess something good had come out of my meeting with Victor — I no longer felt like I held the moral high ground when it came to calling other women sluts. I vowed to never do that again.

"Anyone else?" I looked at the gaggle, one at a time.

Lynette said, "Mariella made us some delicious strawberry bruschetta. You're all going to love it. Warm straw-berries and crunchy sugar -- the girl knows how to caramelize! I'll be right back."

Then Lynette took her lily-livered self into the kitchen, just as my burner started to buzz.

I glared at the girls, smiled at Theresa, then joined Lynette in the kitchen.

She turned around, surprised to see me.

"Why did you do that?"

"Do what?" Lynette asked, like she didn't know.

"Why would you invite Theresa here just to make fun of her? It's bad enough that you do it at school. But asking her over so that you can make fun of her in the comfort of your home is cruel." I shook my head, getting angrier by the second. "I don't even know what to say, Lynette."

She set down a tray of admittedly gorgeous strawberry bruschetta, then turned fully around and gently set a hand on my arm. "Let me give you some friendly advice."

I was already angry, her hand on my arm made me angrier. I shook it off. "I don't need friendly advice. I need you to keep me out of shit like this."

She reached out to touch me again, wisely thought better, then sighed and said, "Natalie, you're beautiful. You don't even realize how much you have going for you. Or how perfect your life is. You need to protect that at all costs because it won't get easier as you get older."

Then she glanced back at the kitchen door. "Theresa? She doesn't have what we have. Her husband left her and now she's scrambling and desperate. She dresses that way for a reason." She lowered her voice to not quite a whisper. "Would you really feel comfortable leaving a woman like that alone in a room with your husband?"

No, I wouldn't. But I didn't blame Theresa for that.

"I would have no problem trusting Theresa because I don't make assumptions about people I don't know."

"You'll change," Lynette said, so smug that I wanted to slap her. "You'll get older, and then you'll better understand how important it is to be aware of the company you keep."

I stared into her eyes and said, "You're right, Lynette. I should be *much* more aware of the company I keep."

Naturally, she didn't get it.

I wanted to go back out there and rescue Theresa, but I didn't even know where to start. Whatever Lynette was up to with dragging this poor woman through the mud, it wasn't my problem. It *couldn't be* my problem.

Money was my problem, Alec and Lena were my problem, and Ryan was my motherfucking problem for sure. Same with the burner phone that wouldn't stop buzzing, and that I would have to throw in the garbage as soon as I left Lynette's.

"I'm leaving."

"Wait! I'll be nice to Theresa tonight, I promise."

"You better be," I said, grabbing a piece of bruschetta, because there was zero chance that I was leaving without one. "But I'm not going to stay here and babysit you. I'll check in with Theresa tomorrow."

Lynette stood there with her mouth open as I stormed out to the foyer, grabbed my purse, and slammed the door on the way out.

Then I shoved the infuriatingly delicious strawberry bruschetta — drizzled with balsamic glaze and perfectly caramelized like Lynette had said — and promised myself that was my last Girls Night ever.

OLIVIA

I'D BEEN LEANING against my Mercedes for a while, wondering when Natalie was going to get home so I could get on with my night.

I hated little suburbs like this, with their tacky McMansions and manicured lawns. I liked nice things, of course, but places like Cherry Hill were sleepy at best and robotic at worst. It reminded me of a Hollywood backlot, with little inside the empty facades of all these phony lives. Families telling themselves stories of who they were, bending and twisting the truth to make themselves look better. I knew, because my time was often paid for by husbands from families like these.

Natalie's silver Volvo slowed as she approached the house.

I smiled and looked at my watch. I wasn't running too late, but I'd still waited a lot longer than expected. Not that I could blame her. It wasn't like I had told Natalie I was coming.

The Volvo stopped and the lights died, then Natalie scrambled out of her SUV in a panic. I don't mind admitting that her alarm delighted me.

She cast a wild glance over her shoulder, both sides of the street then back at me. "You can't just show up here."

"I think I totally can. And Jesus, where were you? What does a stay-at-home mom have going down on a Monday night?"

"You know Frank Wilder, the entertainment lawyer? I'm friends with his wife."

I had to throttle my laugh. Frank Wilder? Holy shit, if she had any idea.

"What do you want, Olivia?"

She was breathing heavy, deeply upset. Just like she should be.

"I like the neighborhood. It's dark, so I can't see all the

details, but I've seen so many that are exactly the same, it's easy to imagine."

She motioned toward her house. "Inside. Now!"

"I thought you'd never ask," I said, following Natalie toward the door.

"Wait in the entry while I kill the alarm."

"Definitely. We need to keep your family and all of your things safe."

She opened the door and walked inside, ignoring me.

It was kind of sad, really. So far as I could tell, Natalie was a pale reflection of who she used to be. The contrast between our lives was startling. I had designed mine around fun and freedom.

I'd been doing well for a decade, and I was hitting my stride. Jobs were getting more luxurious, and more lucrative. I had an upcoming trip to Spain that would begin in Barcelona, stop in Seville, and end in Ibiza — a dream come true that somebody else would be paying for.

But that's how you could describe most of my life.

"You're really lucky that Ryan and the kids aren't home," Natalie said.

"I'm lucky, or you're lucky? Because I would love to see them. It's been a while … about twelve years, right Natalie? Plus another nine months?"

"Are you going to tell me what you want? Or did you just come over to make me feel guilty?" She seemed to register what I was wearing, then eyed me up and down and said, "Jesus, did you just come from a job?"

"I'm on my way to one," I said as I walked toward the mantle, making a beeline for the neat row of family photos.

The one of them all together at Christmas.
The one of them all together on vacation.
The one of them all together at the beach.

Maybe she would want to add some of her newest photos to the collection.

It couldn't stop the stabbing jealousy I felt. This is the life I was supposed to have.

The life I could have had with Ryan.

"Why are you stopping here on your way to a job?"

"Because it's *your job*, Natalie. The one you flaked on. Victor's been trying to contact you all day. You're making me look bad, like you promised you wouldn't. I went out on a limb for—"

"Nobody ever said I *had* to take a job. It's still my decision."

"Are you kidding? Do you not remember signing a contract? You have to take at least ten clients, or buy your way out."

"This isn't fair, Olivia. You know I was drunk during all of that. I can't sleep with ten men. Besides, the business is illegal, so he can't enforce the contract."

"It just says *parties*."

"What?"

"The contract. It says *parties*. That's what you signed up for. It's like a modeling contract. And yes, you can fight it, but Victor will drag it out. That will cost you time and money. But worse, I can't imagine how hard it would be to keep a secret like that, fighting a lawsuit in private."

It was work, trying not to smile.

I offered her an audition because every new girl who worked out earned me a bonus, then kept on paying. There was no way to lose. If Natalie landed the gig, then I made a lot of money and would keep on making it, with my former friend cranking the karmic wheel. If it didn't work out, I wasn't losing anything, while Natalie would get some well-earned comeuppance, and I'd have a front row seat.

"You were totally shitfaced when you made the promise, so I guess I can understand your amnesia, but a contract is a contract. And besides …" I stepped closer to Natalie and made my voice more domineering. However bad she was feeling right now, it wasn't enough to make up for stealing Ryan. "Don't you think you owe me this? After what you did to me? You should be thanking me, *begging* for ways to repay me, to make karma right. Because even though you betrayed me, I was still a good friend and let you know that your husband was cheating."

"You did that to punish me."

"No, not at all." Okay, yes. "But that doesn't mean that I didn't believe you wanted help, or when you thanked me for the 'awesome opportunity.' It's up to—"

"So now you're my pimp?"

"Call it what you want, Natalie. But the two things I value more than anything else are my time and my reputation. You've now stolen one and soiled the other. I went out of my way for you with Victor. But instead of showing your gratitude, you ignored his texts all day, not giving a shit as to how that might affect my relationship with him, or the fact that I have to work tonight when I had other plans."

"Fine, Olivia. What do you want? How do I make you feel better about my not wanting to fuck someone for money tonight?"

"Don't you get it? This isn't about me. This is about Victor. You need to buy him out of your contract, or he will ensure that you or your family pays in some—"

"How much is the contract?"

"Twenty thousand dollars."

"How can it be that much?"

"Simple math, Nat. Ten clients times two grand each."

"That's the gross receipts — why should I have to pay a hundred percent of that to get out of the contract?"

"Because that's what you agreed to," I reminded her, trying not to smile. "We talked about all of this, in between your sixth and seventh drinks."

"Fuck you, Olivia."

The poor thing looked like she was going to cry. "Someone else is going to do that for you in about an hour and a half, so can we wrap this up?"

"You know I don't have twenty thousand dollars right now. That's the whole reason I was willing to talk to Victor."

I looked at Natalie's horrified expression, bleached of both color and faith. A sharp contrast with last year's Christmas photo, displaying her blushing cheeks and ignorant eyes.

I held the moment, let it inflate with her fear.

Her fingers are trembling. I wonder if she's more angry or scared, then realize that I don't really care. I did what I came here to do, and now it's time to get on with the rest of my night, and then the rest of my life after that.

I stared until she blinked.

Then I said, "Victor hates it when people waste his time." I let my expression turn hard. "And so do I. I'll take care of this for you, but if you ever screw me over again …" I waited three beats before finishing. "*I will ruin you.*"

Just as I hoped, Natalie looked terrified.

I turned back to the family pictures. Then, looking at them rather than Natalie, I said, "You might want to reconsider, if not now, then soon. It definitely looks like you could use a little fun, and it's never too late to redesign your life."

Natalie clenched her jaw, stood straighter, and crossed

her arms. "I'm married. Ryan and I will fix this, whatever it is."

I raised my eyebrows. "You think so?"

"Leave, Olivia. Now."

"You're not even going to say thank you?"

A tear slid down her cheek.

And *fuck*, that shouldn't make me feel bad, but it did.

I walked to the door, but turned back toward Natalie as I opened it. "When he texts you the next time, do the right thing and respond. For your sake. And for your children's."

Natalie turned away from me.

She shouldn't have done that.

"And Natalie?" I called out.

She turned back around.

"I took the first picture of Ryan a year ago. He's been doing this for a long time. Your love story is over for good, whether you want to admit it to yourself or not."

Natalie might have said something after that, but I didn't care.

I closed the door and I was gone.

NATALIE

THERE'S *no way in hell I'm sleeping with ten men.*

The thought kept looping inside my mind, getting louder every time I closed my eyes.

My home was filled with luxuries I couldn't afford, and the only one I wanted was sleep.

It was almost two in the morning, and all three attempts at silencing my parade of thoughts long enough to let some shut-eye find me had failed. So I got up to sit at the kitchen table with a mug of tea.

I loved our kitchen table. Long, with blond wood and shapely legs.

Like Olivia.

My family had eaten so many meals at that table together, but the context of my life had changed, and now I couldn't help but see everything differently, through a filter of betrayal and treachery. How many forkfuls of lies had been shoved down my throat without my even knowing it? And how many of those lies had I swallowed?

How is this my life?

Why was Olivia doing this to me? How could she still be mad after twelve years?

At least Ryan hadn't been home. I had no idea how I would've explained her sudden appearance.

I also had no idea how I would've stopped him from screwing her behind my back. Because the way my life was going right now, that's exactly what he would've tried to do.

More than anything, it hurt to admit that I didn't know my husband.

I didn't recognize him, because he was no longer the man that I married.

So if that changed everything, then who would I have to become to get my life back?

Who *could I even be,* with things the way they were? I had a measly $143.91 in savings, and that was a galaxy away from a fuck-off fund.

I couldn't afford to leave Ryan or pay off Victor.

I couldn't even afford to exist.

My stupid anthropology degree wasn't going to get me anywhere, except maybe as a salesgirl at Anthropology. They might think that was cute, if I put it on the application.

That was the third time I'd had that thought in the last

hour or so, and like the other two times it made me want to cry.

Then I thought all of our debt. That made me feel desperate for breath.

So. Much. Debt.

Sure, Ryan gave me enough to pay the minimum on my credit card bills each month, maybe a hundred dollars over. After doing that for years, the damage was now catastrophic. They were all maxed, and the truth was that I couldn't stop pickling in guilt and shame and the absolute humiliation that I had no one to blame but myself.

For my selfishness.

For my plastic wants.

For letting shopping become my narcotic.

Because now I had overdosed.

And I didn't know how to fix it.

Most of the stuff in our house I couldn't actually give a shit about, even though it had all felt great while the boxes and bags were still in my hands. True wealth was supposed to lie not in great possessions, but in very few wants. I was the opposite. I'd bought plenty of uncommon objects and artifacts to display our success throughout my married life, and yet that had only served my longing for more.

For so many years, and for too many things, I kept telling myself that I was doing right, giving my family exactly what they needed. But did Alec and Lena *need* the best schools, music and language lessons?

Of course, if we wanted them to have every opportunity.

Did they always need new clothes, and pretty much whatever they wanted?

And did I need my constant rotation of new clothes or spa days? How were they opening doors for our children?

The numbers made me hate myself.

But I forced myself to do the math.

I grabbed a blank notebook — I can't resist grabbing one whenever I'm at the bookstore — and tried to create a budget, assuming my total lack of work experience would land me a minimum wage job. Because — and this thought more than any other right then was making it really hard not to cry — I wasn't even qualified to be a barista. Though thinking about my total spent at Hill of Beans each day, and adding it up over the last twelve years, I'd paid for at least one employee's annual salary myself.

If I moved the kids into a shitty one-bedroom apartment, sharing a room with Lena so Alec could have his own ...

If I put the kids in public school and cancelled their tutors ...

If I traded the car in for a bus pass and if Alec watched Lena so I could pick up extra shifts ...

I gave up. There was no way I could keep my life on track as a barely employable single mom, even with a full-time job.

And that was assuming Ryan took complete responsibility for all the debt he'd taken out in my name. If he decided to stop paying, I'd spend the rest of my life with wages attached, unable to support my kids after the banks took their share. Or I'd have to declare bankruptcy.

My vision tunneled and tightness clamped down on my chest, making it hard to breathe. Panic or heart attack? And would it be so bad if it was the latter?

Except that I couldn't leave Alec and Lena to be raised by the kind of man who'd do this.

I grabbed Ryan's laptop and logged into his bank account again, hoping to see that fifteen thousand dollar deposit.

It wasn't there.

For the first time, I realized he might have a separate, secret account.

Panic squeezed my chest harder. I felt like my heart was going to pop.

Why would he need a separate account unless he wanted to be sure he could leave me without fear of retribution?

Ryan was a liar and a cheater, not of the garden *I made a mistake* variety. He was doing this professionally. It wasn't a question of *if* he would leave me saddled with debt, it was a question of when.

I wanted to kill him.

I had no one to turn to for help. My parents died in a car crash when I was in my early twenties. My grandparents on both sides were also gone. Ryan's parents would be glad to see me out of his life — I'd always been the slut who'd trapped their son into marriage by poking a hole in the condom. They'd loved Olivia, of course. Another of life's awesome ironies.

I had no friends outside of the circle of moms at school. Lynette and the gang would turn on me just like they'd turned on Theresa. Sticking together, that's what they'd call it. But it would just be more mean girl bullshit.

You could make all of this go away by working for Victor.

Ten nights, ten sexual encounters, twenty thousand dollars. And I'd be free to do whatever I wanted the rest of the month.

I'd be letting ten strangers use me.

Or would I be using them?

How did it even work?

Olivia and her friends had called me a whore, but if I did this, that's what I'd literally be.

In our women's studies class, the professor had talked about how our capitalistic patriarchy commoditizes women's bodies, then punishes women for taking control of the transaction. She'd told us about sacred harlots, the temple prostitutes who'd served as avatars of ancient goddesses like Inanna and Aphrodite. About the courtesans throughout history who'd wielded political influence during eras where women were literally the property of their fathers and husbands (in other words, almost all of them) — from Aspasia, lover of Pericles, to Veronica Franco, courtesan to the French king Henry III. About how women's sexuality shaped history behind the scenes, and how women bargained with their bodies, for money, education, and power.

We'd even had a former prostitute as a guest speaker. She told us a horror story about running away her abusive parents and living on the street before getting rescued from near-starvation by a pimp who'd been both her savior and new abuser. Half the class had been in tears by the time she'd finished, but in the discussion group later, as we'd prepared to write our papers, there'd been a sort of tacit agreement that *we'd* never stoop so low, no matter how bad things got.

What a bunch of judgmental bitches we were.

My paper concluded that although technically prostitution is a victimless crime, it contributed to the degradation of women and encouraged men to objectify women sexually, and therefore it should be legalized but frowned upon.

If I decided to honor the contract I'd made with Victor, I was going to find out if my middle-class college self knew what the fuck she was talking about.

I sincerely hoped so.

Chapter Four

Tuesday Morning ...

I PULLED into Constellation the next morning, looking out of my car window and deciding which of the two annoyances I wanted to ignore more. I could see Lynette, waiting for me to get out of my car. But I wasn't about to indulge her. I'd slept less than ninety minutes total last night, and after that shit she pulled with Theresa, I still wanted to deck her.

The other annoyance was Ryan: He wouldn't stop texting. Every message was another apology steeped in the lie that our marriage had become.

He's sorry for leaving things the way he did?

He's not saying that it isn't his fault, but work has really been stressing him out?

He misses me and loves me and can't wait to be back home?

Lying motherfucker.

He could wait until the weekend for an answer. Let him wonder if I'm mad.

And Lynette could go to hell.

I turned back around and looked at my children. They'd been subdued all morning, almost as if they knew that their beautiful little lives were about to crash. I'd done my best to keep them from seeing my anger, but we're all animals, and children instinctively know when Mommy isn't herself.

"I hope you two have a wonderful day," I said, smiling so hard my cheeks hurt. "I can't wait to hear all about it when I pick you back up!"

As soon as they were out of the car, I threw it into reverse, ignoring Lynette, who'd gotten out of her own car and started to walk toward me.

I was tempted to wallow. I couldn't afford to indulge in retail therapy anymore, and if I started on a bottle of Chardonnay this early in the morning, I'd be useless all day. I needed a plan, and I couldn't make one until I got some answers.

So I hopped on the highway and headed toward the only place I could think of where I might be able to get them.

The Conquest offices weren't far, located in a section of one of the larger buildings in one of the nicer office parks in that part of LA. A twenty-minute drive without any traffic, and probably just over an hour now.

Ryan had been working at Conquest since college when the founder, Dr. Ambrose, found and hired him. Ryan became his protégé, helping the good doctor to develop the Ambrose Method of Psychological Assessment.

I'd never cared for Ambrose. The guy could be perfectly charming, especially if he was about to be quoted, but he was also an attention whore, and unwilling to let the people around him take their fair share of credit. No matter how much my husband had contributed to developing the doctor's methodology, Ambrose never gave him an ounce of acknowledgement. At least not publicly.

Ryan always shrugged it off. To hear him tell it, Ambrose was all compliments and back slaps behind closed doors. And, of course, the money was excellent. Ryan said it was enough, but it never felt right to me. People should get credit for their work. Would it really hurt Ambrose to say a few thank yous every time he won an award?

As I took the elevator up to the fourteenth floor. I tried to remember the last time I had been there. Had it really been three years?

But some things hadn't changed: The same receptionist sat behind the same desk I remembered. I felt an odd and unsettling déjà vu, because although Nora looked happy to see me, she also looked awfully surprised in the most disquieting way.

"Mrs. Monroe! Can I help you with something?"

Her smile looked genuine, but slightly askew, as though it was hard for her to hold. Maybe she knew Ryan's secret and it hurt her to keep it. Or maybe she was just afraid of getting fired if she allowed me to figure it out.

"Ryan's away on his business trip and he forgot something in his office," I lied, "so I told him I'd swing by and grab it."

A shot of Nora's face in that moment would have made the perfect emoji for *whatintheactualfuck?*

"I'm sorry, Mrs. Monroe … Ryan hasn't worked here since December of last year. He left just before Christmas."

The moment that followed was long and tense. Utterly silent. Almost theatrical. I imagined an audience leaning forward in their seats, like magnets to the ore of our performance. That flipped a switch inside me.

I started laughing. Inappropriately. Almost hysterically.

Ryan had quit his job ten months ago without telling me. But that lie paled in comparison to the rest. It was almost anticlimactic, really.

"Are you okay, Mrs. Monroe?

Nora wasn't asking for me; she was asking if *she* was okay -- probably wondering if I was less than a minute from totally losing my shit and somehow taking her with me.

I tried to stop laughing. It was harder than you'd think. All the rage and frustration and hopelessness that I'd been bottling up were trying to use the door that the laughter had opened in my heart. Any minute I was going to be screaming. Or bawling. Or worse.

I slammed that door shut on my seething emotions and forced myself to take a deep breath.

"I must be completely brain dead today. You'll have to forgive me," I managed to say. "I meant to go to his new office and came here out of habit instead. I'm such a ditz!"

She smiled at me with relief and said she hoped I had a good day.

Fat fucking chance.

I'd gotten the answer I needed, and I had my plan.

I called Olivia.

Chapter Five

Tuesday Afternoon ...

I SHOULD HAVE GONE with the landing strip.

Danni, the bubbly esthetician at Pretty Pretty Pussycat had done everything in her power to dissuade me, but I refused to listen.

"You don't need to do this. There are other perfectly acceptable alternatives that won't hurt as much," Danni had said. "Since this is your first time, I would suggest a landing strip."

But no. I *had* to go with the Brazilian. I *had* to overcommit. I *had* to prove to Danni and her perfectly waxed collegiate vaj that my MILF bits were up to the challenge.

If I couldn't handle this, how was I going to handle having sex with a man who wasn't my husband?

By the time Danni ordered me into downward dog, thus stripping me of all remaining dignity, I had half a mind to scream that this biscuit wasn't going to bring home the bacon.

Okay, I never would have said that.

But there was no doubt that I would never be the same woman again.

I closed my eyes, counting the seconds until Danni finished dashing powder on my snatch, punctuated with despondently aggressive comments.

Well, I guess we can get the rest next time.

It usually takes a few rounds.

I don't want to irritate the skin by going over it again now.

My pain was a nine out of ten, and I'd given birth twice. I thanked my daily yoga practice throughout the ordeal; I probably would have died without it. Not really, but seriously, *fuck.*

And this was something I was supposed to *get better at.*

I would have to come back for a second round that would supposedly be easier to suffer through than the first, to finish what I couldn't tolerate this time. Danni promised that it would get easier after that, and that my hair would grow back thinner and lighter as well.

I thanked Danni, thinking that was bullshit while I was doing it, then got myself out of there.

It got worse after that. I had to walk, okay *limp,* through the waiting room packed with women and one lone man, who sat dead center like a bullseye among them.

This was peak humiliation.

I told myself that I'd better get used to it.

I had to call Ryan — I mean on the phone, not just *motherfucker* in my mind like I'd been doing for two days.

I hobbled out to my car, dialing him on the way.

"Hi honey!" the asshole practically chirped, laying it on even thicker than honey. "What are you up to?"

"Oh nothing. Just having lunch with the girls. How's New York?"

... You lying pile of shit.

"It's good. I miss you … and I wanted to call and apologize for the way we left things yesterday morning."

"I understand, the way work is riding you … Ambrose is a taskmaster."

Then I shut up, giving him a chance to correct me, tell me the truth.

But Ryan refused to take it. "I'm looking forward to being back home. Just another couple of days."

"Is that it?"

I wasn't trying to be short with him. Honestly, I didn't even want him to know I was pissed off, since that would make what I had to do that much harder to execute. But I couldn't help thinking that he had Kong-sized balls, and I wanted to cut them off and drop them into the blender for my morning shake.

Of course he kept right on lying.

He told me some bullshit about having dinner with the CEO and I had to pretend I was impressed and that I wished I could be there with him.

Fuck him for putting me in this position.

I had never been so humiliated, never felt this much pain and impotent anger.

I wanted to fall apart, painful as that was to admit. But I couldn't afford to do that. I had my children to worry about, and the rest of my life to rebuild.

Places to be and strangers to fuck.

"Thank you for calling," I practically cooed, trying to extricate myself from the call without making him suspicious that I was onto him. "Your sorry means a lot to me."

Ryan was silent on the other end, likely my sudden enthusiasm had thrown him. I guess I'd laid it on a little thick too.

"I'm always disappointed with myself when I let you down."

I sighed, like I was really feeling sorry for that bleeding hemorrhoid of a man. "I should be doing a better job of taking care of you at home."

He could have told me that I was enough, or said anything other than, "I know you try your best."

He did *not* just say that.

"What do you mean?" I kept my tone curious, almost playful, like I didn't want to scratch his eyes out.

"Nothing?"

More silence.

With perfect timing I got a text on my burner. "Sorry, I've got to take this call. Love you, bye!"

I checked my secret phone — Victor, giving me my last chance, a client in LA on Thursday night. Show up or fork over twenty thousand dollars to break my contract.

He also made it clear that if I decided to ignore him or bring lawyers into our relationship, I would regret it in ways that I could not imagine.

Victor also wanted me to know that Olivia had convinced him to give me one last chance. So if I fucked him, I would also be fucking my friend.

There weren't any details about the client, only that I was supposed to meet him at the Alliance Hotel, at nine p.m., sharp.

Two grand for an hour. Victor and Olivia would split twenty percent off the top, but the rest would be mine.

I texted back: *I'll be there.*

And suddenly it was real.

In a little over two days I would have sex with a man who wasn't my husband.

He'd be a stranger. But it would be an honest exchange, his money for my body. No lies, no cheating, no broken promises.

You can do this, Natalie.

I kept swallowing my nerves and telling myself that everything would be fine.

This was a one-time thing. A means to an end. I was doing this to get the money I needed to leave Ryan and protect the kids.

I was in.

But first, I needed some goddamned aloe.

Chapter Six

Thursday Night ...

I WAS IN THE ELEVATOR, trying not to be sick.

It wasn't like the motion of the elevator was getting to me, even though I was going all the way to the penthouse. The nausea was coming from the motion of my life that had brought me here. I could no longer pretend I wasn't about to hit a very personal point of no return.

I'd spent the day before throwing up every little thing that I ate. I was hoping that this client — I still had zero information about him from Victor — didn't want to drink. The way I was feeling as the elevator doors dinged open to the top floor, a couple of drops might be enough to get me drunk.

My phone buzzed.

I took it out of my purse to check, stalling.

It was Olivia:

Don't make me look bad.

Thanks for the encouragement, Olivia.

Not sure what I would do without a friend like her.

Besides being safe at home with the lie, and not about to sell myself for money.

I shoved the phone into my purse and walked faster down the hall, toward the large white double doors at the end.

What if this guy is like Victor?

It doesn't matter if he's just like Victor or not. You don't have to like the guy; you just have to fuck him until he's satisfied, or until his time is up.

I knocked on the door, heart pounding, waiting for it to swing open from the other side.

Nothing happened, so I knocked again, not sure how much more my poor heart could take.

Third time's a charm.

But before I could knock, the door swung open and I couldn't believe what I was looking at.

I tried to say *hello*, but nothing came out. I'd realized that my client could be well-known — Victor was catering to Hollywood in the aftermath of the Rosebud scandal, after all — but I still couldn't have imagined that it would be one of my favorite actors.

Bennett Cole had been voted the Sexiest Man Alive twice in the past decade. One of my favorite pictures was of a two-year-old Alec holding a *People* magazine with Bennett's sexy self on the cover, pretending to be reading.

Bennett Cole was about to pay me to fuck him.

I was suddenly worried that I wouldn't be able to do it, but for an entirely different set of reasons.

Bennett appeared amused. He opened the door wider and stepped to the side. "Would you like to come in?"

"Of course," I finally managed, then entered. Bennett closed the door and I offered him my hand.

"Elle," I said as he kissed it.

His smile turned into a laugh. "Is this your first time, Elle?"

Well, that was humiliating. I was so apparently terrible at this that the truth was tattooed on my expression, or maybe my body language. It might have been my total lack of voice.

"I guess it's not yours," I responded after a beat, then wondered if that would be rude.

But Bennett just laughed harder. And still, it sounded kind.

"That doesn't bother me," he said, gently taking me by the arm and leading me over to the couch. "Would you believe me if I told you that the thought of my being your first is thrilling?"

That sent a warm flush through my center. "You're very direct."

Bennett gave me another smile, his best one so far. "Do you know why you're here?"

There were many reasons, but I wasn't sure which he was looking for.

"So that we can have sex?" I said, like I was auditioning for the lead in Unsexy Escort. "So you can fuck me."

Another smile, this one soft, followed by a tiny chuckle. "I meant you specifically."

"I have no idea."

"I'm sure you've heard about the security leak at Rosebud, and I'm sure you can understand that discretion is my number-one priority. I asked Victor for the girl he thinks would be best at keeping a secret. Did he make the right decision, Elle?"

I nodded.

Bennett eyed me up and down. "You do seem like

someone with something to lose." He kissed me softly on the back of my neck and removed my coat like a gentleman. More like we were coming home from an anniversary date than being mere minutes from me debasing myself for money.

"And, you look stunning," he finished.

"Thank you."

He gestured toward the sofa. "Would you like to sit?"

I nodded and sat, figuring that was what I was supposed to do.

"Would you care for something to drink?"

I felt the emptiness in my stomach again, but then heard Olivia in my head.

You do whatever it takes to keep the client happy. You got it?

I wanted Bennett to be happy with me. "Yes, please."

It's not just about the sex, Natalie. It's about the companionship and the conversation.

"What would you like?"

"Whatever you're having," I said.

But I had no idea what he was having, and just about shit when I saw that it was a bottle of Château des Rêves Bordeaux. I'm no connoisseur, but I've seen that same bottle selling for hundreds of dollars.

I wondered what Lynette would think if she saw Bennett Cole pouring me this glass of overpriced wine.

She'd probably shit her pants.

He handed the glass to me. "2009 was a great year for Medoc Bordeaux."

I took the glass and inhaled, then nodded, looking up at Bennett with appreciative doe eyes. "Thank you."

"Do you prefer Cab-dominant versus Merlot-dominant wines as well?"

"I do," I lied, not because it was untrue, but because I had no idea what I was actually saying.

Not that it mattered. I was here to be Bennett's dream girl. So yes, I definitely preferred Cab-dominant wines.

We clinked glasses and I took a sip.

The wine was velvety on my tongue, almost syrupy with the taste of dark cherry, tobacco leaves, and spices I couldn't quite identify. I smiled.

So far, so good.

Half an hour later, we were both deep into our second glass, and I was getting anxious for the main event. It took me a while to realize that Bennett was not. For him, this *was* the main event, and I needed to slow down enough that I could start enjoying it along with him.

I was feeling looser by the sip, willing to open up that much more. Bennett seemed to enjoy peeling away the layers, and always like a gentleman. It made me a little uncomfortable at first, realizing that he was genuinely enjoying watching *me* enjoying *myself.*

But then I heard Olivia yelling at me again, reminding me that it's not just about the sex, but the conversation, and that I needed to do whatever I could to keep the client happy.

So I answered all of Bennett's questions as honestly as I could.

That honesty got easier. Not because of the wine, but because he actually listened, unlike Ryan. At first I was worried that I shouldn't be talking about my family, or the many problems in my marriage, despite the fact that he asked.

But it didn't take long before the box was open, and all of my grievances came spilling out.

And he understood. While emptying the remaining Château des Rêves into our glasses, Bennett said, "Sharing your thoughts and feelings is a vulnerable moment for you, and when your husband refuses to give you his full attention, it leaves you feeling rejected. So it's not your fault when you pull back. That's instinct, to avoid more rejection. Honestly, it sounds like it's his fault for letting you recoil, rather than pulling you into his arms, looking into your eyes, and letting you know that he's there to listen. If he did that, I imagine you wouldn't be here with me now."

And that was all it took to get me wet.

When was the last time I had felt like this? So sexy and desired, even though he had yet to lay a finger on me.

"I want you to get undressed now ..."

I hadn't been wearing much under my coat. Now I was wearing even less. Just the thinnest gossamer blush-colored slip up top, and matching panties below. But for some reason, I was no longer worried about those few extra pounds.

How could I be, the way that one of the most famous movie stars in the world was eyeing me?

Like he wanted to devour every inch of my body.

I looked down at myself. Yes, I'd had two children, but I still looked good.

Even better, I *felt* good.

Lit by a genuine spark. Confident. Self-assured.

More like myself than I had felt in a long, long time.

Maybe it was the wine; maybe it was Bennett's seemingly genuine sympathy.

Or maybe it was all the times I'd fantasized about Bennett while I was fucking Ryan.

Except that in my fantasies, I wasn't his whore.

WE WERE forty-one minutes into our hour, according to the gorgeous Perigold wall clock I kept trying not to look at. Was I supposed to make the first move, or was I supposed to wait for him to?

My body had been warmed on a molecular level. I felt like I could come from the sound of his voice alone. I couldn't even begin to imagine what it was going to feel like with him inside me.

And I couldn't believe that I was going to have the chance to find out.

Or that my first time getting paid to fuck would be with one of the world's biggest movie stars, a man I couldn't have even imagined as a john just a few days before.

At least not a john for a Plain Jane like me.

I reached over and touched his face, stroked his cheek with my thumb. I'm not sure why I started there. It just felt right. I wanted to kiss him long and hard on the mouth. Forget Julia Roberts and what she said in *Pretty Woman*, I wanted to taste him. But maybe she was right, because that didn't feel quite right either.

My fingers fell to his lap, then to his zipper.

But then his hand fell on top of mine, and I looked up to see Bennett shaking his head.

"You first."

I wasn't sure what he meant, but I couldn't let him know that, so I said, "But I want to taste you."

He let me take his cock out of his pants.

It was hot in my hand.

I tightened my grip.

"Kiss the tip," he told me. "Then put him away."

Put him away?

But I kissed the tip, with a little sweep of my tongue around the top, then down and back up his shaft. It was more than what he told me to do, but I was really wet. That's probably why I went back to the top, pursed my lips at the top, and slowly lowered my mouth all the way down the base, before sliding back off of the top.

Bennett groaned. Then he murmured, "Put him away. *It's your turn.*"

And then I got it.

I thought.

He wanted to watch *me* pleasure *myself.*

But I couldn't do that.

This was supposed to be a duet, not a solo. I was frozen.

How was I supposed to perform with stage fright?

I finished putting Bennett's cock back into his pants. It wasn't easy, with him being so hard. I wondered if he was in pain, and if maybe that was part of the pleasure.

"I want you to make yourself come."

I wanted *him* to make me come — in my fantasies, he made all the moves.

But the customer is always right, especially when that customer is Bennett Cole.

Blushing and hoping that he didn't notice, I leaned back on the sofa, peeled off my panties, and dropped them onto the polished hardwood floor.

Then I spread my legs, imagining Bennett inside me, and using my fingers to play pretend.

He smiled, still so obviously hard in his pants, but made no move to touch me.

That was hot too. I was starting to understand the appeal of this *wanting to watch* thing. Ryan and I had never done it, probably because Ryan wanted to get in and get off as soon as he could. Even when we first fell in love, Ryan had never appreciated looking at me the way Bennett seemed to.

Bennett said, "Put them inside you."

I assumed he meant my already-glistening fingers. "How many?"

"Two," he said.

I slipped a pair inside myself, made a little hook, and moved it around, my legs spreading wider, eyes rolling back into my head, toes curling.

Then just like that, and totally unexpected, I came, surprisingly hard.

"Good job," he said.

I held my two fingers in front of his face. "Do you want to taste me?"

He did. But Bennett swatted my hand away, and went for the real thing.

It was even better than in my fantasies. It took everything inside me not to scream.

I wondered if maybe I was supposed to. I moaned, and he got more enthusiastic.

Then I did scream a little.

Bennett stood and slowly undressed, starting with his shirt to reveal his chest. Next came his belt, and his pants falling to the floor. No underwear, just that impressive cock.

No condom.

And Olivia in my head: *For the money they spend, most of them aren't going to want a condom. Technically, you can refuse.*

I reminded myself that this was why I was here, to give him whatever he wanted.

I wasn't sure where to look.

Part of me wanted to watch him enter me, but the other part wanted to stare right into his eyes.

Did he want that? Or would it be too intimate?

He slid inside me.

The sensation was wrong, and delicious — all the more so, I realized with shock, because of how very wrong it was.

Apparently my vagina has muscle memory, and it could tell that the penis inside me wasn't Ryan's.

It was better.

"You feel amazing," Bennett said. Ryan never talked once he'd gotten inside me.

I wondered what Ryan would think if he saw me now.

That was even hotter.

Fuck you, Ryan.

Bennett started to thrust.

With one orgasm already behind me, the second one followed fast.

This time I did look into his eyes.

And Bennett stared back.

His breathing became heavier as he moved faster. Beads of sweat formed on his lean chest.

He stopped and ordered me to turn around then get on all fours.

So I did.

And then I did everything else after that.

We went over our time but I didn't care.

I wanted to stay as long as he'd have me.

"I'm going to cum in your mouth," he groaned.

I nodded, and he pulled out.

I dutifully put his cock in my mouth.

I ran my fingers over my clit, then two fingers in to fill the emptiness he'd left behind.

I felt my own pleasure rise to the precipice yet again as he finished.

I didn't remember swallowing.

I couldn't believe that I was getting paid for this trip to nirvana.

The bed felt like heaven. I leaned back and looked over toward the bar and another unopened bottle of Château des Rêves.

But reality was a bitch.

"That was wonderful, thank you. There's an envelope

on the counter." Then Bennett pointed vaguely toward the door.

Ouch. It was like being doused in ice water.

But what was I expecting? That because I'd been in lust with Bennett for years, he'd spend a couple hours with me and fall in love?

He just paid you to fuck him; he's not looking to fall in love.

I dressed, took the money, and left without a word.

I needed to be more careful. I couldn't afford to let my emotions get tangled up in this. I'd gotten lucky. My first job had been a man I was already attracted to, and he'd turned out to be the kind of lover who gets off on his partner's pleasure. The next client wouldn't be Bennett Cole.

But at least now I knew I could do this. And now I knew my way out of the mess that Ryan had made of my life.

One down, nine to go.

Chapter Seven

Friday Morning …

MELINDA

THE FUTURE of Blush was sitting right in front of me. I was *certain* of it.

"Thank you again, Mrs. Shelly—"

"Melinda. *Please*," I said.

Seriously. How many times did I have to tell this one? His earnestness was endearing, but I only wanted true subordinates to call me Mrs. Shelly. I wanted Ryan Monroe on board as a partner.

"Sorry. *Melinda.* I just wanted to tell you how grateful I am for the opportunity to work with Shellter this year. You have no idea how much you guys have helped me and my family."

"I think I might have *some* idea. The operative word is *family*. I'm sure you can see that even though we don't have children of our own, Dominic and I treat Shellter as our family. That's why we're having this meeting here, rather than in our offices."

I gestured around our yard to remind him, sweeping my hand across the back of the house, from the patio where we were sitting to the infinity pool with a view butting up against a sprawling view of the city below.

Ryan had a lot going for him, which means he had a lot going for us. He didn't quite understand the power of his natural gifts, but Dominic and I would help Ryan to know himself better, nurture those gifts for our mutual benefit.

He had the unique ability to *see* people. He knew how to look into the heart of their truths, to understand their secrets, and interpret the DNA of their character.

"Really, Ryan, buying you out of your debts to Conquest and Dr. Ambrose was the best decision we ever made."

That was my cue to give the man what he had been waiting for.

I reached into my purse and grabbed my wallet, then withdrew the check, neatly folded for this very moment.

I slid it across the table.

Ryan picked it up, then unfolded it and read the number. His face flushed with relief.

He folded it back up and slipped it into his jacket pocket, breaking into a laugh as he did.

"I'm officially debt-free for the first time since I was twenty!" This was followed by another long and hearty laugh. "I'll never take another loan — especially from an employer — again."

I'd met Ryan last year when Conquest sent him to do some assessments for Dominic and me during a hiring spree. I'd seen his potential and invited him to have a drink. It didn't take me long to learn all I needed to know, that he was in hock up to his elbows to his former boss Ambrose a dozen years ago. He'd started working for the man right out of college, and after struggling to support his new family, he'd needed a helping hand. His debt to Ambrose had been snowballing for a decade. It was easy to see how he had fallen into the trap, and even easier to see how Ambrose had laid it.

By the time I had my first conversation with Ryan, he owed Conquest just over a million dollars.

But he was worth at least ten times that to us.

His work on contracts for Shellter since the beginning of the year had been exceptional. Now, with the fallout from the Rosebud scandal clearing a path for Blush, I wanted him to stay on permanently.

It had been a piece of cake, making that scandal happen.

All we'd needed was a couple of moles within the Rosebud organization, paying them to feed us information. Getting their stories onto *Hollywood Hunted* was simple, especially since Ellis Hunter was always looking for new ways to rouse the Hollywood rabble, and like a fool, he believed that his identity behind the blog was a secret.

These weren't exactly the days of Heidi Fleiss. The world was different, and so was the industry. Sex itself was practically different. In the '90s, Fleiss had run a premium ring that catered to the rich and famous. She'd made more than a million dollars in her first four months, and at her peak, was generating nearly a hundred grand in commissions per night.

We were going to make Fleiss look like an amateur.

Ryan understood none of this. But he knew a good deal when he saw one. One year of work for Shellter, and we'd pay everything he owed.

"Your contract work over the last year has been exceptional. We would be thrilled if you were interested in making a permanent home here at Shellter."

As expected, it wasn't an immediate home run.

Fine with me. Dominic liked his fish to gobble the bait, but sometimes I preferred a slower reel.

I would get my man either way. Ryan's method was revolutionary, steeped in meticulous research. Who cared if it skirted the lines of traditional ethics? And who cared if it cost millions to make this happen? It would be worth the risk, and the cost, in the long run.

"Has your work in this last year fulfilled you?" I asked.

He brightened immediately. "Oh, absolutely. The best of my professional career."

"So you liked working with us here at Shellter better than with Conquest?"

"Oh yes, absolutely."

"Why is that?"

"Autonomy. You guys told me what you needed, then let me figure out the best way to do it. I was able to try new things, and that allowed me to more deliberately develop the method."

"Exactly," I said. "That's exactly the kind of thinking we need. Can you tell me what you didn't like about working with us?"

"Oh, there's nothing like that … Shellter is great. But I don't know how much longer I can keep it secret from my wife. If she knew I'd slept with some of the subjects—"

"But the buyout from Ambrose made it all worth it?"

Ryan smiled. "Absolutely."

"Yet you're not sure if that's the life you would like to continue?"

"Right." Ryan nodded, still smiling.

"I assume that you are open to hearing our offer? You're not *opposed* to working with Shellter again?"

"No, not opposed. And yes, I'm definitely curious."

"Let me just ask you a few more questions. I'd love to understand where you're coming from so that I can refine our offer. Will that be okay?"

Ryan said yes, but squirmed in his seat.

Good.

"I can tell from the things you say that family is important, but I'd like to get a little more specific there. Is it being the provider that's the most painful thing for you? Or maybe not *painful* exactly, but would you say that's one of the biggest sources of pressure?"

"Absolutely."

He answered immediately, almost involuntarily, like a cough.

I could see it on his face — it had been a long time since anyone had acknowledged his sacrifice. I was seeing both the comfort of being understood, and the pain of its rarity. I imagined his wife. Ungrateful. Spoiled. *Ruined.*

Ryan might need a lesson in unanswered prayers.

Leaving his wife might be a blessing. With his looks and his brain, he could have a better life than he was pursuing right now.

"So, I'm trying to understand your objection. I just cleared a year's worth of debt, and invited you to do it again, but better than the first time. What is it that doesn't appeal to you?"

"I told you, I'm not comfortable with all the lies. This last year has been a means to an end."

"What about the next year?"

"I don't need the money now." He laughed uncomfortably.

"We all need money. I'm sure your wife likes a lot of nice things -- a million dollars is a lot to owe at your age, and I really doubt that you spent all that money by your-self, Ryan."

He reddened. That hit home. I'd bet they fought about money all the time.

"Sure, you could be an independent consultant," I continued. "But that's a lot of shit travel and hunting around for work, when you could make five times as much for a quarter of the effort with Shellter."

I let that sink in. There was a long thirty seconds where Ryan didn't know what to say. I used every one to study him. Yes, I was willing to pay, but I needed to know he would follow through on his commitments once a perma-nent part of the team. Blush was a crucial piece in the larger game.

"Would you like another twenty-four hours?"

Ryan shook his head. A pained, conflicting look appeared on his face.

"I don't think I need the twenty-four hours. I'm not going to take the job."

I laughed, wanting him to feel small so that he might need to feel bigger. "You'll never get an easier job for less hours and more money in your life."

"I know," the pained lines in his face deepened. "But I have a wife. And kids. Helping you to staff a lineup for Blush would require me to go too far."

I laughed louder, and harder. "Haven't you already crossed that line helping us out with all the other assess-ments? *For the last year?*"

"Well, yes, that's true" Ryan said, shifting in his seat as though he had an army of worms in his pants. "But only when it was absolutely necessary."

I crossed my arms, looking at Ryan across the table and trying to figure him out.

Was he playing me for more money like Dominic had warned me he might? Or was he earnest like I'd argued?

"Mind if I ask you a series of questions?"

He shrugged. "Shoot."

"Okay, answer them fast. Don't think. First question: What's your favorite ice cream?"

"Cookies and cream."

"Have you ever been to Milwaukee?"

"No."

"Thick or thin crust?"

"Thin."

"Sword or gun?"

"Sword."

"Breakfast, lunch, or dinner?"

"Dinner."

"Book or movie?"

"Movie."

"Have you ever wanted to visit Australia?"

"Yes."

"Have you ever wanted to sit courtside at a Lakers game?"

"Yes."

"Have you ever wanted to sleep with someone other than your wife?"

"Yes." And then he stopped, having realized what he just admitted.

"Don't feel bad," I soothed him. "That's human nature. We're supposed to fuck other people, and if you don't buy that, then we can at least agree that it's a normal desire."

Ryan said nothing, as expected.

So I pressed. "Do you agree?"

A reluctant nod, then, "I guess."

"So stop worrying. I shouldn't need to remind you that

privacy is our top priority. If we can keep secrets for the city's elite, then we can sure as hell keep them from you. Your wife will never have to know what you're up to. Just tell her that you're managing human resources for Shellter, which in a way, you are."

But unbelievably, Ryan still hadn't given me his *Yes*.

"I don't know," he said, his eyes telling me *No*.

But I really, really needed him. More than I wanted to admit.

Ryan Monroe was the only one who could do this right, who could do everything that Dominic and I would need him to do. I couldn't afford to lose him.

"Fair enough. But how about we do one job just to find out if it's something you're interested in permanently?"

Ryan nodded his head. "Maybe. Just give me a couple of weeks to go home and reset. Then we'll talk."

I couldn't afford to let him walk out of there before he'd talked himself into a *Yes*.

So again, I laughed. "You know we move faster than that around here. No pressure, but I think you're right for this, and I wouldn't want to start looking elsewhere until I have a firm no from you. But on the other hand, I know Dominic won't want me sitting around waiting. I'll make you one final offer, and if you like it *great*. If not, no big deal."

His eyes were curious.

My heart was pounding.

"Okay," he said, carefully. "What's the offer?"

"Like I said, one small job to see if you like it. I want you to assess Jess Lindley."

Ryan was already shaking his head. "Wasn't she recently in the hospital for an OD? She might be too fragile. Even if I agreed to enter a 'relationship' or have a one-night stand with a woman under false pretenses, that doesn't mean I'm willing to inflict permanent damage. It just isn't ethical. I do need to maintain *some* professional standards."

He was getting indignant. I didn't like that.

I leaned forward. "Oh, please. I think we blurred the boundaries beyond what's considered ethical months ago. With *your* method. You wouldn't want that getting out now, would you?"

I stared at him, waited for Ryan to shake his head, then continued.

"A hundred thousand dollars for the assessment, then a 250 thousand dollar signing bonus if you want a contract after that. But you keep the first six figures regardless."

He stared at me, unable to believe the offer. Exactly as I'd hoped.

So I brought it home.

"The offer expires in five minutes."

But Ryan didn't even need one.

Chapter Eight

Monday Evening …

NATALIE

I WAS HELPING Lena with her homework before dinner, trying to pretend I hadn't forgotten how fractions work while also ignoring my burner phone, which was — and had been — constantly buzzing for the past half hour.

"Who keeps calling you?"

"It's spam," I told her.

"Like what you get in your email?"

"Yes, but these people are using the phone."

"To sell you things?"

"Right!" I sounded excited, but only because I'd just figured out how to reduce the fraction in front of me.

"What do they want to sell you?"

"Health insurance."

"Are you going to buy some?"

"No, honey." *Someone's going to buy me.*

I had done two more jobs since Bennett, with another seven to go. Apparently word had gotten out that Victor had a new MILF on staff, and I guess people were into the mom thing.

Neither of the other two clients had matched the bliss of my encounter with Bennett. I almost wish he hadn't been the first. But he'd taught me the most important lesson that a girl in my new profession needed to master: *Never get emotionally attached to a client.*

Speaking of people I was no longer emotionally attached to, Ryan walked into the living room and joined us.

He looked down at the math and said, "Need any help?"

"Nope, we've got it."

"Sure, Daddy!"

Ryan smiled and sat on the other side of Lena.

I suddenly wanted very much to answer that last text. Or be anywhere my husband wasn't.

I couldn't even look at him.

He was such a phony, practically smothering me in affection ever since coming back home. Almost like he was a new man. I don't know when was the last time I'd seen him so relaxed and happy. But my skin crawled every time he touched me.

Ryan felt like more of a stranger than the men I was letting inside me. At least my clients weren't pretending to care about me. My time with them felt more honest than my marriage did.

If my clients were cheating, then they were doing it to someone else. Not me.

"Perfect," I said, sliding the homework over to Ryan. "I need a break."

He took the paper and immediately began working out

the problems, while I asked about his trip to New York. I'd avoided the conversation so far — because I knew how much it would piss me off — but I was finally ready.

"So how did the assessments with the startup go?"

He answered without looking up from the fractions. "Really great, actually. The boss for this project is really smart. She has big plans, and she appreciates my work."

"The boss ... it's not Ambrose?"

"No." He shook his head without looking up. "Not for this project."

"So who is it?"

"I'm not supposed to say, but it's a woman."

It's a woman?

Was he baiting me?

"Did you have much time to see the sights?"

He laughed. "No. Not at all."

"Remember when you took me to New York for our anniversary? I had so much fun. All the restaurants. You didn't have time for *anything*?"

"The project is intense, Natalie." There it was, the edge finding his voice. "There wasn't free time for anything. I never got out of the hotel."

"Didn't you grab dinner with the CEO?"

"Yes. In the hotel."

I had to give Ryan credit. He was good, answering every one of my questions with ease. If Olivia hadn't shown me those pictures, I never would've suspected.

He would keep lying. Because if Ryan was to tell me even one truth, then I could pull at the string and unravel his whole ball of yarn.

He finished another fraction and slid the paper to Lena. "Now it's your turn. Follow my example to solve it, but I need to see your work."

"Okay, Daddy!"

Fuck you, Ryan.

Alec entered the room, looking shy like he did when he wanted to ask something.

"What's up?" I asked.

He looked from me to his father, then his shy eyes settled somewhere in between us. "I was just wondering if we could have a family movie night."

"Of course," Ryan responded before me. "But why are you asking like that?"

I was wondering the same thing. Alec sounded like the saddest child alive.

"It's just that you're always traveling, and Mom's been out a lot more recently. Since you're both home ..."

My stomach dropped.

I really wish he hadn't said that.

Ryan's eyebrows bunched together. He turned to me while still speaking to Alec. "You mean at nighttime? During or after dinner?"

"Yes," I answered before either of the children could. "I've been spending a lot more time with some of the moms from school."

Ryan was much too observant. Now he was suspicious. So I had to turn the screw.

Conspiratorially, I whispered, "Sometimes it's fun, but usually it's the worst."

"Then why do you go?" Ryan asked.

I shrugged, acted like I didn't really want to express myself or admit this particular truth, then waited a beat and said, "I guess their company really helps me to deal with the loneliness. Like Alec said, you're always traveling."

That hit him for sure, but I couldn't tell exactly how. Ryan seemed to be studying me, and he was definitely processing. It looked like guilt, and that would make sense, but what did I know? He'd been cheating for a year at

least, and it had taken an old frenemy wanting to manipulate me into indentured servitude for the truth to come out.

Ryan had seemed so happy since coming back home
this time, or at least he'd held the facade. But now he
looked visibly upset.

"I'm sorry I've been gone so much," he said, sounding
like he meant it. "Things will be changing soon."

You bet your cheating dick they will be.

"You're gone so much, it's getting harder for me to
even keep the calendar straight," I said, figuring that I
might as well keep turning the screw, maybe buy myself a
little more leeway if he noticed something else. "I know
you have another trip coming up, but I'm not even sure
where it is, or how long you'll be gone."

"Wednesday," he reminded us. "I'll be assessing for a
firm in Atlanta, but I'll be home by the weekend."

He still seemed suspicious.

Fine with me, I'd been more than that for a while.

And fuck him with his phony trip to Atlanta. This time
I was going to follow him, and see exactly where he went.

Chapter Nine

Wednesday Evening ...

OLIVIA

NATALIE WAS LEANING against the door to my condo.

I saw her a second before she saw me and had just enough time to wonder what in the fuck she was doing here.

Natalie turned toward me, or toward the sound of my clacking heels. She half-smiled, but it didn't keep her from looking pathetic. Quite the opposite, really.

She was dressed like a total mom. Not even a MILF, just a regular old juice box-packing, carpool-driving, PTA-attending mom in jeans, flats, and a cardigan, her hair pulled back like she just got back from her weekly book club, where all the idiot housewives were discussing something insipid like *Fifty Shades of Suburban Bullshit.*

"What are you doing here?" I asked, because she didn't deserve a *hello.*

"I need a favor," Natalie said, though I'm not sure it was too early in the exchange to use the word *beg*. She sounded so goddamned needy.

There was a part of me that loved it, seeing her so low.

"A favor?" I laughed. "Sorry honey, but I don't do favors."

I went to unlock my door, hoping she would just go away, knowing she wouldn't.

"Please, Ol—"

"Aren't you supposed to be with a client tonight?" I stepped inside, but blocked the opening. No, she couldn't come in. I had to admit, the girl was already proving herself to be an excellent earner. According to Victor, Natalie's clients were thrilled, and that extra ten percent was adding up to a nice little bonus for me.

But none of that meant I was going to let the betrayer into my home.

"My next client is tomorrow, and I'll do what I'm supposed to, but tonight I need you to help me."

The way Natalie said that last part actually hurt, the emphasis on *you* serving as a stiff reminder of how close we used to be, before she seduced Ryan away from me. "What's the favor?"

"I need to get into Cameo."

I laughed, long and hard. I wasn't even trying to be unkind. Sure, I could get Natalie inside, but fuck her for asking. Cameo was one of the most exclusive clubs in LA. It was always swarming with celebrities, the kind of place where entry was impossible unless you knew someone.

"I hate it when you laugh at me like that. It's really condescending."

"What do you expect, Natalie? You'll never get in looking like that." I gestured to her sad little outfit. "You do know you're an escort, right? Maybe it's about time you start dressing like one. The soccer mom act isn't fooling anyone."

Stupidly, she said, "Neither of my kids play soccer, which you would know, if you cared."

"Well, clearly I don't."

I stared her down, expecting her to retreat. But instead, she whispered, "*Please.* Let me come inside, just for a minute?"

Hating myself for relenting, I swung the door wide and invited her inside.

Things got better after that, and I wondered why I didn't realize that it would be fun to watch Natalie realize how outclassed she was.

A grand chandelier poured a million points of light into the living room, which was decorated in white and black, chrome and steel, with splashes of color from all of my overpriced art — one of my accountant's many ways of managing so much cash. There was nothing in crayon, and no cheesy family photos either. It was a far cry from Natalie's suburban wasteland.

"You live here?" Natalie asked, clearly awed.

"I sure do, and I'm smart enough to pay for the things I buy with cash, so all of this is actually mine."

Natalie looked slapped.

Get to the point, I said with my hands.

"Ryan said that he was going to Atlanta, but I followed him instead. He's at Cameo right now and—"

"Oh, isn't that too bad? Would you like to know how I found out that he was cheating on me? It's a really good story."

"He wasn't cheating on you, Olivia. You two were—"

"Really, Natalie? You're going to make that argument? Here and now?"

She looked near tears, and I couldn't believe how bothered I felt, annoyed that Natalie couldn't conceal her sadness, and that I was feeling an empathy she didn't deserve. This was why I no longer dated. Or had many friends.

I sighed then said, "Finish your story."

"He left for the airport, but I followed him to the Indigo. It's a luxury hotel in—"

"I know the Indigo."

"Twenty minutes later, he walked out wearing a suit. Then he took a FASTr to the club."

"And why should I help you?"

Apparently Natalie didn't understand the mechanics of betrayal. Once you sold your best friend down the river, you lost all the benefits of that friendship. I'd eventually recovered, of course. I'm a strong woman, but she ruined me for a while with what she did, sleeping with Ryan in college, when he was the only person I had ever loved, and she *knew it*.

So no, people who shit on their best friends didn't get to make demands, no matter how far in the past their betrayal might have been. I couldn't imagine a single reason that would get me to agree.

But Natalie didn't even try to give me one. Instead she just looked at me with her big brown eyes and begged.

"Please. I don't have anyone else." Pathetic. Vulnerable. Desperate.

Why was I feeling *any* sympathy toward this person who had hurt me so much?

I couldn't answer that question. But I did.

I needed to make sure that I got something for helping her because otherwise she'd sense that weakness in me and exploit it again.

"Fine. I'll help you. But I have two conditions. First,

once you're finished with your first ten clients, you'll re-sign with Victor for another three months."

She looked horrified but said nothing.

"Second, you'll take over one of my regulars. He insists on meeting in the afternoons, which is inconvenient for me, and he likes the Broadway, which is closer to you."

He's also the worst of the worst, and someone who could really throw a wrench into Natalie's life, but I had no obligation to warn her.

She shook her head, looking like a beaten dog. Probably couldn't talk without crying.

"So do we have a deal?"

"No!" Natalie blurted, shaking her head. "No way. I'm doing my ten, and then I'm out. There won't be eleven, and I'm sure as hell not taking one of your 'inconvenient' regulars."

"Fair enough." I walked to the door, then held it open for Natalie. "Have a great night. Enjoy never knowing when your husband is going to leave you for another woman."

Natalie braced herself. She was fighting some sort of internal war, and even though my conscience was tugging at me, I couldn't deny that I was enjoying the show, watching her wrestle with herself, and losing the battle on both fronts.

Her jaw set and her fists clenched, shoulders rolling forward as she said, "If Ryan hadn't chosen me, *you're* the one he'd be cheating on right now."

She was right, of course. But she'd already pushed me to the limits of my mercy.

"Two conditions. Take the deal or get out of my condo."

"I accept," she said with a waver in her voice.

Good. Now we were getting closer to even.

95

. . .

NATALIE

EVEN IN MY tiny black dress and matching heels, I felt totally out of place standing next to Olivia.

She kissed the bouncer on the cheek, a guy who looked like Michael Clark Duncan and had an even deeper voice, like rumbling thunder.

I waited a few steps behind her, listening to her talk in a loud whisper, just low enough to exclude me.

Everyone here seemed in love with themselves, which probably explained the giant golden mirror fixed to the building. It should have been tacky, but somehow it wasn't.

I looked at myself, admiring my body in the little black dress, a new addition to my wardrobe that I rationalized by reminding myself that I could afford it if I was going to renew my contract. My makeup was dramatic, in vivid colors I rarely wore. Olivia had teased my hair into suggestive waves.

If I crashed into Ryan now, he probably wouldn't recognize me.

I barely recognized me.

The bouncer ushered us inside. I could hear chatter behind me as I followed Olivia, following the bouncer into Cameo.

Who are they?

I think the blonde is Margot Robbie.

Damn, that dude is big.

Olivia turned to me and said, "Don't do anything I wouldn't do, although I can't imagine what that would be."

She started to walk away, but I grabbed her by the arm. "Wait!"

"What?"

"Aren't you going to help me?"

"I got you in here, now you're on your own."

Then Olivia strutted off.

I felt itchy in my skin and out of my body.

My husband was here with another woman.

I wasn't sure what would happen when I found them, but it wouldn't be pretty. I might kill him right in front of everyone.

I walked through the club, trying not to get distracted. It was dark enough to shroud me in shadows and obscure the identities of the patrons around me, yet it was somehow light enough to see whatever I needed to in front of me, with halos of light where people were clustered.

There were doors everywhere I looked: bathrooms, apparently unisex.

Olivia had already disappeared into the mob. I was in awe of the woman, walking in like she owned the place, then vanishing into its throbbing heart like she'd been there a hundred times before.

She probably had, and made a couple grand per visit.

This was probably a mistake. Best-case scenario, I would see Ryan with another woman and slink off in horror, too injured for a confrontation. Worst case, I'd lose my shit and go viral, because of course someone would film it.

Or maybe keeping silent was the worst case. Maybe losing my shit was exactly what needed to happen.

I swallowed, then started walking the club.

I would have given anything for a friend. It had been a long time since I could use that word with Olivia, but her abandoning me at the door still hit me harder than I would have imagined. I felt deserted, standing solitary in the face of something that was so much bigger than me.

At least I was enjoying the view. Cameo was stunning,

and so was its clientele. The bar was occupied by a long row of wealthy-looking men. Tailored suits, polished watches, gorgeous dates that had only been legally drinking for hours.

Whoa.

If Aldo Barr and Sebastian Swan were casually drinking a few feet away from me, then this place was even more exclusive than I thought. How could Ryan afford to come to a place like Cameo?

And how was he able to get in?

"Whiskey on the rocks," I told the bartender, who looked like Brad Pitt's better-looking little brother. He smiled as I paid for my drink and dropped a twenty into the tip jar.

By the time I finished my drink, I still hadn't caught a glimpse of Ryan, so I went back to the bar. I wanted another whiskey, and some more of the bartender's smile.

After being served, I returned to wandering, but I still wasn't finding Ryan.

So I had another, then another after that.

I didn't see Olivia anywhere and figured maybe she had left. Abandoned me again.

Soon enough I was *that* girl: drunk, sad, and alone at the bar.

Brad's kid brother offered me another whiskey, but I waved him away.

"This one's on the house," he said, setting it in front of me a minute after my refusal, probably figuring I couldn't really mean no if I was still at the bar, and it was the least he could do after sixty dollars in tips.

I finished that one off, even though I really shouldn't have.

Now I was officially fuckered, with a swimming head

and my equilibrium about to go on strike. And — dammit — I might have to throw up.

"Where's the bathroom?" I asked like an idiot, only remembering Cameo's layout after the words left my mouth.

He laughed. "Just spit and you'll hit one."

"Thanks," I said, then wobbled over to the nearest one.

It was locked, and so was the one after that. The third was open. I went in and locked the door behind me.

I looked at myself in the mirror, wondering how those perfect women all managed to keep their makeup so perfect while my eyeliner was smudged under my eyes, awful enough to make me look like a crack-whore.

I didn't have to throw up, once I had a closed door between me and all that chaos. But I did splash cold water on my face and fix my makeup as best as I could. Then I stared at myself in the mirror long enough to collect myself, reaffirming my mission to find Ryan, before leaving the bathroom.

I took two steps before there were arms at my waist, grabbing me and spinning me around.

I was expecting to see Ryan, but instead I was staring into the eyes of someone else.

"Elle! I thought that was you."

IT TOOK me a moment to realize who I was looking at, and to register how weird my life had become.

Bennett Cole held me close, looking down on me, concerned.

"What's the matter? Have you been crying?"

I wanted to lie, but I couldn't. Not with the way he was looking at me.

"Just a little," I said, wiping at my eyes. "But it's no big deal."

"Sure it's a big deal. Do you want to talk about it?" Bennett looked at me like he had on his sofa, in a way that made me feel seen.

It was light amid so many shadows.

"I was stalking my husband, but now I'm just drunked."

"Drunked?" Bennett laughed.

"Something like that." Then I laughed too.

I know I shouldn't have let my guard down. But I was still a little hurt over the way he'd kicked me out of his hotel room, and he was being so nice to me now.

"Do you know what helps when I'm drunked?" he said.

"What?"

"I'll show you," Bennett said, holding out his arm for me to hook mine through.

"Where are we going?"

"Upstairs. Have you been?"

"I didn't even know there was one," I admitted.

Bennett didn't say anything else as he led me into an elevator that took us up to the rooftop.

I wondered if he'd done this with other women he'd hired out, approaching them in public off the clock and taking them somewhere isolated. Did he want sex from me now? Or was he just being nice?

Or maybe he just feels sorry for you.

That brought me back to the question I'd been working hard not to think about at all.

Why hadn't he booked me again?

I couldn't stop wondering, even though I scolded myself for caring every time I found myself doing it. This time was no different, but there was a chill in the night air kissing my naked skin, and unlike Cameo below, the rooftop was brightly lit.

I felt exposed. Practically naked.

"Do we have a plan for when we find your husband?" Bennett asked, clearly amused.

"Kill him, of course." I laughed, but I was drunked enough to almost mean it.

"Of course."

Bennett let that settle. He didn't try to touch me, even though I wanted him to. He stayed a respectful three feet away, but he was still looking at me, *into* me, more deeply than Ryan ever had.

He finally spoke. "So you followed him here?"

"He's supposed to be on a business trip in Atlanta."

"And where are you supposed to be?"

"That's not the point," I said.

"I'm only asking you the questions that *he* is going to ask you, if you choose to have this confrontation."

"What, you don't think I should talk to him if I see him?"

"I can't tell you what to do, Elle. But I can tell you that if I acted on every impulse, my life would be a mess. Know when to let things go, so your actions matter when you take them."

"What's that supposed to mean?"

Bennett raised his eyebrows and looked at me expectantly. "Is this fresh air doing you any good?"

He was eyeing my body; why wasn't he doing anything else?

Fuck, even his voice was sexy.

"You need a plan," he said.

"I'll be fine." I turned around and started walking toward the elevator.

Bennett stayed right beside me.

"Don't do anything that you're going to regret," he warned me in the elevator, his warm hand on my cold shoulder.

"Mm-hmm."

"Information is power. Take what you learn and do something with it," he suggested on our way back to the bar, his large palm on the small of my back.

"Mm-hmm."

"I think you've had enough," he cautioned as I ordered another whiskey neat, his strong arms around my waist, leading me over to one of Cameo's dark corners.

I wondered what he might want to do to me once we were there.

"I want another drink," I slurred, faux-pouting.

"Not tonight."

I was about to argue when I saw my husband. In the corner, sitting at a loveseat in one of Cameo's few illuminated areas. Practically framed, at a small round table under a decorated arch, inked with ivy that looked real from where I was standing, almost trompe-l'œil.

If we weren't in a tangle of shadows, or if I wasn't painted and dressed like a whore, Ryan could certainly see and recognize me from where he was sitting with that stunning blonde. She had movie star looks. Or at least TV.

That's where I'd seen her before.

Jess Lindley. She played Allison on *Adulting*.

They were close. So close.

It shouldn't have surprised me since Cameo was a Hollywood hotspot, but the lighting in this place was unreal. My husband entertaining a beautiful former actress, young but already done, seemed almost backlit for my horror.

My face was hot, and the hairs on my arms were all standing on end.

I lurched forward, but something yanked me back.

Bennett's hand on my arm. He pulled me toward him, squeezing.

"Don't, Elle." He nodded toward the loveseat. "Is that your husband? With Jess Lindley?"

I nodded.

"But you have no idea how they know each other?"

"No. That's why I'm here. Why are you making that face? Do you know her?"

He didn't tell me why he was making that face, and kept right on making it as he said, "No. But we have people in common."

"Why do you care whether I go over there and confront him?"

"Because I don't want to see you hurt. This place is still very public, as exclusive as it is. A woman like you should be well-practiced in the arts of discretion."

"What's that supposed to mean?" It came out sharper than I wanted, but also kind of 'fuck him.' That sounded like an insult.

"It's supposed to mean that you traffic in secrets." Bennett said it gently and in almost a whisper. "Restrain yourself now and you'll have all the power later."

He squeezed my arm again before letting me go.

"Okay," I said, desperate to have some sort of closure about something, hating how impotent I felt. If I couldn't interrogate Ryan, what could I do?

I reeled around on Bennett. "Why haven't you booked me again?"

His body straightened. His jaw firmed. His hands fell to his sides.

And it was all my fault.

I was soiling his fantasy by making this real, trying to hold him accountable for a relationship that didn't — that *couldn't* — exist. I was being overly emotional, and that was more than he had bargained for.

"Compose yourself. You're acting like a child."

I flinched. The last time anyone had told me I was behaving like a child, I actually was one.

I opened my mouth to protest, but the sound of familiar laughter made me whirl around in time to see Olivia greeting Ryan with a giant hug.

I strained to hear her above Cameo's racket, a soundtrack of celebrities, wannabes, and the dripping rich. Her laughter was louder than her talking, but it was easy enough to imagine.

Oh my god! What are the odds that we'd run into each other here?

The hug broke and Olivia sat.

Then the bitch looked *right at me.* Her eyes were an arrow and mine were the target.

Her lips were twisted in menace. She wanted me to wonder what she was doing.

"Do you want to go?" Bennett asked.

I couldn't tell what he even meant by that. Did I want to leave Cameo with him? Or was he hinting that he wanted me to go away?

I didn't care, I *couldn't* care. Not right now, not while I was watching this scene play out like a bad joke.

What happens when Natalie's cheating, lying, fucker of a husband sits down with a washed-up actress and her oldest friend-turned-foe?

"I need to see this," I whispered.

Ryan looked smitten to have run into his former girlfriend, turning his attention from Jess to her with a smile that I haven't seen him wear in years.

It hurt, like a blade between my ribs, but mostly because the light of that gleaming knife illuminated the truth. There was a natural ease and connection between them that Ryan and I still didn't share, even all these years later.

I was dying to know what they were saying, but their body language made it clear: they were happy to see each other, their hands on each other's shoulders, and a lingering embrace that was more intimate than friendly. Familiar, and from my place in the shadows, perhaps even tinged with longing.

I could feel myself starting to spiral into rage.

Fortunately, I was a slightly different person than I had been the night Olivia first showed me those photos. Or at least I now had access to a different *me*. I knew where to go, because it was the same place I went whenever I was getting paid for a party. Before, during, and after, because in that place, I called the shots, even if someone was calling them for me.

I took Bennett by the hand and made a beeline for the nearest bathroom without any line, hoping for a vacancy, and not giving a shit whether or not Olivia saw me.

He knew where we were going and clearly liked the idea. He tried the door for me.

It was open, so we went inside.

Bennett locked the door and pressed his back against it, his hands already at his belt.

I was on my knees, that little black dress riding all the way up my ass.

I took Bennett in my mouth to get Ryan out of my mind.

What happened next had nothing to do with pleasuring him as a client. It was about me being desperate to take back some little bit of control over my unraveling life.

Bennett grabbed me by the arm, hauled me to my feet, and led me over to the sink.

Then he bent me over so that my palms were flat on

the tile. He lifted my little black skirt up above my waist with one hand, while he hooked his thumb into my panties and lowered them with the other, and sank into me.

I bucked back, wanting him as much as he wanted me, trying to lose myself in the unbridled pleasure of feeling wanted by *someone* to consume me.

He finished in less than a minute, then left without a word.

When I emerged from the bathroom, Ryan was gone.

Jess and Olivia too.

Chapter Ten

Thursday Afternoon ...

"DON'T LEAVE us with Anna! Anna's mean." Alec sulked as I secured my earring. "Lena hates her."

That's how put out Alec was. He was using his sister to manipulate me into staying home instead of heading out for another client date.

"Why do you say she's mean?"

He hesitated. "You're always gone, and so is Dad."

He wasn't wrong.

I was trying not to feel like a terrible mother. I missed spending time with them — movie nights and popcorn, board games on Thursdays after dinner, playing catch at the park on Sundays. But I was doing this for them. Even if I couldn't explain what I was doing to Alec, I needed him to understand that I didn't want to be away.

"You're right, Alec. But *please*, I need to take care of a few things tonight, and so that means that I need you to behave for Anna, and to set a good example for your sister. Can you do that for me?"

Silence.

"Alec?"

"Fine."

I grabbed my purse, then kissed him on the forehead as I passed by on my way to the door.

"Ew, gross," he protested half-heartedly.

"If Anna tells me you've been good, we'll go for ice cream this weekend. As many scoops as you want."

There was a time when the promise of unlimited ice cream would've made my son cheer, but tonight it earned only a skeptical grunt.

As I got into my car, I promised myself that I would make it up to him soon.

I'd been an absentee mother ever since Cameo. Catching Ryan in his web of lies had rattled me. Okay, it had *depressed* me. And empty sex with Bennett had made it worse — ironic that when he'd been paying, he made me feel cared for, but when the sex was free, he'd made me feel used.

I'd dealt with the emotional aftermath by asking Victor to set me up with as many bookings as possible. My calendar was suddenly packed, so Alec was right to be upset. I was starting to have regulars — several clients had booked me on repeat, except for Bennett — so with my full permission, Victor had scheduled three clients in a row, from lunch through late dinner. Two of today's were new.

But at least that kept Bennett mostly out of my mind. Even thinking his name hurt. It wasn't like I was a school-girl pining for his affections. I wasn't in love or anything like that. But I was still reeling from our exchange because he'd made me feel so small.

Bennett left me in the bathroom without a word. It had

felt like the most honest sex of my life, but it also felt like I would never see him again, at least not for another booking.

Maybe I'd run into him again the next time I was stalking Ryan.

But at least I knew I'd made the right decision to accept Victor's offer. Seeing Ryan with Jess Lindley drove that home like a spike through my heart.

He'd been quietly reconfiguring his life to get rid of me.

My client was waiting when I arrived.

Berto Reyes wasn't as famous as Bennett, but he was a celebrity on the rise, having elevated himself as a small-time actor in his teens on a web series called *F the 90s!* to writing, directing, and starring in a series of blockbusters, most of them featuring a man in his late twenties who suffers from smoking way too much pot.

Just like Berto in real life, except few would say he was suffering.

This was the actor's second call, and if it was anything like the last time, my stomach would be hurting from laughing by the time I left. The only thing I hadn't enjoyed during our first go-round was that Berto kept calling me *Mom.* He thought it was hilarious, both before and after we started smoking.

But Berto was otherwise a blast. His droll punchlines had me laughing hard, and he was an easy client to please. He wanted to get baked, make jokes, order room service, and fuck. I couldn't tell if he was more interested in *Adult Video: The Movie!* streaming on the hotel TV, or my tits swaying in his face as I straddled him. He paid ample attention to both, managing to laugh, while indulging my body like he actually cared.

Hollow fun that left the client happy. Berto even paid me to finish watching the movie with him. Since it was cash and off the books, neither Olivia or Victor needed to know.

I wished all my clients could be like Berto, but unfortunately my next one, Guy Vernon, wasn't fun at all.

Victor had pitched the guy as an easy client -- a Hollywood agent who had more stress than time, and was always in need of relief. "I hear he's fast. Twenty minutes, and you should be out of there."

But the man was a monster, who only wanted to hear himself talk.

I tried to greet him as I entered, but his glare shut me up.

I tried to entice him with the same dirty talk I'd been using to great effect with other clients, but he ordered me to shut the fuck up.

I tried to tell him I was sorry, and that I would be happy to please him however he wanted, but he told me if I opened my upper cunt again he'd fuck it until I was tongue-tied for good.

Guy wasn't just uptight and controlling, the man was a beast. He made me undress, then kept me on my knees for half an hour while he paced circles around me in his ten thousand dollar suit, ranting and raving about actors and contracts and things I didn't understand, saying nothing specific, but all of it came with an angry spittle that flew from his lips to dampen me.

I hated him and desperately wanted to leave. So I did some math in my head and figured that even with Victor and Olivia's cut, I was still making more than twenty-six dollars for every minute I spent on my knees.

But I also didn't want this asshole bitching to Victor, and I wasn't willing to stay a minute longer than he'd paid for. I still had to get the guy hard, and I wasn't sure if that would require me to read Variety while twiddling my twat and telling him that he was the greatest agent in Hollywood or something. So forty minutes in I dared to speak into a lull in his diatribe.

"You seem so stressed. Are you sure there isn't any way I can help?"

Without a word he marched over, unzipping as he approached, and shoved his cock into my mouth.

He apparently didn't mind the sound of my gagging.

Guy was also fast like Victor promised, but only after he got started. After three minutes of barely being able to breathe, he finally unloaded and I was able to swallow while he walked away, zipping up his slacks and muttering something ugly under his breath.

I thought he was going to be my worst client, until I met the third one for the day.

Damon Pierce, money man to the stars. He wasn't a misogynist or a terrible person like Guy. But Damon was a family man, and thus sent me into the deepest place I'd had to travel so far. A bit like my time with Bennett, but so much blacker. He wanted me to role-play a cheating wife who hated her husband and wanted to vent her anger during sex.

In other words, I was supposed to act like I was revenge-fucking my husband.

For the first time I could scream all the things I'd been keeping inside. My rage for Ryan sent angry words flying out of my mouth like knives, but they cut me as they left. I had to pretend that everything was about Damon, stoking the embers of my client's fantasy, keeping him at arm's length while showing him the ugliest side of myself, hoping he couldn't tell that I meant everything I shrieked.

I yelled and yowled and bellowed as he bucked.

You're a selfish liar and this is all your fault.

You're not just cheating on me, you're doing this to our entire family.

Then one for him: *You'd rather be an accountant to the stars than a decent husband and father.*

You could have been home with the children and spending more time with me, but instead you're sticking your dick into every slut you can find.

And another: *You have to pay women to fuck you.* (He asked me to say it, but to me it felt like just another way to call me a whore.)

You're a lying piece of shit who broke all of his promises and broke our family.

I can never trust you again!

I'm leaving!

By the time he finally came, I was crying real tears of anguish. It was like I'd had a wound in my soul that he'd ripped open so he could stick his dick into it. I couldn't get out of there fast enough.

As I snatched the envelope from his hand, I swore I was going to earn the money I needed to be safe — to keep my kids safe — as fast as I possibly could, and I was going to get the hell out of this business.

Move to another part of the country, someplace where the cost of living was less and I could live for years on what I'd earned. The kids would adapt, once they got over the shock of the divorce, and we'd be happy together.

That's why I was doing this.

On my way home from Damon's I gave Victor a call.

"Thrilled to hear from you," he said after the first ring. "It's always the other way around."

"Don't book me with Guy Vernon again. Or Damon Pierce."

Victor laughed like an asshole. "I've heard stories. So he likes to hear himself talk and—"

"I'm serious, I won't see either of them," I repeated, firmer this time.

"Fine. What can I say? I'm thrilled with your work. Or at least the clients are, and that's what matters."

"What else do you have for me?"

Victor said, "You want some fast money?"

No hesitation. I needed to get through this as fast as I could stand to. "Yes."

"It's not the sort of thing I would normally offer you because you've been clear on your preferences, and Guy is now noted, but I could send you on something tomorrow if you're interested."

"I already said that I was."

"Yeah, but there's a lot not to like on this one … even though the money is good."

"Get to the point, Victor."

"They're two guys, and they're both nuts. Not dangerous, just loony. Oddest pair you've ever seen. One is skinny and pale. The other one is a few hundred pounds."

Great, so now I'm going to be fucking Laurel and Hardy.

But what did I expect if I asked for *fast money?*

"Okay, fine. Whatever. How much does it pay and how long will I need to be with them?"

"They always book three hours, so you'll clear over 5K for the time, and they're generous tippers. You know I don't touch what's yours."

"What do they want that's loony?"

There was a pause, and I pictured him shrugging. "Different stuff, I dunno."

"You don't know, or you don't want to say?"

"All I know is that they regenerate fast, and take turns. And you're not allowed to clean yourself until it's all over."

Ewww. But five grand would get me a lot closer to moving out before Ryan could screw me. For all I knew, he was already working with a divorce lawyer.

"Right. Fine. Sign me up. I can handle them."

"Ha. You continue to impress me."

"Thanks. And Victor?"

"Yeah?"

Don't say it. You're better than this.

But my bank account wasn't.

"Never mind what I said about Guy."

"Good girl," he said.

I hung up, exhausted from the labor of taking strangers inside me, and the harder work of not hating myself for it.

My mind drifted until I found myself pulling into my driveway.

The house was silent as I entered.

I paid Anna and apologized for being late. She told me that I was fifteen minutes early.

I checked on Alec and Lena, both of them sleeping and looking like angels, making me feel like the devil's wily daughter.

I went to my room, taking the phone out of my purse on the way, then turning it back on now that Elle was off duty and Natalie was back.

Four missed calls from Lynette.

What could she possibly want?

Whatever it was, it wouldn't get me away from Ryan faster, so it didn't matter.

WEDNESDAY NIGHT, *Six Days Later* …

JADE

I COULDN'T BELIEVE IT.

I sat on the edge of my bed, in the room I shared with one of the other girls here at Victor's. I'd just finished my first real job, and to make it feel even realer, I'd fanned out all the money in front of me.

I shook my head, staring down at the most money I'd ever seen in one place.

I was filthy rich and just getting started.

My dreams were about to come true.

I had a place to stay and money in my pocket.

I was safe.

And trying not to cry.

I had a new name — *Jade*.

But before I celebrated any more, I needed a shower. Like, *asap*. I felt disgusting. Not the sex part, though that wasn't as bad as I thought it might be.

It wasn't my first time. I lost my virginity to one of the kids that worked with my dad at the shop. He was twenty and an artist -- the first person to ever buy me a box of colored pencils. They were the expensive kind, the kind that lasted a long time and didn't sound all scratchy when you used 'em.

But it was my first time getting paid for it.

I was getting two grand, minus a fair cut. That was a life changer.

Still, I felt sorta hollow and was trying hard to pretend like I wasn't. This wasn't exactly what I had in mind when I left for Los Angeles. I'm not stupid; it's not like I thought I would slide down a rainbow into a river made of chocolate, then find myself the star of some Hollywood fairy tale. But I hadn't had much of a plan, thinking that being eighteen and a day was enough. So I got on a bus after cashing my last paycheck from Wendy's — 237 dollars — thinking I'd figure out what to do next once I was in sight of the Hollywood sign.

But maybe it was fate. Maybe if I had stayed behind a little longer and planned a little better, I would never have needed to do the thing that was going to make everything else come true. Maybe Victor was right, and this really was like getting one of those FastPasses, except that I would be skipping to the front of my Hollywood dreams.

I met him outside an open audition. He was sweet and handsome. He looked like one of the guys who would hang around my father's shop, either looking for work or just getting off a shift. I was hoping to land the lead in some much-too-serious indie film that I didn't even really want, anyway. Victor bummed a smoke, and then he sorta took my breath away.

"Mind if I …?"

He didn't finish his sentence, but he nodded all sexy toward the cigarette, dangling from lips I'd painted to get told I was wrong for the part. I handed him the pack.

It was in his mouth like magic. Victor moved so fast, the pack was back in my hand before I knew what had happened. Then it was lit and he said, "They have no idea what they just lost in there."

He eyed me up and down, taking a drag, then he exhaled with a shake of his head. "Damn shame. You radiate everything that matters."

I shrugged, not sure what I should say to a sudden rush of compliments from a total stranger. "They're right. I'm wrong for that part."

He smiled in a way that seemed to light his stubble, turning the blond nubs brighter. "But I'd bet my life that you're perfect for something."

"Thanks," I said.

"Are you hungry?"

Starving.

"I could eat."

"How about we grab a burger?"

Thank God for that. After four days of living off ramen and breath mints, I was starving times ten.

Victor could tell. He let me order whatever I wanted, and I wanted a lot. We went to Perfect Burger and I ordered everything, meaning a burger and fries and a drink, except he said I could order a shake so I got that instead of a Coke. He seemed really concerned about me.

"Crashing on a couch isn't a permanent solution, Amanda. What are you going to do?"

"I don't know." I stuffed several fries in my mouth.

I'd known I was ill-prepared for life in Los Angeles, but sorta expected to figure it out. But if it wasn't for Victor I'm not sure what would have happened. We spent the whole day together. He took me everywhere. We even got donuts from that place with the big giant donut on top of the shop. He paid for everything, and didn't try anything, even though I would have been okay if he did. I even kind of wanted him to.

I didn't know what to think when he called me *his girl*, except that I liked it.

Then he offered me a job *and* a place to stay. Of course I said yes.

I didn't know what the job was until we got back here, and by then it was too late to back out. I didn't want to disappoint him; that wasn't any way to say thank you to someone who'd saved me. It's not like he needed me. He already had so many beautiful girls working for him.

Yeah, I realize that he played me, but I also know that he helped me.

I could be hoarding a roll of breath mints right now,

stretching them out to last all night and wondering if my parents would buy me a bus ticket home, if I begged.

"Knock knock," Victor said as he entered.

He came in and stole all my nerve. I didn't know what to do. My hands were like giant pancakes.

I looked down because it's too hard to look at him.

I can't believe that I ever thought he might want me. He'd probably laugh if I asked.

Yes, I'm his *his girl*, but he has a houseful of 'em. As nice as this room is, it's just one of many.

I glanced at him sideways.

I watched him reach for the bills, counting them, take his share, and toss the rest back onto the bed.

I was one deep breath away from crying.

What the hell is wrong with me?

Then Victor's finger was under my chin, tipping it up. "There's my girl."

My eyelashes fluttered, something they'd never done before.

"You made Mr. Welty very happy tonight, you know that? Most of the girls who come through here, they're all looks. But you?" He shook his head, and looked for a second again like he really cared about me. "I know you're special. I want to be the one to show you how special you are."

He crouched down and met my eyes.

"I can't imagine what it's been like for you. I bet where you come from, nobody ever appreciated you. I bet you've spent a lifetime being treated like a girl with a beautiful body. Let me guess …"

I was already trembling, but then he leaned in and made me tremble harder.

"You just got used to your daddy's friends staring at

you like they wanted to fuck you, finding excuses to be alone with you, touching you?"

Now I was frozen.

"Well, now you're my girl. I'm going to make all your dreams come true. Do everything I say, and you're going to be my star. You—"

"I don't believe we've met," said a voice from the doorway. "I'm Natalie."

NATALIE

THE GIRL LOOKED young enough to break my heart twice.

She had to be eighteen because Victor was way too careful for her to be even an hour less, but she barely looked legal, which, I supposed, only added to her value.

I didn't like the way Victor was looking at her, or the way the girl — Jade, I thought her name was — glared at me, like *I* was being inappropriate for interrupting.

Maybe I was.

It was hard not to imagine that she was judging me.

You're pathetic. Gross. You've got kids, lady. And a husband. Go home.

But I wasn't there to see Jade, I just wanted to give Victor his cut and get the hell out of there.

I gave Jade a friendly nod, but she ignored me, if that's what you can call a barely perceptible rolling of her eyes.

Victor didn't even count the cash I handed him. He just folded the bills and slipped them it into his pocket with an appreciative smile.

"Always good to see you, Natalie."

I didn't like that he was so frivolous with my real name. But I liked to believe that everything happened for a reason, and maybe the poor girl sitting on her bed, looking lost to all the world, needed a friend. If that was the case, then our friendship shouldn't start off with a lie.

I walked over to Jade, holding out my hand to her.

"Jade, right?" I was just off another tour de clients — exhausted and dying to get home. But maybe I could help her.

Or maybe I was a hypocrite.

That might be what Jade was thinking, the way she was eyeing me.

Victor looked between us, seeming ever so slightly amused. He smirked, said, "I'll leave you ladies to it," then disappeared from the room.

Jade hardened the second he left. Her eyes, mouth, and posture all told me to get the fuck out of her room. I wondered if I had made a mistake. I probably should have left with Victor. I could be in my car already.

The silence weighed a ton, and I was thinking that I should probably just leave when Jade finally spoke.

"I've heard about you," she said, her tone antagonistic, like a teenage daughter rebelling against her mother, the kind of tone I'd not yet had to suffer from Lena. "You're the MILF, right?"

"I guess."

"That's what I figured."

"Do you have a problem with that?" I asked.

Even though she sounded like a total bitch, I couldn't help but feel sorry for her.

Then the drawings tacked to the wall beside her bed caught my eye. Four of them, done in pencil. But they were delicate and beautiful. Her sketchbook was open to the start of her fifth drawing, what looked like a young woman sitting on a park bench, staring at a pond full of ducks, trying not to cry. The shadows were there, and I felt

Tell Me No Lies

a sudden longing to see the whole thing filled in. Jade had clearly poured herself into them.

"Don't think you're going to boss me around. I'm a legal adult and free to do as I please."

"Did you draw these?" I asked.

She shrugged. "They're just sketches."

"No," I said. "They're incredible. You're *really* talented."

Jade shook her head and gave me another shrug. "They're stupid, and it doesn't matter anyway."

Then she fell silent again, obviously wanting to be left alone.

But I didn't want to go, despite my fatigue. I thought of Lena, considered the karma in my account if I were to simply leave this young girl to her fate. There were so many things I wanted to say.

Why are you here?

You have all the potential in the world.

You're too young to settle for this, can't you see that?

But then, couldn't she level all those same arguments on me?

Jade finally said, "Are you planning to stay in my room all day, or did you actually need something?"

"I just wanted to make sure you were okay."

"Gucci."

I didn't know what that meant, so I just kept looking at Jade, hoping she might elaborate.

One more try: "I guess I just want to make sure that this is what you really want to be doing."

She sat taller, and leaned forward. "They warned me. Said that people would feel threatened, and that they might even try to chase me away. So good luck with that, Mom, but it isn't happening."

The *Mom* hurt, more than it should have. "Who

warned you?"

"Some of the other girls. There are only so many jobs and—"

"I'm not trying to take your job, Jade. I have plenty of work on my own."

"Well, whatever."

I shouldn't care, but I genuinely couldn't help it. Seeing Jade, defiant and lost, was pulling me out of my own drain of despair. She needed someone to care.

And Victor sure as hell didn't.

I took out the little pink Moleskin I kept in my purse, double-checked the number for my burner, scribbled it onto the first blank page, then ripped the sheet from the notebook and handed it over to Jade.

"You can call me. Anytime. If you ever need anything."

"I'm good," she said, with another harsh and almost scathing gaze. "I can't imagine needing something from you."

I didn't know what else to say. I tried to smile, but I'm sure it came out looking like sorrow stretched across an awkward face. I wasn't sure why this girl was affecting me so much, but I couldn't deny that she was.

I left her room, and it was easier to put her out of my mind. She didn't want my help and I had plenty to worry about.

On my way out, I saw Victor giving shit to a girl, one I'd never met. I hesitated. I shouldn't stick my nose in.

"—then fine. Don't. There will be another bus full of beauties better looking than you by this time tomorrow. So you decide, but I doubt you're going to be earning this kind of money at Walmart, which is where you'll be if you don't start listening."

I should've walked out before he noticed me listening.

Gotten into my car and driven away. But as I looked from him to the girl — a tiny thing with red hair and freckles and a girl-next-door appeal — I couldn't stop the ugly thought.

He's going to use her up, way too fast.

"Everything okay?" I asked, not looking at either one. I meant the question for her, but of course Victor assumed I was talking to him.

"Angelica here needs a lesson in enthusiasm, isn't that right, Angelica?"

Angelica nodded.

Victor continued, "She doesn't quite understand that *confidence* is the key to making this gig work. It's a simple formula — well-groomed, comfortable, and confident in your skin. It's a vibe that men are paying for, not the pussy itself. They want you to be energetic and professional; they want to know that they're needed and wanted. *That* is most men's actual fantasy."

Angelica looked like she was going to cry.

"So why are you yelling at her?" I asked.

Victor shook his head at me, "Not that it's any of your business, but I'm not yelling, I'm instructing, and hopefully, helping Angelica keep her job. But I can't have clients calling me after her job telling me that it didn't seem like she was into it. She needs to make her guy think she wants him bad and that she's enjoying him, even if she isn't. *That's the job.*"

"I can do that," Angelica whimpered, trying to sound strong.

"You heard her," I said. "She's got it, Victor. Now back off."

And to my surprise, he did.

Angelica thanked me with her eyes.

Victor did not.

Chapter Eleven

Thursday Evening ...

THE HOUSE WAS BLESSEDLY QUIET.

My nerves were shot. I kept thinking about Jade and her drawings. I'd assumed that all of Victor's girls were like me — short-timers needing to earn money fast — or like Olivia, who'd confessed to me that her family had lost most of their fortune, and she was socking away most of her earnings toward an early retirement fund that would let her recover the wealth of her childhood. I hadn't realized that Victor was also recruiting barely legal runaways and grooming them into a career.

Jade was a talented young woman. She should be going to college and dating boys her own age and stressing about her grade point average — not learning to fake enthusiasm about sucking a stranger's dick.

I wondered how many of his escorts had been brought in young enough that they knew nothing else? How many had never even had a chance to fail at something they cared about before they'd fallen into this?

As I shut the front door, I shrugged that thought away and focused on how good it felt to be home.

That lasted about two seconds. Then I heard Alec and Lena fighting. Again.

At first I couldn't make out what they were saying, but then Lena yelled, "Stop it!" and started bawling.

Dammit.

I pushed myself up from the counter and traded the solace of my kitchen for conflict in the living room.

"What happened?"

Lena cried harder, but Alec stared me down, obviously not sorry at all. "It's her fault!"

"What's her fault? What did she do?"

"She wouldn't give me my space!"

"What do you mean, *she wouldn't give you your space?* You pushed her for that?"

"She had the whole living room to play in, but she kept coming over to my side of the coffee table." Alec pointed an accusatory finger at the glass top. He was trembling mad.

"Your sister was just trying to be closer to you. You didn't have to push her."

"You didn't see, you weren't here." There was a pregnant, horrible beat, where I knew exactly what Alec would say next. "You're *never* here."

I ignored Alec and went over to Lena, who'd transitioned from sobbing to shrieking.

"It's okay," I soothed her, holding Lena's head against my chest, and rocking her back and forth.

"You always take her side!"

It had been like this lately — Alec acting less like a big

brother and more like a sulky toddler who needed just as much coddling as Lena did. He felt neglected, I understood that, but I was working so much for him, as much as for his sister, and I needed him to step up and act his age, since I couldn't depend on his father for help. Or anything else.

"You come over here and tell your sister you're sorry."

"No."

I knew he was pissed, but I didn't expect that. Alec had said *No* to me maybe five times in his entire life.

"Alec."

He stared at me. "What?"

"Tell your sister that you're sorry."

He shook his head. "She should say sorry to me."

"Shhhhh …" I soothed Lena, her sobs now soaking the front of my shirt. "She should say sorry for what, loving you? Wanting to be closer to her brother?"

"She kept poking me and poking me and poking me. And she wouldn't stop! How would you like it if someone kept poking you, even when you didn't want them to?"

I sympathized. That's exactly what servicing asshole clients was like — having someone poking and poking you, and having to keep your mouth shut and even pretend you liked it because that's what they were paying you for.

And Victor enjoyed poking us too, poking holes in our self-esteem so we'd be more willing to take the shitty jobs he needed us to do.

But if you poke the bear often enough, she might bite off your finger.

As Lena's sobs faded into hiccupy whining, I wondered if I could afford to slow down. I was obviously hurting my children, especially Alec. Lena wouldn't be this needy if everything was okay, and Alec wouldn't be acting like a little dick.

I was ready to spend more time being a mother instead of a MILF.

Starting right now. I pushed aside my exhaustion and resentment and pasted on my Mommy's-got-a-surprise smile.

"Who wants to go to the Galleria?"

The look of hope on Alec's face made my heart ache — that was all it took to make him happy?

"Can we have dinner at the food court?" he asked.

I'd really rather not. "Sure."

In a trembly voice, Lena asked, "Can I get a rainbow mermaid blanket?"

I had no idea what that was. "Of course."

Less than five minutes later we were on our way to the mall. I was on full mom duty, doing what I apparently did best, pacifying my children with shit they didn't need to assuage the guilt I was heaping onto myself. Every penny I spent on my kids now meant more time spent away from them later.

But I couldn't tell them that and push the burden of guilt onto them.

I didn't expect it to be the best shopping trip of my life, but it was, because for the first time ever, I didn't make a single charge on the cards. I hadn't been carrying them for more than a week, though I did have at least a thousand dollars cash on me at all times.

For the first time I had money of my own to buy my children the things that they wanted, and I wouldn't be fighting with Ryan about it.

Alec got his dinner at the food court, but he also got a new pair of Air Jordans, two games for his PS4, and an archery set that Ryan wouldn't be happy about, which was half the reason I bought it.

Lena got her rainbow mermaid blanket — it was actually cute, and exactly what it sounded like — along with barrettes from Claire's, a stuffed rhinoceros she immediately named Gollypalooza, and a bag of crap from Bodyworks, including a lotion that Lena thought "smelled like a meadow."

Things were definitely better by the time we were all driving home.

But I couldn't escape the feeling that I hadn't done the right thing at all. I was teaching my kids to make the same mistake that had gotten me trapped between Ryan and Victor — making them think they could go shopping for happiness.

But this was a short-term thing. I'd be with them all the time once it was over. Then we'd figure out how to be happy, together.

I just needed to make enough money to leave Ryan, then everything else would be fine.

Chapter Twelve

Monday Afternoon ...

I WAS USED to being uncomfortable at CPA meetings, just not like this.

I couldn't afford to be here — I'd already seen one client and had another book for this afternoon. But I couldn't afford to skip another meeting either, not with the rumors going around. Lynette has to be behind all the odd looks and whispering behind my back. Probably still hasn't forgiven me for calling her out on her bullying of Theresa, who I noticed was sitting in a corner of the room, surrounded by empty chairs.

It was paranoid, but I had the sinking feeling that they knew. Everything.

Knowing I was being paranoid didn't stop me from sweating or wanting to squirm every time someone looked my way.

There's no way they could know. Olivia, who I hadn't seen since she ditched me at the club, lost out on her cut of my income if I had to quit. Ryan had been out of town almost nonstop since that night, so he couldn't know either — unless Olivia decided to tell him to hasten the breakup of our marriage out of spite. For all I knew, he'd already moved in with one of his other mistresses, and this current business trip would be his version of going out for cigarettes and never coming home.

But I still couldn't imagine him doing anything that would hurt Alec and Lena. And telling the rich bitches at their school that their mother was an escort would definitely hurt them.

That left Alec and Lena themselves. Maybe they'd told their friends that I was never home, or even that I'd been out with Lynette's pack of bitches when Lynette would know I wasn't.

I felt a flash of fury that my own children — the reason I'd agreed to work for Victor in the first place — might be running their ungrateful little mouths and starting whatever rumors had obviously taken root.

In the next moment, I was horrified at myself for that reaction. How could I be angry with Alec and Lena for wanting what every child wants: their mother's love and attention?

They had no idea the line I was trying to walk, or what it was like to be treated like a pariah, or why I had so little time to spend with them. And I couldn't tell them.

So this, whatever this was going to turn out to be, was my cross to bear.

Lynette was staring at me the hardest, but with suspicion instead of admiration, like she used to. If she ever discovered the truth, I would be ruined.

The meeting adjourned and I had no idea what we even accomplished, except that Eileen Patrelli is an idiot because even after her son has been caught stealing — *six times* — she still stood there with her hands on her hips, declaring that it was the school's job to teach her children right from wrong.

I turned toward the door and found Lynette blocking my way.

"Natalie," she gushed with obvious insincerity. "You look *so good*. What have you been doing? You have to tell me. Is it that keto diet? I thought you gave that up."

What could I say that would get me out of here fastest?

The most boring thing.

"Nothing, really. I've just been super conscious about what I eat, and I'm always moving around."

I'd been eating kale instead of cookies and doing Pilates videos before the kids woke up and replacing my mochas with that weird coffee with the butter and coconut oil. My tips depended in part on how good I looked naked, so I'd made it a priority to lose those ten pounds of baby pudge.

"Well, you look fantastic." She smiled at me like the strawberry bruschetta incident had never happened. "So where have you been lately? I've barely seen you."

Shit, the kids probably had complained. And now I was backed into a corner I wasn't sure how to get out of.

Theresa was also backed into a corner, all the way across the room. Her shoulders were sagging, and it looked like she was trying hard not to frown, to appear cheery in the face of a friendly berating by another concerned Constellation parent trying to save Theresa from herself.

I had to deal with Lynette, so she was on her own this time.

I forced a smile that I meant to be apologetic but probably looked condescending, and said, " Ryan has a lot of stuff going on at work, so I've been running around for him. He's about to get some really big promotion, and there's a lot of little things to take care of before he hands things off to his successor."

Lynette gave me a knowing little smile. "So, are you looking forward to Family Day?"

Family Day? Fuck! NO.

But then I realized I could throw Ryan under the bus to get out of Family Day.

"Of course! I really hope that Ryan doesn't have anything last minute. His schedule is like stupid unpredictable these days. Alec would be so disappointed."

"Oh, you *can't* let that happen, Natalie! Drew is so looking forward to it. Frank, too. Everyone is."

I laughed, just enough to reassure her. "I'm sure it will work out."

Theresa walked over and Lynette immediately stiffened.

"Hi, Theresa," I said.

She looked relieved, like she wasn't sure I'd acknowledge her presence. "Hey, Natalie."

Lynette said hello too, and clearly didn't mean it.

"Hi, Lynette!" Poor thing, for a moment Theresa looked hopeful. "Do you think that new lighting in the auditorium is really worth all that money?"

"What I think," Lynette said, swaying her neck like a cobra, "is that you should consider what you're saying about yourself when you come to school in that uniform."

Take that, Slut Mom, I could hear Lynette in my head.

Theresa looked like she'd stopped breathing.

She fired again. "I'm sure this isn't the first time that someone has told you your uniform is inappropriate."

"Lynette!"

"Can you believe yesterday my son asked me to explain the Rosebud scandal to him? Apparently your son told him about it." Lynette continued, ignoring me. "We need to set the moral example. Pay attention to things — what we say, what we do ... what we *wear*."

I wanted to slap Lynette. "I don't think Theresa's wardrobe had anything to do with the Rosebud scandal. But I do think we should all probably be better at minding our own business."

I smiled, turned around, and went to the back of the room to get a cup of coffee that I didn't even want, hoping that Lynette wouldn't follow me.

A soft voice beside me said, "Thank you for that."

I looked up from my coffee and saw Theresa.

Lynette was already gone from the room, and good riddance.

"Fuck Lynette," I said. "She's just threatened by anyone who might be half as pretty as her, and she doesn't know how to not act like a bitch when that happens."

Right now my act of sticking up for Theresa had everyone in the room pretending not to stare.

But I stood by that. Fuck Lynette, and everyone else. I was sick of the other moms picking on Theresa. I wished now that I'd given her a chance when we'd first put Alec and Lena in this school. I could've been hanging out with a decent human being instead of Lynette's bitches.

I thought back to my sorority days, and what Olivia had been like before I'd stolen Ryan from her, and I realized that I've spent my entire life hanging out with mean girls.

Because I'd been a mean girl.

Well, no more.

I put a friendly hand on Theresa's shoulder. "Don't let them get to you."

"I won't." She shook her head, still smiling, still appreciative. "I usually don't. Thanks again, for sticking up for me."

"Of course." I wanted to give her a hug, but that felt like too much, so I told her to have a great day before slipping out of the room, feeling too many eyes on my back.

When things calmed down a little and I had more time, I would ask her if she wanted to have lunch.

She needed an ally as much as I did.

I WAS on my way to Olivia's regular client, the one I'd agreed to take in exchange for her help getting into Cameo. It was an afternoon appointment, just like she'd said, so it was as inconvenient for me as it was for her. But at least the Broadway was beautiful.

I pulled up to the valet, got out, and sauntered into the lobby like a starlet.

Then I went up to the desk and told them I was here to see Frank Sinatra, just like Olivia had told me to. What kind of arrogant asshole would use Sinatra's name as a pseudonym?

The clerk called to double-check, although the way he was looking at me and trying not to smile, I was sure that he'd made similar calls more than a few times before. He gave me a card key and sent me to the gorgeous glass elevator, the one in the middle that went straight to the top floor.

Five minutes later I stood in front of the penthouse suite, my heart beating hard as I raised my fist to knock. I wanted this appointment to go well so that Olivia would be happy with me.

I opened my coat so that my lingerie-kissed body was on full display, then I knocked and waited, trying not to tap my feet.

The door opened, and I peed myself.

The most vile creature I knew in real life stared right back at me.

Frank Wilder, Lynette's husband.

I hadn't known it was possible to dislike the guy any more than I did. I wondered if Lynette knew he was cheating on her. Maybe.

Maybe that's why she was such a bitch.

Or maybe she was relieved that he wanted to have sex with someone else.

Frank was sloppy and slovenly. The kind of guy who didn't care if he had tufts of hair growing out of his folds from spots he missed shaving, or food from lunch still in his teeth. His hair was usually greasy, just like the rest of him. Everything about him was big — probably except for his dick — and he wanted the world to know it. And apparently, Frank was good enough at his job that none of that mattered.

It took him a moment to recognize me, but once he did, Frank actually licked his lips and said, "No shit."

"Exactly what I was thinking."

We stared at each other. I didn't know what to do.

What would Olivia do if I welshed on my deal to take Frank over for her?

What if Frank decided to tell someone that I was working as an escort?

Would my walking away make that more likely to happen, or less?

But we couldn't just stand there forever, with me in the hallway and him in the penthouse, neither of us knowing how to react to such an unfortunate pairing.

Except it was only unfortunate for one of us.

Frank opened the door wider. "I always thought you were the best looking out of all Lynette's friends, and you've never looked better than now." He raked me with his eyes, making me feel like I deserved my hourly rate just for that, then added, "Now we'll have a little secret to share whenever you swing by the house."

Just hearing him say it made me want to take a shower.

Disgusted but trapped, I went inside and let Frank close the door behind me.

"Would you like a drink?"

"Yes, please." I smiled, but it wasn't easy. "Whiskey, neat."

I had to get my shit together. Frank was a client and I had a job to do. I went to the bar as he finished pouring my whiskey.

"Mind if I take this off?" I asked

Frank looked at my jacket and nodded with a predatory smile. Then he waited for me to doff it before handing me the drink. I felt more naked in my lingerie than I usually did. I turned away for a swallow of whiskey so that he wouldn't see me wince, then I turned back around and said, "How can I please you?"

I don't want to talk about what happened next, or think about it ever again. I'll just say that sex with Frank should be against the law. It's like fucking a greased elephant that reeks of body odor, eggs, and human shit. Worse, the asshole loves to make a mess — all over and inside me. All around the room. It wasn't just sticky, it was disrespectful. How was I supposed to walk through the lobby with my eyelashes glued together and the rest of the goop crystallizing in my hair?

I wanted to wash up, but I wanted to get out of there even more.

I wanted to kill Olivia, but I couldn't blame her for being desperate to hand off her worst client.

I wanted to tell Frank to fuck off, but he was a client, and the client was always right.

Except, fuck that last one.

"What the hell is wrong with you?" I yelled at him.

He looked at me, confused. "I'm sorry?"

"You should be!"

"What did I do?" Frank asked, as if he didn't know.

"Look at me!" I pointed to my face and my hair and my body, then to the mattress and the mirror. "Look at the room!"

He didn't seem sorry at all. "But isn't that what I paid for?"

"No, Frank. It isn't." *But yes, it totally was.* "And you're cheating on your wife!"

He stared at me, flummoxed. "Aren't you cheating on your husband?"

I was speechless, because yes, of course I was. It was a sinking moment, realizing that I was fostering the same destructive cycle in someone else's marriage. I tried so hard not to think about that, each and every day. But this time it was staring me in the face. I'd had coffee with this man's wife, traded recipes, and ...

Had Family Days.

Like the one that was right around the corner.

"I'm really sorry, Natalie," Frank said, seeming to mean it.

He went over to his jacket coat and pulled out an envelope, then reached into his pants pocket, his hand emerging with a wad of cash fastened with a money clip. He peeled a bunch of hundreds from the top of the pile, and added them to the envelope. It was hard to know for sure, but it looked like a thousand dollar tip.

"I promise to be better next time," he said.

There was still cum on his hand, so that probably meant there was cum on my money.

But of course, I took it anyway.

Chapter Thirteen

Monday Evening ...

"NO WAY, Victor. I'm not seeing Frank Wilder ever again and—"

"I said okay, Natalie. But you need to stop yelling."

He was right, for both of our sakes.

I'd had to pull over three blocks after starting my car — I was shaking so hard that I'd nearly clipped a Mini-Cooper by accident. I got the finger from somebody's grandma as I swerved around.

"I'm sorry I'm yelling, I'm just really upset. I know him."

"I understand, and believe it or not, that sort of stuff does happen. But it isn't my fault. How was I supposed to know that you knew him?"

I bet Olivia knew.

"You're trying to draw a line in the sand that doesn't need to be drawn. We're on the same side. You say *No*

Frank, we figure out a way to make that work. But you can't just—"

"What do you mean, *we figure out a way to make that work.* How hard is it to figure out, Victor? You tell him *No, Natalie doesn't want to fuck you.* How hard is that?"

"I'll do that with Frank, sure, I get it. That's sticky." *Fucking right it's sticky.* "He'll understand. But it isn't good practice to tell a client that a girl don't want 'em, Natalie. And believe me, there are a lot of guys that our girls don't want. So what kind of business would I be running if I told our customers that they weren't good enough to purchase our product?"

"That's not what I'm saying."

"It is what you're saying."

No harm in being blunt. "I'm your most requested girl, is that right?"

"What are you getting at, Natalie?"

"My first-timers all become regulars, and I only just started." No need to mention yet that I'd be quitting soon. "So I ought to have some input into who those regulars are."

"I'm not saying that we can't. But that doesn't mean—"

"If you want me to keep working for you, then I get to know who the guys are before the jobs. No more mystery dates from now on. And I have the right to refuse. Nothing, *nothing* is worth what I just went through."

"Are you done?"

"I'm done."

He didn't sound pleased. "Then I hear you, and good-night. I'll email you."

The line went dead, and I immediately regretted my tantrum. I didn't have enough set aside yet to leave Ryan and be sure that we'd be okay.

How mad was Victor?

Was he going to let me go?

After everything I'd put up with so far, would I end up slaving my face off at Sloppy's anyway, knowing that I'd blown my chance to give my kids everything they needed?

I drove home, asked the sitter to stay until I got out of the shower, and once I was clean, spent a satisfying night with my children watching movies until they fell asleep. Alec was on my left, and Lena on my right, each with their heads on my chest. I'm not even sure what we were watching, since I was drifting in and out of sleep the whole time, but we were together and we were safe.

I cuddled them on the couch, telling myself that at least for this little moment my world was okay, and that my work was helping to make it that way.

I don't remember going to bed, but I thought about my call with Victor the second before I opened my eyes.

I reached for my phone, unplugged, opened Victor's email, and laughed out loud.

He'd sent me a list of all my requests, restating everything I had ranted about the day before in terms that were clear enough to validate my concerns but while also meaning nothing in court. Basically, he was letting me know that yes, I could pick my clients, and yes, I would get to know who every one of them was beforehand. Even if secrecy was a part of his promise, he could swear that their secrets were safe with me. He also warned that I was not to share the details of our agreement with any of the other girls, for the sake of "keeping discipline." If they found out, the deal was off and Frank would be one of my regulars.

My lips were sealed.

Chapter Fourteen

Wednesday Morning ...

MELINDA

"YES, MA'AM."

"Please, Ryan. Never call me that again. Melinda, or we can't work together. We really should be closer than that by now, considering the secrets we're keeping between us."

As usual, Ryan was a delight.

If I was using him for other things, I might even call him delicious. He was too pretty to be so unassuming. And it wasn't just because we were sitting outside by my pool. Dominic was inside, pretending he didn't give a shit, though he could hear every word and was probably already dying to check in.

Small talk was over. The first few beads of sweat were beading Ryan's brow. He didn't seem nervous, but he was probably overly hot in his collared shirt, especially with the

sun as warm as it is. That's why I was wearing my swim-
suit. Well, that, and because I liked to watch Ryan behind
my sunglasses, trying hard not to stare at my tits.

"So, what was your general impression of Jess?"

He looked almost grateful to be getting down to business. He opened a folder, looked down on the page and
then back up at me. Blinked, probably because he got a
flash of my cleavage. He really was adorable.

"My notes are all here." He closed the folder and slid it
over to me.

I didn't say anything, enjoying his discomfort, not
because I'm a sadist, but because it was necessary before
we reached a place where we both could be happy. Right
now he was feeling a medley of emotions, including the
holy trinity that would help Dominic and I to get our way:
guilt, excitement, and regret.

"I can read those later. I would love to know *your*
thoughts, Ryan. What do you think of Jess Lindley?"

He shook his head. "It doesn't matter what I think. It
matters—"

"Aren't you the one who assessed her?"

"Well, yes, of course, but I followed the criteria. It's
checking boxes, and all of my work is there." He pointed
to the folder, as though that might stop me.

Lightly laughing, I took the folder and put it under-
neath the tablet sitting between us. "Like I said, I'll read
that later. Right now I'd prefer that we talk it out. Fair for
the amount that Shellter Productions has paid you, yes?"

"Yes ... Melinda."

Looking at him now made me want to pitch an idea to
Dominic, a web series where great-looking guys were
caught completely off guard. It wouldn't be good for more
than a dozen episodes, but sometimes even that was eleven
more than enough. He was probably cursing himself,

hating the way he was responding, without any way of knowing that we saw Ryan as the right guy *because* all of this made him so uncomfortable.

"Can you maybe start with a specific question? I feel a little lost."

"Of course." I smiled. "Let's start in the simplest place possible. Why don't you give me a summary?"

"What do you mean? Should I—"

I pointed to the folder under the tablet. "Summarize everything there into a paragraph."

He looked like he wanted to argue, so I told him to, "Go."

And then he blurted, "Jess Lindley's addictions are manifesting in a variety of ways, through overt drug use, perfectionism, and catering to others. She has her issues, of course, but Jess is committed to recovery, and she has positive notions about the future. She ... well ..." Ryan gestured toward the folder. "Like I said, it's all in the write-up."

He looked down at the table, avoided my eyes, even though he couldn't see them behind the shades.

Because he knew what I was really asking, before I asked it.

"No," I pressed, all business, no bullshit. "I want to know what you thought about *fucking* her."

Ryan's torment intensified. "She was good?"

"Just good? If I have something that's just good, I send it right back."

"She was ... eager."

"Eager?"

"Committed. I don't know." He shook his head. Desire for Jess was tattooed on his face, so was the pain of confession.

"Tell me more."

"Why?"

"Because it's your job, Ryan. My questions are perfectly reasonable, considering the amount we paid for this job. I'm sure your report is thorough, enlightening, and insightful. Meticulous. Like always. But this is a very human business, so I need you to be a little more human with me."

I leaned back to stretch, both my body and the moment, to raise the roof of Ryan's discomfort while he kept trying not to look, squirming in his chair.

"Be descriptive. You're not telling an employer, you're telling a friend. Because Blush clients will want to boast. Our girls will be the best in the world, and you're helping us to make sure of that. We aren't just building the best of the world's oldest business, we are changing the culture around it. Turning the taboo into an extravagance. Blush customers will *want* to tell their friends about their time with our girls and boys. Eventually. So …"

I leaned forward, ample cleavage on display.

"Pretend you paid good money to fuck Jess Lindley. How was she?"

I settled back in my chair, crossed my legs, and waited.

"She was … uninhibited. Open. Playful I guess. She was fun to … you know, have sex with. She was comfortable in her skin. Some people exude sexuality, and Jess actually doesn't outside the bedroom, or at least it isn't the same. But behind closed doors, she's wasn't exactly a wildcat, although I'm positive that she could be if that's what her client wanted. But what made her great is that she was excellent at reading my mood. That's her super power."

"And that's why you're suggesting that we keep her."

"As long as she stays sober, you won't want to lose her. Jess Lindley is an asset to what you're trying to build."

"What was *your* mood? What was it that she was so excellent at reading?"

"She reminded me of an old ex-girlfriend," he admitted, and it seemed to come with relief. "Someone I still think about every once in a while. She was like that ... uninhibited. In control, unless I wanted to be. Great at reading my mood. That was sort of her super power, too."

"So an ex-girlfriend? Not your wife?" I smiled. "No shame in that. We all have fantasies. I'm just trying to understand."

"And my wife, of course. But more in the early days of our relationship. We've been married for twelve years, we have two kids. It's just ... different than it used to be. You know how it is."

"Of course."

For you.

I knew how it was for a lot of people. But Dominic still made me wet with a look. We each had our extracurriculars; with a stable of willing stars and starlets we would be silly not to indulge, but things were still a smoldering constant between us. Regular married people were so depressing.

"What was something she did that deeply pleased you? Something that isn't in the write-up."

Ryan knew the answer, and his red cheeks were proof. He looked down and then away.

"It's okay," I prompted. "Just tell me one thing, and then we'll be done."

He took a breath and held my eyes. "She thanked me. Before we did it, she bent over, looked over her shoulder, and then whispered in the sexiest possible voice, *Thank you for fucking me, I know how good this is going to feel.*"

"Wow. That's hot."

"Yeah. It was."

"Okay, last question."

"You said that your last question was the last question."

"This is a follow-up question. Was there anything that would have improved your experience with Jess, or made her better in some definitive way?"

Ryan looked far away as he thought, taking a moment to answer.

He could take all the time that he needed. This was important.

"I don't know how to say this exactly …"

"I'm sure you'll find a way."

"I'm married … and I think that bothered her."

"Did she say that it bothered her?"

He shook his head. "No. But you paid me to read her, right? Because that's what I do. Well, it bothered her that I was married."

"Why did you tell her you were married?"

"I didn't, but I left my ring on, and I did that because ninety percent of your clientele, at least to start, is going to be married. That's an area to navigate, not just with Jess, but with every one of your girls."

"That's an excellent answer, Ryan. Thank you. I'll look over the rest of the report with Dominic, then we'll determine the best way to go forward."

"Of course." He nodded toward the cabanas. "Do you mind if I use the restroom?"

"Be my guest."

I waited until Ryan was out of sight, then I tapped the tablet glass and made Dominic appear.

"You're still sold on this guy?" he said, a second after I could see him. "I mean, a hundred percent?"

"I am. Why aren't you?"

"He hesitates, and I know that's one of the things that you like about him, but it strikes me as maybe too much.

I'm not sure that he has enough faith in us to see the big picture, to understand what we're trying to do."

"You can't expect that to happen overnight."

"I don't. But ultimately, this is about changing culture on a global scale. We can't run an operation like Rosebud. They were fast and loose and putting everyone involved at risk. The girls *and* the clients."

"We've talked this into the ground, Dominic. We agree."

"Not about Ryan."

He was right. We rarely disagreed, and it was always like splinters in my skin when we did. But he was wrong about Ryan, I was certain.

"Ryan is the one who helped us to exploit the gaps, he's the number-one reason that we were able to take Rosebud down. We could end up running some second-tier operation like the one guy Bennett was telling us about."

"Hence, *Blush.*"

"Exactly, but we have to do it the right way. And Ryan is a part of that. He's important to the launch, if not downright essential. He's what's going to keep us from making mistakes we can't afford to make. Trust me on this, Dominic."

"You know I don't trust anyone else in the world as much."

"I do. So hear me on this. And do it now, he's coming."

"You have all my faith," he said, a second before I turned the tablet to black.

Ryan sat across from me once again.

"Thank you for all of your candor," I said. "I know that wasn't easy."

He shrugged. "It was more than fair. You and Dominic have been good to me."

"We want to keep being good to you, if you'll let us. Do you realize how much I trust you, Ryan?"

He looked unsure, but curious. "I guess."

"You signed an NDA before taking the job, but that's just paperwork. *Trust* goes much deeper than that. Working with Ambrose put you close to something extraordinary, didn't it?"

Ryan nodded.

"In some ways that was the best time of your life, right? Being a part of something remarkable? Helping to build something substantial from nothing?"

Ryan nodded again.

"And there's a part of you that's afraid that time is behind you forever, that you'll never be a part of something that important again."

I could tell from his expression that I'd guessed right. I'm not too bad at reading people, either.

"That's why you got into this in the first place, isn't it? To help people."

"Of course," he replied.

I made my final offer.

He asked for a little time to think it over, but I already knew exactly what he'd decide.

Chapter Fifteen

Wednesday Afternoon ...

NATALIE

RYAN SURPRISED me by coming home early.

The children were still in school and I was in the bedroom, getting ready for a client. I heard him a second before he appeared in the reflection behind me, and I couldn't help jumping.

I turned around and could immediately see that something was wrong.

I wondered what it was, but didn't want to care.

He collapsed into me with heaving sighs.

Ryan wasn't crying, but I couldn't help but feel like he recently had been. Stress seemed to be seeping out of his pores.

Maybe he got in a fight with one of his little girlfriends, broke up with Jess Lindley, or lost a nonexistent promotion at his imaginary job.

Whatever it was, I doubted it had anything to do with me.

Ryan gave me a deep hug, heart to heart, like he used to.

Time to put some of the acting ability I've been learning on the job to good use. If I could pretend to like Frank for an hour, I could pretend to still love my husband for a couple more days.

"Are you okay, sweetie?" I asked, petting the back of his head. "I'm surprised to see you home so early."

He pulled away. "The job finished early. I'm just glad to be home."

I bet you are.

Then Ryan lost some of his daze and seemed to really *see* me. He must have been really out of it to miss that I was nearly naked. Either that, or was just one hundred percent taking me for granted.

I was wearing lingerie at two in the afternoon on a day when he was supposed to be out of town. I was fucked if I didn't fuck him, make Ryan think that he'd spoiled his surprise.

"You look amazing."

"Thank you," I said, looking coy, lightly licking my lips. "I wanted to be ready for you when you came home." My voice fell to a whisper, sex a suggestion between every sylla- ble. "*I was practicing.*"

I could already feel his arousal.

These days I kept mine at a constant hum.

"What were you practicing?" His words came out a little too fast.

I looked in the mirror and then down at my body. "Looking like a present so that you'll want to unwrap me. Do you want to unwrap me?"

Now he looked almost comical, his tongue practically wagging out of his mouth like a cartoon character.

"Yes."

"Then what are you waiting for? I've been thinking about you all day …" I took a step closer and found his hands. "… waiting for you to come home so that I can fuck you."

He started panting as he reached for me.

Every bone in my body wanted to hate him, but in that moment, I couldn't. I'm not sure if it was because somewhere deep inside I couldn't help but still love him, or because I was getting so much experience lately in separating my emotions from the sex.

And the sex was hot. *Scorching.* Blazing enough that I didn't think of Bennett and our first night together until halfway through the encounter with my husband.

"Take off your shirt," I ordered him.

I lowered the straps on both sides of my teddy until my tits were fully exposed and Ryan was staring at them like he hadn't in years.

"You look beautiful."

"Shut up," I said, surprising us both.

I peeled off my panties and ran a finger idly over the blushing swell between my legs. "I got waxed, and I've been dying for you to see it. What do you think?"

Ryan looked gobsmacked.

"I can't stop touching myself." And then I showed him.

"*Jesus.*"

"If you'd be so kind as to take your pants off, I'd like to put your cock in my mouth."

The sex was hard and fast and filled with more passion than our bed had seen since the mattress was new. Ryan was mesmerized. This wasn't the wife that he had grown accustomed to.

Taken for granted. Lied to. Betrayed.

Revealed his most disloyal, unfaithful, adulteress self to.

This Natalie was confident, adventurous, playful. Neither his eyes nor his body could seem to believe it.

But then, something unexpected.

At first, Ryan was all smiles, stealing glances at my freshly waxed snapper, and then his face was suddenly full of something that I couldn't understand and didn't want to see. Something that made the moment a little too real.

Guilt. His pain was obvious. I'd seen flashes of the same self-loathing on the faces of clients. I didn't want to figure out where it came from, or even how to take it away, because fuck Ryan and his infinite lies. But I knew enough to get through this moment, and help him to finish — if I was reading the look in his eyes right, he was going to need it.

This is what I was good at, maybe even *best at*, even though I hadn't been doing it long.

It's what I did each day now, figuring out exactly what a client needed. Strip them of their pants and strip them of their pain.

In that moment Ryan was no longer my husband. He was a client, no different or better than any other.

I was a filthy, dirty whore, doing the job I was paid for.

And as I finished him off with that in my mind, Ryan seemed to like it that way.

"That was amazing," he said, clearly wanting to luxuriate in the afterglow.

But I didn't. I had another client waiting.

I hopped out of bed, walked over to the closet, and began to get dressed.

"Come back," he said.

"I have plans."

"You have plans? I thought you were waiting for me to come home."

"I was. But you came home and we had a good time. Now I can go out with the girls."

"Haven't you been going out with them a lot? Stay with me." Ryan patted the mattress, and I hated him again. For making me feel guilty about doing what I had to do to protect myself, when he was the one who'd put me in danger.

"Sorry," I said, forcing a smile as I tugged a pair of low-rise jeans up over my ass, wondering how I could get my sluttier getup into some sort of go bag and out of the house without Ryan seeing it.

"It's hard, being cooped up all the time while you're gone. But this is great for us both. We've already connected —" I glanced at the wet spot to remind him "—and now I can have a little fun with the girls while you bond with the kids."

"Okay," he said, sounding defeated.

I confess that I enjoyed that he was taking it as a rejection. It made seeing him at Cameo with Jess and Olivia sting a little less.

He picked up the remote from his nightstand and aimed it at the TV, no longer paying attention to me.

Good, I thought, crouching in the closet, stuffing clean lingerie and fuck-me pumps into a bag.

Ryan was scrolling through the channels, still distracted.

I looked at myself in the mirror, wanting to laugh at what now looked like a costume. I remembered Olivia mocking my mom clothes, and how much that made me want to change. But now I was like Superman, dressing as Clark Kent, pretending to be less super than I was.

I walked from the closet to bedroom door, set my bag

on the hallway floor, then returned to our bed and kissed Ryan goodbye. He was no longer scrolling, having settled on something he wanted to watch. *The Emerald Escape*, starring Bennett Cole, because of course.

"I fucking love that guy," Ryan said, smiling at the TV. Then he turned to me with big eyes that looked full of remorse and added, "But I love you more."

"I love you too," I said, then kissed him like I meant it, but I was thinking about how Bennett had fucked me in the bathroom at Cameo and abandoned me. Somehow, that made it hotter. I can't explain why.

As I headed out the door, I wondered if I'd always been messed up, or if the job was making me that way.

Either way, I didn't know what I could do about it.

Chapter Sixteen

Saturday Evening …

THERE WAS a constant aching like an echo inside me.

I desperately missed Alec and Lena, but with Ryan home, I couldn't stand being around the house. Part of it was that I didn't want to be anywhere near him. But another part of me wanted a confrontation, wanted Ryan to ask where the hell I was going. So I could finally say some of the things I'd been carrying around since that awful night when Olivia walked back into our lives.

I'd taken five appointments in between when he came home early and this morning. Yet my husband hadn't questioned a single one of my domestic escapes. He sprawled in our bed all day, watching movies. Every time I asked him when he was going back to work, always casually, and never nagging of course, he would say something like:

I'm not sure. Ambrose will let me know when he needs me.

They're reshuffling some things, but this is going to be good for us.

I'm on break until Conquest gets their next contract. Isn't that great? We can spend more time together!

A few years too late, asshole.

Now it was Saturday night. Not only had I been gone all afternoon, thanks to a series of unexpected events (Victor texted me the wrong time by an hour, the client wanted extra time and was a generous tipper, but he was also messy and I needed time to shower, but since his wife was coming into the hotel any minute, I had to book a room on another floor just to clean myself) I was much later than I promised I would be.

But I opened the door and no one seemed to notice.

I usually came home to a chorus of greetings, especially lately.

Maybe Ryan and the kids were playing. That thought should have made me happy, but it was almost impossible to have any positive thoughts about him, even when I wanted to.

Then it hit me. The scent. Downright sumptuous, and coming from the kitchen. I couldn't remember the last time Ryan had cooked. The last couple nights he'd had takeout delivered — pizza, then Chinese. I'd figured tonight would be burgers from Sloppy's, still one of his favorites.

He used to come in and eat there when I was on shift, back in the days when he was pursuing me behind Olivia's back.

I heard happy laughter coming from the kitchen. So hurried into the living room — and froze.

This couldn't be good.

Olivia sat at the table coloring with Lena. Behind them I could see Alec helping Ryan with dinner in the kitchen.

What the ever-loving fuck?

Had she told Ryan? Or a better question, *what* she had told him? Because she had to have told him something.

I wondered if life as I knew it was over.

But then I realized that life as I knew it had been over for a while.

"Hi everyone!" I said, announcing my presence, my heart full of thunder and lightning.

Ryan looked over from the kitchen, definitely a deer in headlights.

Olivia smiled, looking smugger than a sommelier.

Ryan tousled Alec's hair and whispered something in his ear, probably about keeping the stirring going, then he trotted out into the living room, grinning wide with a smile full of lies.

"Look who I ran into earlier today! Can you believe it? After twelve years? I insisted that she come over for dinner."

What a deceitful cocksucker of man. I *saw* Ryan run into Olivia after twelve years, just a few days ago.

"Hi Natalie!" Olivia said, still holding her sommelier's smile.

I wanted to kill her. Kill *him*. Bury them both in my backyard, and do yoga on top of their graves.

"Olivia!" I rushed over to greet her. "How long has it been?"

It might be hard to believe, but the next hour and a half was worse than fucking Frank. I would have rather curled into a ball and let him beat off on me. That would have been better than pretending that I wasn't dying inside, watching Olivia laughing with my husband, turning around to smile and wink and shrug and show me in every possible way that she was the queen and I was a pawn in a game that she planned to keep playing until I surrendered in full.

We went through a bottle of wine during dinner, but I only pretended to sip.

NOLON KING

Olivia noticed. "You're not drinking?"

"It makes me too sleepy," I said, though the truth was that I couldn't trust myself with more than a few drops. There were too many things that I wanted to say, and they might pour from my mouth like wine from the bottle.

We talked about Alec, his grades in school, and how he was about to start karate; Lena's favorite books (*A Tale Dark and Grimm, Holes*, and — of course — *Harry Potter*) and her essay on "Why Family is Important" hanging in the hallway outside of Constellation's front office; Ryan's job, most of it centered around the last year so I knew every word out of his mouth was A TOTAL FUCKING LIE; and Olivia's job, which she referred to as "Rolodexing" before explaining that she was a professional networker, which I had to admit was a great way to describe what we do.

Then the conversation turned to me. Olivia had thirty-seven thousand questions about the CTA and all my girl-friends at Constellation, curious as she was about how a modern housewife raised a wonderful family like ours.

I wanted to vomit the entire time.

"That was amazing!" I blew my husband a kiss. "You really can do anything when you put your mind to it. Thanks for putting your mind to something for our table tonight."

Ryan looked like he didn't know how to take that. I wasn't even sure what I meant, except fuck him and every word out of his stupid lying mouth.

He finally said, "Thank you," then invited Alec and Lena into the kitchen to help him with the dishes, just like the perfect husband he wasn't. "You girls should stay out here and catch up."

FUCK YOU BOTH!

Ryan stood and began to gather dishes.

Beaming up at him: "I couldn't do this without you."

Looking at me, slightly unsure: "Same for me."

Olivia watched us, smiling.

The children were making silly faces at each other.

As soon as I had her alone, I hissed at Olivia, "*What are you doing?*"

"Taking a stroll down memory lane." She looked appreciably around the living room, studying it all with a steady gaze. Framed and hanging, polished and waxed, ordered and shipped and displayed. "This is a nice life you have here. Reminds me of Page 27 in the Restoration Hardware Catalogue."

"Cut the shit, Olivia. This is my family we're talking about. Why are you—"

"You only have a family because you stole it from me, Natalie." Olivia had drunk most of the bottle but she was holding it well. Her words were clear, and her smirk sharp enough to cut them. "Ryan's gotten better-looking with age. He was a perfect fit then, and with all of his experience now?" Olivia laughed, shaking her head in pity. "I can't believe you'd rather fuck strangers for money when you have that waiting for you at home. Poor thing, he probably feels so neglected. And I can't imagine what that's done to your self-esteem … To think that you were heading right into frumpy town before—"

"Get. Out."

Olivia laughed. "Sorry, sweetheart. I'm not going anywhere."

"Like hell you're not."

"What are you going to do, Natalie? You're not holding a single card."

"What do you want from me? Why did you show up out of nowhere to ruin my life? I don't under—"

"You know exactly why I'm here. And you always knew

that something like this would eventually happen, because you can't outrun karma. *You* used to say that, Natalie. Not me. But you're right, you can't. So here we are."

"What about when karma comes for you?"

Olivia shrugged. "I'm good at settling my debts. That's what I'm doing now."

I was boiling. Good thing we weren't anywhere near the knives.

"Tell me how to get you out of my life forever."

Those words appeared to hit Olivia the same as they hit me, with a sort of yawning hurt, haunting her face in an immediate shadow. She lost her smile.

"I'll get out of your life when you pay me back."

"Pay you back for what?"

"You stole my life."

I could see in her eyes that she meant it.

There was no way to argue with her, not without her announcing to Ryan — in front of my children — that I was a whore.

She'd screamed that at me before, but now it was actually true.

"How are you girls doing out there?" Ryan called out from the kitchen. "Anyone in the mood for some ice cream?"

A chorus of *Yes!* from the children.

"That sounds great!" Olivia said, while glaring at me.

"Sure!" Then, "How am I supposed to pay you back for *stealing your life?* What's the price tag on that? I've never seen it at Target."

"Like you shop at Target."

"I shop at Target all the time!"

"Are we going to Target?" Lena yelled from the kitchen.

"You should lower your voice," Olivia said.

Goddammit. "Tell me what you want."

"I want twenty-five percent of whatever you're taking home."

"Fine, Olivia. If an extra five-percent is really worth all of this to you, then please enjoy an extra Benjamin every time I'm taking another dick in one of my two available holes."

"No." She shook her head. "It's not an extra five percent. I want another fifteen, on top of the ten that you're already giving me."

"WHAT?"

"What?" Ryan echoed from the kitchen. "Did you need something?"

"She's fine!" Olivia said, her smile still fixed on me.

The first tear fell down my cheek. I couldn't stand to let Olivia see me wipe it, or for anyone from my family to see it at all. I dragged my sleeve across it as one fell down the other side.

"Why are you doing this to me?"

"You know why."

"I don't even want to be doing this." Now I was softly crying, and doing everything I could not to bawl. "I just want to pay off my debts and get out."

"Then work more."

"I *can't* work more."

"Then raise your rates," Olivia said.

"I can do that?"

"Of course you can. My best clients pay me five grand, but for them I charge by the encounter rather than by the hour. It's twice that for overnight. Although I could see how that particular service is out of reach for you. So, you give me a quarter as my cut, and I'll keep all of your little secrets. Then I'll leave you alone for the rest of your life once you're out, just like you want. Do we have a deal?"

I gathered myself as best as I could, then drew in a breath and held it before exhaling.

"Deal," I said.

Then I got myself ready for ice cream.

Chapter Seventeen

Monday Evening ...

LYNETTE

"WOULD YOU LIKE A REFILL, LYNETTE?" Roberta asked.

"Sure." I held out my glass and let her fill it.

She finished, smiled, then set the pitcher on the table between us. Susan went on with her bleating.

I was grateful for the Long Islands because Susan hadn't said anything interesting in the entire time that she had been over, because there was nothing interesting about her oldest son, unless you were one of the unfortunate few fascinated by arrested development. That kid was a thirty-year-old nightmare. Roberta wasn't helping, leaning forward with her chin on her knuckles, listening to Susan's stories as though they were in any way absorbing.

I looked around my backyard, wondering if I'd rather be alone.

Probably not. Frank was inside, and he'd probably try to get on me. This time of day that meant watching some sort of financial reports while he grunted from behind.

Finally, Susan said something worth caring about.

"I saw Natalie over the weekend …"

I hated the way she always trailed off when she actually had something to say. Susan never did us that favor when discussing gluten, grades, or Owen's tantrums (they were never his fault, nor hers, just an even mix of no sleep, hunger, and schedules gone haywire).

"You know how I started counting my steps and trying to get ten thousand—"

"Yes," I said, twirling my finger.

"Well, I haven't been able to get more than seven thousand on average, even with all my running around and Owen's—"

"So you figured it was the weekend, what the hell, you'd go for ten," I finished.

"Right?" Susan looked at me, the smile half-hanging from her face. "So I was walking a little further than I normally would, and—"

"*Farther,*" Roberta corrected. "*Further* is metaphorical. *Farther* is distance. You meant distance."

"Thanks!" Susan chirped, because she actually liked that shit. "Anyway, I was walking *farther* than usual and ended up over on Dalton."

"Where Natalie lives."

Roberta had an unhealthy habit of stating the obvious.

"Right!" Susan gave Roberta a look: *You know me!*

"So I was over by where Natalie lives and I thought—"

"Oh my God, Susan! Will you *please* get to the point?"

Then she looked at me, blinking like a child who'd peed himself. Maybe she was imitating her son.

Her voice a lot quieter than it had been a few seconds before, Susan said, "I saw Natalie walking a beautiful blonde woman out to her car."

I sat up straighter, instantly curious. And jealous. I hated to admit to that particular emotion, but I couldn't lie to myself about what I felt. Natalie didn't have time to have lunch with me, but she had time for this blonde?

"What did she look like?"

I was glad Roberta asked so that I didn't have to.

"Not the kind of woman I would ever want around the house, that's for sure." Susan shook her head. "No. Way. Natalie's beautiful, don't get me wrong, and youth is on her side. But this woman?"

Susan took a moment to exhale in appreciation. For the first time I didn't mind.

"She was one of the most beautiful women I've ever seen in real life. I wouldn't trust her around my husband."

Roberta said, "And you just know that Ryan could have any woman he wants."

I didn't disagree. If Frank had an exact opposite, it was Natalie's husband.

"I bet it gets lonely on the road, with all the traveling he does," Susan said, then lowered her voice to a conspirator's whisper. "Do you think he's ever ... you know?"

"I don't know, and it seems mean to say," Roberta said, "but can you imagine sex with him?"

"Yes," I said, laughing.

I probably wouldn't have said that without the three glasses of Long Island iced tea, but the girls laughed with me.

"No," Roberta clarified. "I mean with a psychologist. The way he must know people ... and *things*. It must be so ... *intense*. And yes, the way he looks. Because oh my God, I don't mind bitching to you girls, and I know I don't have to tell you, but he is *nothing* like my husband."

"Well, yours is older than your father, right?"

Roberta shook her head like always, an uncomfortable laugh as usual. "Only by a year."

"Seriously," I said. "*Do* any of you think that Ryan could be cheating on Natalie?"

An uncomfortable silence settled among them. None of them wanted to break it. My money was on Susan, but Roberta proved me wrong.

"I just wonder if she knows what she has." She looked at Susan. "You and Steve are like peas in a pod. He's just as high strung as you are, and don't look at me like that because you know it's true." Then she turned to me. "You seem to genuinely appreciate Frank and the life that he's given you. Same for me and Walter. Our sex life isn't great, or really even good." She laughed. "But I love Walter. He makes me laugh and he takes great care of us. I never, ever have to worry. And I appreciate that."

"But you're not sure that Natalie does?" I said.

"Right." Roberta nodded. "Men *need* to feel appreciated. It's in their DNA. So if she's not appreciating it, then things are going to break, and if they break in the bedroom, then most men are going to at least *think* about getting it elsewhere. And with all of his traveling?"

"I'm more suspicious of Natalie," Susan said. "All of a sudden, she's always busy. But she's a stay-at-home mom? How much stuff can she possibly have to do? What is it that has her missing CTA meetings and volunteer days and—"

"I want to know why she looks so fantastic lately," I cut in. "Mark Krieg's dad was *staring* at her during drop-off the other day. I mean, I don't blame him.

"But" Roberta said, "there's gotta be something else going on there, right?"

"Well, whatever it is, I hope Natalie realizes how good she has it. With Ryan."

Roberta looked wistful. "If he had a practice, I'd book office hours for sure."

I thought about what office hours with Ryan might be like, and wondering if he and Natalie had ever role-played that particular fantasy, or any fantasy at all.

I leaned back in my chair, stewing, sucking on the end of my straw, slurping to the bottom of my Long Island iced tea, stuck in a cycle of illogical thoughts that I couldn't seem to escape.

Why did I care so much that Natalie had been avoiding my calls for a while now?

Why was I so bothered that she was hanging out with another woman? We were barely friends, although not for lack of trying on my part.

Why on earth did it matter if she was losing weight and looking great, with her calendar and heart both apparently full?

I was tuning the girls out and considering filling my glass one final time, when Frank came outside.

He appeared more buoyant than usual. The sort of mood I knew well enough to be suspicious of.

I reached for the pitcher.

Frank looked at the three of us and said, "No Natalie today?"

He probably thought he sounded nonchalant, but if anything I thought he sounded eager.

I traded a look with the girls. They could hear him lying too.

"No darling," I said, saccharin sweet despite the souring of my stomach, "Not today."

Frank looked disappointed, and I was suddenly hungry to know why.

Natalie Monroe was up to something, and I was going to find out what.

Chapter Eighteen

Tuesday Afternoon ...

NATALIE

I WAS RACING down the freeway, headed toward Constellation, hoping I wasn't going to get pulled over, and thinking that I probably would since everything else about this afternoon had been total shit.

Alec was in trouble, and I was on my way to go get him, an hour and a half after getting the call. I'd been with a client when Principal Butler called. It was forty-five excruciating minutes before the client finally rolled off me and I was free to check my voicemail. Three messages, each one sterner than the last.

I checked to make sure I was clear, cut across two lanes of traffic, drove another three-quarters of a mile, then barreled down my exit. There were six lights in between me and Constellation. If half were red, I might be able to make myself presentable by the time I arrived.

I wish it had been a hundred red lights. That would keep me from having to face the inevitable.

Not what Alec did, but what *I did*.

I would have bet every stitch of clothing in my closet that I wouldn't be getting called into Mr. Butler's office if I'd been doing a better job as a mom. Disciplining my son rather than bribing him. Doing the hard work instead of spending so much of my time taking the easy way out.

That's because you're trying to get out, period. And there's nothing easy about what you do.

Alec had gotten into a fight with Drew Wilder, and as much as I can't stand Lynette's little twat demon, I was shocked when the school receptionist told me that Alec had thrown the first punch. He'd never been in a fight, even in third grade when one of the other kids had tried to make him hand over his lunch money.

Clearly he was having more trouble dealing with my absence than I'd realized.

And again, I knew it was all my fault.

I parked, killed the engine, then marched up the front steps and into the office where Lynette was already waiting.

She looked up at me, her eyes darker than I'd ever seen them, especially when directed at me. Coldly and quietly, she said, "Thank you for finally deciding to join us."

I couldn't quite bring myself to apologize to her. "I was stuck at an appointment."

She said nothing, and we sat through a few minutes of silence, cut mercifully short when the principal opened his door and invited us inside.

"And you're sure that Alec started it?" I asked.

"That's not what I said," Mr. Butler shook his head. "Alec did strike Drew first, but both boys agree that it was in response to something that Drew said."

Lynette suddenly looked a little less smug. "What did he say?"

Mr. Butler clearly wasn't looking forward to answering, shifting in his seat, and working hard to avoid my eyes.

"Yeah," I prompted. "What did he say?"

"I'm sorry, Mrs. Monroe, but Drew called you a hooker to Alec's face."

I gasped. So did Lynette. Both of our jaws could have been swept up off of the floor.

That was so ... *specific.*

I started to panic, wondering if I was sweating, sure that the guilt was like red paint all over my face. Probably all over my body. Maybe they knew where I had just come from and what I'd been doing.

What if I had cum in my hair and didn't even know it?

Drew had called me a hooker, told my son how I was spending my time. How did he even know? If Frank had said something, I was going to kill him.

But it seemed crazy that Frank would spill the beans and risk the consequences for his own actions.

Maybe I was panicking. Boys talked shit, and calling your friend's mom a hooker was probably typical pre-adolescent shit talking, nothing to be worried about.

Except that it was true, and if Alec was upset enough to hit his friend, then maybe he knew deep in his heart that it wasn't a lie.

Mr. Butler watched us, probably wondering what would happen next.

Me too.

Lynette turned toward me and I braced for the worst.

Her hand found my arm and I was flooded with panic.

But then, shaking her head, she said, "I am so, *so* sorry, Natalie. There is absolutely *no* excuse for that. I am so embarrassed."

I couldn't believe it, or stop myself from straightening my shoulders and acting at least a little bit miffed. I mean, I had to if I expected to sell the role.

"That really is a horrible thing to say, but boys are boys, and it's not like Alec is innocent. He should never have hit Drew, no matter what he said. So I'm sorry, too."

We settled back in our chairs, both of us looking at Mr. Butler.

"So, what's next?" Lynette asked him.

"As you know, we have a zero tolerance policy on fighting at Constellation, regardless of who started the fight."

"We get it, Alastair," Lynette said, using his first name in a way I wouldn't dare. Maybe you could do that when you covered tuition for children that didn't belong to you. "Now can you please just tell us what we're supposed to do with our boys?"

"Both Alec and Drew will be suspended for two days."

Lynette turned to me. "Sound fair to you?"

"Sounds fair," I agreed.

"Two days. Anything else?" Lynette looked at Mr. Butler expectantly, clearly done and wanting to go.

"No, Mrs. Wilder, there won't be any other punishment. But I would strongly suggest that you spend the next couple of days talking to Drew about what language is and is not appropriate, in or out of school." He turned to me. "And Alec needs to understand that intelligent men do not solve problems with violence."

"I promise we'll have a nice long talk, tonight. And then another tomorrow. Where are they now? I assume we should just take them home with us?"

"They're both spending some quiet time with Ms. Dougherty." Then after the subtlest glance my way, he added, "They've been in there a while."

We walked toward the Quiet Room, a rather cavernous space on the far side of campus that only a school like Constellation would be pompous enough to have. I usually appreciated such things, but right then a trip to Disneyland might have annoyed me.

We were silent enough to be practicing for our own spell in the Quiet Room, when Lynette finally broke the quiet.

She stopped walking and said, "Why haven't you answered any of my calls?"

I stopped too, then turned to Lynette. Her eyes were big and wet.

"I'm sorry," I said, feeling suddenly and inexplicably terrible. I couldn't think of anything that didn't sound lame, but I tried anyway. "Things have been hard with Ryan, and I … I've been doing a terrible job of managing my time."

Lynette looked at me like she didn't believe a word I was saying, but was trying her best to figure it out.

"I'm trying really hard to be your friend, Natalie, but I'm sick of you making it so difficult."

Then she walked ahead of me without another word, and went to pick up her demon spawn.

Chapter Nineteen

Friday Evening ...

MY BODY HAD ALREADY BETRAYED me.

Bennett booked me again, and as I got ready to see him, I was already wet.

I changed into a fresh pair of panties, feeling even guiltier than usual. Weird, since I was also over the moon and halfway to Mars. Plus anxious, excited, and a little afraid of how much I liked him when I couldn't afford to like any of my clients.

Also, a little embarrassed about our prior encounter. I worried that the booking was a punishment.

I'd never had all of these feelings together, but it had been a long time since I'd felt even half of what I was feeling now, getting ready to see a man with the sort of aroused anticipation I'd once reserved only for Ryan.

I was pretty sure that I was going to enjoy tonight more than I should.

It wasn't safe, and that was turning me on, too.

Seeing him again would be awkward, and exhilarating. I was grateful for the closure. After feeling so desperate and confused in the aftermath of our last encounter, he'd been a constant itch in my brain. I would think of him at the oddest times.

I had given it up for free in a restroom. If that wasn't the bottom, then it was inches above. Why would Bennett pay a premium for what he had already gotten for free, and in the most undignified way?

Mostly, why was I staring in the mirror, acting like a fucking teenager?

Because Bennett had become *my* fantasy. My escape, in the same way that I was an escape for the men who paid to be with me.

I imagined our evening as I drove to meet him, picturing things that would never happen, and that didn't need to. There was beauty in the fantasy. Why shouldn't I get what my clients got? And wasn't I lucky that someone was actually paying me for the experience? I didn't care *what* happened with Bennett. I couldn't imagine an order of his that I would refuse to follow, since he already told me that he wasn't into the one thing I told him I wouldn't do, and I was already wet enough for anything else.

He wanted to meet at the Mill, an odd place for a tryst. The shopping is great, and so are the restaurants. It's the best place in the city to see a movie. But unless he's wanting to fuck in public, which I couldn't imagine, considering his high profile, I didn't really get the location.

But the customer — Bennett — is always right.

Meet me in front of Crossroads.

There he was, standing in front of the shop like he wasn't one of the world's most famous men, holding a bag like it was no big deal, just like any other shopper. He wasn't perfectly lit like he was in movies, but the sun did a nice enough job, even if it made him look glossy rather than matte. And handsome wasn't a strong enough word to describe him. Bennett was rugged but beautiful. Chiseled, yet silken. Fire and ice and all the degrees in between.

I approached with a coquettish smile. "Are you waiting for someone?"

I wasn't sure whether to kiss him on the cheek or the mouth, or nothing at all. I was so used to meeting my clients in private that I had yet to learn the protocol for greeting one publicly.

"I feel like I'm always waiting for someone," he said with a smile, and I wondered exactly what he meant.

I nodded at his bag. "Did you go shopping without me?"

"I did not." He raised the bag and shook it. "This is just stuff I needed to get."

"So what's in the bag?"

"Underwear."

"Just underwear? That's a big bag."

He shrugged. "I wear a new pair every day. I knew I was getting low and I don't like other people buying my underwear for me, even if I'm okay with them buying everything else." He laughed. "It's stupid, I know."

"It's not." I didn't want to say what I was thinking, that Crossroads was expensive, the kind of store I'd never even dared to go inside. I bet that underwear cost well over a hundred bucks a pair, and to him they were disposable.

"So what are we going to do?" I smiled to let him know that I would be happy with *anything*.

"We're going shopping."

"Great." I could hardly believe that he was paying me to go shopping with him. "What do you need?"

"I don't need anything," he said. "We're shopping for *you*."

My hand went to my breast. "Me? Why are we shopping for me?"

"Because I want to."

Then Bennett held out his arm, waiting for mine.

My heart was doing somersaults.

We went into Mirror Mirror. It wasn't my favorite place to shop in the Mill because the prices were too prohibitive for me, but it was my favorite place to *look*. I'd been in there a few times and only made a single purchase: an indigo scarf with the most delicate edges, spatters of lavender and black and a dusting of white. Half off, the scarf was almost 500 dollars. Stupid idiot purchases like that are exactly what had gotten me into this mess. I felt sick, considering the compound effect of all my impulsive, impetuous behavior.

Then I thought, *These days, five hundred dollars is twenty minutes' worth of work.*

Still, I was watching every dollar. With Olivia demanding her devil's ransom, I had to be stricter with my spending than ever.

As soon as we were inside the shop, he said, "Pick anything you want."

"Anything?"

"I always say what I mean, Elle." He raised his bag to remind me. "Remember how much I just spent on underwear. I'm not stupid with my money, but the small things stopped mattering a long time ago. Anything in this store is still a relatively small thing to me."

I stepped closer to him, blew my lightest breath in his ear, and said, "Underwear is important. I'm glad you buy the best."

Bennett liked that; I could hear his breathing speed up. I continued to whisper. "But I can't wait to take those boxers off of you so that I can put your cock in my mouth."

I reached down to check my work, found that I'd done a serviceable job, gave his semi a pet just to let it know that we'd be getting better acquainted later, and kissed him on the cheek before pulling away.

"Thank you," I said.

And then I went shopping.

I was ready to go after the first thing I tried on, but Bennett was not. I couldn't believe that he really wanted to sit there in Mirror Mirror while he was paying me. Ryan would never do that, not ever, even for free.

I tried on seven things. *Seven*. I stopped feeling bad after the third one because Bennett was going to buy something for me, and that's what test drives were for.

The fifth was my favorite. Bennett's too.

It was black, but with a sort of sheen as light washed across it. The straps were thin, two on each side and woven together like lovers who couldn't bear to part. The fabric fell to just below my knee, and felt like someone was kissing the skin there. Silky and soft, thin but not in a way that exposed me.

Holding it in my hands, I wanted to cry. "It's the most beautiful dress I've ever seen."

"It's yours," he said.

There had to be a catch.

"Why are we really here, Bennett?"

"Why are you having such a hard time believing that I really wanted to go shopping?"

"I don't … it's just, there's gotta be something more, right?" I laughed and touched him playfully on the arm. "I want to make you happy. If you tell me, I can do a better job. Do you want to rip this dress off of me? I'll be sad, but okay." I laughed again. "Same if you want to cum all over it. Really, I just want you to see you smile, and know that I'm the one who put that smile there."

He shook his head, lightly laughing. "It's nothing like that."

"Then what is it like?"

"I did have an ulterior motive."

"Of course you did." I smiled. "Can you tell me more?"

"I can tell you that I wanted you to pick out something to wear for an upcoming business meeting."

"What else can you tell me?"

"That was all I was planning to tell you for now." Then he stared at me, like he wanted to devour me.

So when was he going to do it?

"Can you change your plans?" I asked.

"If you can change yours."

I didn't know what he meant, or why he was looking at me like that, still like he wanted to reach down and slip a couple of his digits inside me, but also expectantly, as if waiting for me to understand.

"What do you want me to change them to?"

"I want to book you for an entire weekend. Next weekend. Will you do that for me?"

I didn't know what to say. The thought of a week away with him weakened my knees and made every cell in my body start to tremble.

But what was I going to tell Ryan? And should I leave the kids when Alec was getting into fights at school?

Tell Ryan you're sick of his shit. You don't have enough to leave, but you do have enough to hire a great divorce lawyer.

But spending the money meant working for Victor longer.

"I have a family," I waffled.

"I know. It's a big ask. I'll make it worth your while."

You already have.

"Where are we going? How long will I be gone?"

"I'll get you details soon. I'm still working it out, but I need to know if you're in."

I was desperate to say yes, but any excuse I could use to get away from home for a weekend would come off as thin at best and absurd at worst. "What *can* you tell me?"

"That I'll pay you twenty-five thousand dollars." He smiled. "Plus the dress."

I might have peed myself.

It was already *Yes* in my head, but I didn't want to seem too needy or excited. I was a service provider, and Bennett a client. I couldn't forget that, especially not now.

"Soon. But I really want you to do this with me." Then he took my hands and reminded me of my place. "You're Victor's best, and I don't trust anyone else."

"I'll do it."

"I can't wait." Bennett grazed me with his eyes. "Go in the dressing room and put that back on. I'll meet you in five minutes. We're going to have some fun before we buy it."

I whimpered my excitement, both because I was happy and because it made Bennett happy.

I went into the dressing room, donned my new dress, and then waited for Bennett on my knees.

Chapter Twenty

Saturday Evening, Eight Days Later ...

MELINDA

"PARDON ME, MRS. SHELLY?"

I turned around. A server was holding a platter of drinks. "I thought you might like a Stoli Doli. They're delicious."

"Please," I said, reaching out to take one. "And it's Melinda."

I hated *Mrs. Shelly*, even from the staff.

It was a divide-and-conquer night for Dominic and I. We were attending the premiere of some second-rate studio's upcoming lineup, a watering hole for actors who had felt success on the tip of their tongue, but had yet to truly taste it. A great place to scout for potential candidates for next year's Onyx List. While Dominic was doing that, I was here for a different reason, and one I still seemed to believe in more than him.

I had my own shit to conquer, and that involved meeting my good friend Bennett and his date.

There weren't many people in the world who knew what Dominic and I were planning with Blush, but among those select few, Bennett was one of the biggest supporters. Especially after the Rosebud leak had exposed so many of their clients.

Bennett wasn't the first person to tell me about Victor and his little ring of girls, but he was our only client on the inside. Not that I'd sent him to infiltrate the place. Bennett is a buyer, preferring the professional performance and total lack of strings. He likes having a secret. He loves sex with women who love what they do, and paying them handsomely for their time. Escorts were his fetish, and being the friend that he is, Bennett was always happy to share.

I'd asked him if there were any girls over there who he thought deserved better. At first he said that he wasn't too sure, probably not. But then he called me up and told me that he'd found someone special at Victor's. Someone he thought I should meet.

I needed someone to handle these girls, but she couldn't think like a typical madame. We needed someone smart but maternal, and able to blend into any social setting. Organized yet flexible. A woman who could see the biggest picture in the tiniest details and could also see things from the other side without having to ever turn around. And most important of all, she needed to believe in what we were doing.

Supposedly, Bennett's date might be that person.

I saw them walk in before he saw me. So I had a moment to study her first.

She was pretty without being ravishing. Her cheeks were round, but her dark hair hung long on either side and made them look thinner. Her smile was true; this woman practically glowed. Her dress was stunning, and if Bennett had done as I suggested and had her select both the shop and the gown herself, then she'd proven to have excellent taste.

She did look a little starstruck, but that was absolutely as it should be at this stage, and also, how could she not be? Even from across the way, I could see it in her eyes, that this was equal parts fantasy and business opportunity, shaken and stirred.

Perfect.

Bennett saw me, waved, and brought her over.

"Melinda!" He kissed me on the cheek and whispered in my ear, "She is a *treat.*" Then louder, "I'd like you to meet Elle. Elle, this is Melinda."

"It's good to meet you." She shook my hand.

Elle was … mature. But not in an old or stuffy way — I didn't see a single line on her face — and she didn't look a thing like the MILFs that littered all of those lesser porn sites with fake tits and toddlers at best. The woman looked like an actual mom who I would like to fuck.

And she was elegant, the way that dress draped her very real body. She looked like a blast in the bedroom after a dignified dinner, and a gourmet at both the blow job and breakfast the next morning.

"How long have you been an escort?" I asked, trying to catch her off guard.

"Either too long or not long enough," she said without hesitation. "I haven't decided."

I laughed, then let that one go. "Have you been to the raw bar yet?"

I'd asked Bennett, but she answered, just like I hoped that she would.

"I dragged him there first. Raw oysters sound good.

With my schedule, the closest I've come to fish lately is sticks." She laughed. "At home I can dress whatever with my sauce, it's the best you've ever tasted, but here you don't need to. Everything is *so* fresh."

"What's in your sauce?" I asked, not because I cared, but the woman lit up at the mention.

"A little mayo, ketchup and brandy. Tiny bit of mustard." Another smile that looked like a wink, followed by a swipe of her hand. "And, of course, a little bit of me."

I couldn't have written myself a better opening.

"I get the feeling that you put at least a little of yourself into everything you do, is that right, Elle?"

She blushed like a good girl, stealing the slightest glance at Bennett beside her, a flash of her eyes and nothing more. "I try to. Otherwise, why do it?"

Bennett put his hand on her back. "Elle is one of those people who cares."

"I can see that," I said. "Tell me Elle, if it isn't too gauche to be interrogating you at a party."

"Bennett said that he wanted me to meet someone. I'm assuming that was you, and I trust him." Another glance at her dream date. "So go ahead and ask, what is it you want to know?"

"The same thing from you that I always want to know about everyone else: *What are you best at?*"

It wasn't what Elle expected. She pursed her lips, thinking, appearing to give my query some serious thought.

Then finally she said, "Listening."

"Lots of people listen," I nudged her. "Why is that special?"

"I mean *listening.* Because people *don't* do that. Not nearly enough. I always know what people need."

"Be specific," I had to keep pressing. "Which people?"

The first time Elle looked uncomfortable, but then she

said it anyway. "My children. My husband, when he's not being a lying asshole. Everyone at school."

"What are you worst at?" I asked.

"Making time for it all," she admitted.

It was hard not to like her, and I was looking for reasons.

"Are you organized?"

"Oh yes, but flexible." Then, "Excuse me, but is this a job interview?"

Yes.

"Not at all. Just curious."

I kept my questions light after that, observing her with Bennett, and feeling better and better about Blush. Every instinct was telling me that Bennett was right, this girl would be great; I had to capitalize on this opportunity.

Like always, I was willing to spend. But first I had to know what I was buying.

Elle, or whatever her name was, because it sure as hell wasn't that, would need a full evaluation. Whether or not Ryan agreed to a full-time position, I would make this job worth his while. A detailed write-up on this woman — similar to the one he'd provided for Lindley, albeit for an entirely different role in the new company — would give me the green light required to get Dominic fully on board. Even if he didn't necessarily believe that Ryan should be part of the permanent team, he had never questioned the quality of the man's recommendations.

Bennett gave me a knowing smile and whispered, "*I told you,*" into my ear before escorting her back over to the bar.

I walked over to a quiet spot on the far side of the tennis courts and dialed Ryan.

"Hello?" He answered on the second ring, children laughing in the background. In the distance I heard, "*Shhh*

… I'm on the phone." Then louder, "Hi, Melinda. Sorry, I'm with my kids right now. What's up? I still have until tomorrow to decide about the job, right?"

"I have something else for you, if you're interested. A special psych assessment. High priority. Are you interested?"

"Maybe? Do you have any details?"

"Absolutely. And that's the prize for telling me that you're interested. You say yes, then I get back to you with the specifics as soon as I have them. Right now, I just need to know if you're in."

So on cue he said, "Then consider me in."

Chapter Twenty-One

Sunday Evening ...

JADE

LAST NIGHT'S party was the worst so far.

Not to say that they've all been bad, because they haven't at all. Some are fun, and they all paid me really well for my time, even the ones that are sorta hard to stay excited for because the guys are yelling at me or telling me to do things I don't wanna do, which Victor told me at first that I wouldn't have to do because this was a better class of gentlemen and all, but now he's telling me that I should just *roll with it.*

That's what I kept telling myself during my time with Nelson Bragg. He maybe had the most appropriate last name of any guy I ever knew, and for sure anyone I ever had to sleep with. He was lucky his stupid show, *Out of My Mind* was still on the air. I only saw it once, but it was dumb, even though it was hard to follow. I didn't know anyone who watched it. Critics said it was boring, tone-deaf, and tried too hard.

I'd looked it up after leaving Nelson because reading how much everyone hated him made me feel a little bit better. I didn't know much about *Out of My Mind*, but the review sounded like a critique of Nelson himself.

Nelson talked like he was more successful than God, but he spent like a parishioner on the dole. Instead of springing for the penthouse like a lot of actors — it hadn't happened yet for me, but I kept hearing the stories — he dragged me into a dingy motel on the wrong side of the hills.

Some of the guys like to make small talk ahead of time, or at least try to be nice to me. They're paying and all, so they don't have to, but still, it's not hard to know that if you get a girl in the mood, it's probably gonna be better for you.

Unless you're a guy like Nelson Bragg -- then that's not what you want at all.

We'd been in the shithole for about five minutes when I realized that he wasn't just being cheap, that was part of the turn-on for him. And I was okay with that, until he refused to wear a condom. That was my one thing. I didn't want to end up pregnant, or with something nasty that I'd have for the rest of my life, and maybe even pass onto my babies. I heard that could happen. It was one of the first things I asked Victor, too.

I don't have to go bareback ever, right?

And he promised me that I wouldn't.

But Nelson wasn't listening when I told him that I wasn't gonna do that, unless he only wanted me to use my mouth.

"I paid for your pussy or your asshole or wherever else I want to fuck you!" I could see him all hard through his pants.

I said no, so he started to rough me up. First grabbing me hard by the arm, then shoving me onto the bed after I said *no* even louder.

He took off his pants and his cock was throbbing.

He ordered me to put it in my mouth and I did, even though I didn't want to and I felt scared, my heart beating all fast and almost sorta violent. I kept doing that for a while, until I thought it was time to change, then I went to get a rubber.

He slapped it out of my hand, and then he slapped me.

"What did I say?" Nelson yelled at me, my spit still dangling down from his dick.

That's when I realized this was how he got off. He wanted to watch me be hurt.

I'd been there before. I just didn't expect it from the sort of gentlemen that Victor said would be better behaved.

I wanted the condom, but Nelson didn't, and I'd been with men like him before. So I knew what to do, and did it while crying, both to let it all out and because that's what he wanted.

I tried to tell Victor on the phone, but he said I was being hysterical, and that he didn't want to discuss it over the phone. So now I was going to tell him, but he was surrounded by a handful of other girls. I wasn't sure if that would make talking to Victor better or worse. Most of the girls were fine, but that MILF was there too, and I really didn't want her in my business. She handed Victor an envelope, same as I was about to do. She wasn't better than me, even if she thought she was.

Victor saw me, and started walking over.

I couldn't help myself, and started right in, hoping that I'd emptied my tears onto the pillow in that shithole, while Nelson took me sans condom from behind.

"You said that—"

Victor shook his head. He already had my arm gently in my hand and was leading me over into a quiet corner.

The girls were all watching, especially the MILF.

"Nelson Bragg is an asshole!" I said, trying to keep my voice low, but knowing it was louder than it should be. "You can't book me with him ever again."

"Okay. But I need you to be quiet right now, and when this sort of thing happens in the future. You got it?" He stared into my eyes, releasing my arm only after I nodded.

"You promised me I wouldn't have to wear a condom."

"Bragg made you go bareback?"

I nodded, still trying not to cry, or notice all of the other girls watching.

"What'd you say?"

"I told him no. Then he shoved me ... and he hit me. I was scared. And he liked that."

"Okay, I'm sorry about that. I'll take care of it. You'll never have to see him again."

But what did that mean?

Was Victor going to book him with another girl?

"Will he still be a client?"

"Probably," Victor shrugged. "I'll tell him what is and isn't acceptable, but we got a lotta girls, and you're all into different stuff."

"No one would be into him."

"You'd be surprised. But it doesn't matter. You don't have to see him again, isn't that what you're asking for?"

Not exactly. "What if someone else doesn't want to use a condom, or wants to hurt me."

Now he looked impatient. "You can do anything for an hour, especially for that amount of scratch. Just tell me when it's over and I'll take care of everything, okay?"

No. But if I told him that, would he fire me? "Okay."

"Great." Victor held out his hand and I filled it with money.

He counted the cash, gave me a smile, then slipped his cut into his pocket before handing the rest back to me.

I turned to go.

"One more thing," he said.

I turned back around and he finished.

"Make sure this stuff just stays between you and me, you got it?"

"Of course."

I had been keeping secrets, especially about stuff like this, for most of my life. What the hell, I could always keep more.

I left the common area and headed for my room, wondering if I should go inside or keep on walking and pretend I was going somewhere else. Because the MILF was behind me, and if she was like every other nagging busybody mom I'd ever known, I didn't want to be anywhere near her, let alone be on the wrong side of what would surely be her conversation.

But by the time I reached my room I figured *fuck her,* so I unlocked the door, went inside, and closed it behind me.

A few moments later, she knocked.

"No one's home!" I yelled, then picked up my tablet and started to draw, hoping that the MILF would give up and go away.

She waited another minute or so, it was almost sorta respectful. I even thought that maybe she had gone away, just a moment before I heard the second knock.

"Please, Jade. I'm a friend."

Um, no, you're not even close. We don't even know each other's real names. Besides, I only have a few friends in this world, and if any of them were over twenty years old, then it wasn't by much.

"Go away."

"Give me five minutes and I will. Otherwise, I'm camping out in the hall."

I didn't really think she'd do that; she'd probably have to go home and make mac and cheese for her stupid rug rats. But I wanted to draw in peace.

I went to the door, opened it, and said, "Five minutes," then went back to my bed.

Elle closed the door behind her, and for a moment, the look on her face made me feel bad for thinking of her as a MILF. In that second, she looked like just another one of the girls.

I pressed the home button on my phone to light the screen, then showed her the time. "Your five minutes has started."

She sat on the edge of my bed, filling me with déjà vu, watching me draw without saying a word.

"I'm serious about the five minutes," I said to remind her that I wasn't feeling especially social.

"I wanted to talk about what you and Victor were just discussing."

I looked up from my drawing, more embarrassed than I expected or wanted to be. "You could hear that?"

"Not the whole thing, but I understood enough."

"What do you understand?" I sounded like a bitch, but she was the one who wanted to sit on my bed.

"Some of the other girls have been coming to me, telling me about some of the awful jobs that Victor is sending them on."

"Yeah, so?"

"So, it's your body. I know you're granting people access for an hour at a time, but that's *your* choice, Jade. Do you understand the difference? You don't ever have to take any job that you're uncomfortable taking."

"What makes you think I'm uncomfortable?"

"You sure looked bothered to me when you were giving Victor his cut. Did I misread that?"

"Maybe."

She looked at me again with that pity in her eyes. I just couldn't stand it.

"That's all I wanted to say. Just please, take care of yourself."

I laughed, hoping that it might make her feel stupid. "I'm not doing anything I don't want to do."

"Okay. I just wanted to make sure."

"You don't need to, and you shouldn't. Hasn't anyone ever told you to mind your own business?"

"All the time. But like I said, some of the other girls have been telling me some stories, and I wanted to reach out."

"Consider me reached." Then I rolled my eyes. "It's not my fault if the other girls are taking parties that they don't want. Victor promised to look out for me, and so far he has."

She went from sad to angry, and I expected the MILF to maybe say something cruel — I guess I would have deserved it — but we were interrupted by a knock on my door.

"Jade?" I heard from the other side. "It's Kristi. Can I come in?"

"Sure," I called.

Kristi poked her head through the threshold, then

smiled. "Elle! Perfect. Just who I was looking for. Angelica and I need your help."

NATALIE

I CAN'T EXPLAIN why I felt so desperate to help Jade. It broke my heart when she said she *wanted* to be an escort.

Maybe because I hated the idea that someday Lena might make the same decision.

But it wasn't like she was going to listen, so I followed Kristi out of the room. Lately, some of the girls had been treating me almost like a den mother, asking for advice, and occasionally even looking to me for the resolution of small disputes. Probably because I'd stood up for Angelica when Victor had been giving her the lecture about enthusiasm.

I was back from my weekend with Bennett, but while I was gone, Ryan had dropped the kids off with his mother and disappeared. Probably pouting with one of his many mistresses about how I'd abandoned him. We'd had a huge fight before I left.

I told him that I was getting away for a well-deserved spa weekend.

"Money's going to be tight for a while," was his opening gambit.

"Olivia offered to foot the bill. She said that I really looked like I could use a break and that she'd be happy to help out, so I wouldn't feel stretched thin with you being gone all the time."

"I had plans for the four of us."

"Reschedule. I have to do that all the time. It's part of being a parent, especially when your spouse is out of town."

"What if work needs me?"

"You'll figure it out."

"You're being selfish."

I couldn't believe that one. "*Selfish*? Because I want something for myself?"

He gestured around, apparently at the house and everything in it. "All of this isn't enough?"

"Is it enough for *you*?" By that time we were both yelling, behind closed doors so the children could only hear an unintelligible rumble. "Because if it was, you probably wouldn't be *constantly gone*."

"I'm *working*."

"Whatever, Ryan."

"Everything I do is for you and the children. I'm not gone because I want to be; I'm gone because I'm supporting you."

Right. I'm sure you're sticking your dick into Jess Lindley for me and Alec and Lena. Thank you so much.

"Fine. I'll try to be less selfish in the future. But I'm going to this. Everything is paid for and I already said *yes*."

And *fine* was just what I meant. A switch had been flipped inside me.

I finally saw my relationship with Ryan for what it really was.

My husband was a client that I couldn't afford to fire, not yet. I couldn't call Victor and tell him to block Ryan, so he was the only party that made me feel trapped. It was a trial to realize that I had more freedom as an escort to choose what I did and didn't want than I did in my own marriage.

I followed Kristi into a room where Angelica sat at a desk, watching something on her tablet. She looked up and took out her earbuds. "Hey Elle! I was just doing my French for the day."

"She's always learning a new language," Kristi explained. "She just started French."

"What else do you know?" I asked.

"Spanish and Italian," Angelica said. "I'm starting with the romance languages. Farsi was too hard."

Kristi closed the door and said to Angelica, "Tell her."

Angelica look nervous.

"We've been noticing that a lot of the younger girls are coming back upset," she said, "and we think it's because they're being sent out on parties with this one group of guys. Victor's not doing anything about it."

Why were they coming to me with this? Did they think I was going to force Victor to intervene?

I had enough to worry about without also being their union rep.

But could I say no when Angelica looked at me like that? Like she thought that I was going to make everything okay?

"What else?"

Angelica hesitated, then said, "These clients are livestreaming sessions with the girls, Elle. And taking live requests from the audience."

"THEY'RE WHAT?"

In a squeak, Kristi echoed Angelica. "They take live requests, and stream the sessions."

I couldn't believe that Victor was on board with that, unless he was getting a cut of the profits. In which case, I might be on board with killing him.

"Thanks for telling me." I forced myself to march out of the room despite my red haze of fury. In the hallway, I leaned against the wall and forced myself to breathe. In and out, in and out, several times, until the red began to fade.

Then I marched right into Victor's office.

I didn't even knock, and that pissed him off, because he was getting blow in both ways.

April scrambled up off the floor, half from surprise and the other because he shoved her.

Victor stuffed his dick down into his pants, fuming, glaring at me as he buttoned up. "You better be about to inform me of an alien invasion."

"We need to talk about a client. Alone."

He turned to April. "Outta here. But don't go far."

Victor waited for April to leave, but there wasn't so much as a second of silence after the jam settled in place before he said, "This isn't your business, and you have no right to interfere. You're lucky to go with the grace that I give you."

"Fuck your grace, Victor. You need to do a better job vetting, so that you're not sending the girls out to assholes who are going to take requests from a live audience and stream them. That's not a party, it's free porn."

"What?"

I dropped that bomb for maximum damage, and from what I could tell, it seemed like genuinely new information to him.

"You're supposed to be protecting them, Victor. That's part of the agreement."

"No one said anything to me about livestreaming."

"Maybe they're afraid that if they complain, you'll send them someplace worse."

I couldn't tell if he was furious because someone was making money off of his girls that he never saw, or that the girls who'd been sent on the job didn't mention it to him.

I was pretty sure he wasn't furious that the girls hadn't felt safe.

Victor was an asshole, but putting a stop to the

livestreaming made business sense, so I was pretty sure he'd take care of it.

"Tell the girls that I want the client's name, and I won't consider it a complaint if they come forward." He fell back onto the couch and unzipped. "And tell April she's got a job to finish."

Chapter Twenty-Two

Wednesday Afternoon ...

LYNETTE

LYNETTE, *we should drive out to the Mill, or down to Cielo del Mar. Do some shopping.*

Susan had been nagging me forever. She had a bug up her butt for the two of us to spend some quality alone time together, and I finally ran out of excuses for not going. So I agreed to hang out, and buckled up for every one of her insipid stories about Owen and how she couldn't let him poop without getting his feces all over her bony fingers. Metaphorically, of course, but that was more than enough. No CPA, no Natalie, no anyone else. *Just. Us. Girls.*

But no, I didn't want to go shopping. I wanted to people watch. My favorite place to do that was the Broadway Grille, the restaurant inside mine and Frank's favorite hotel. It was one of the best, and I had sampled from the top. They made a tableside Caesar that I couldn't stop thinking about for a week each time I ordered it, and a surprising wine list for a restaurant of that size.

I liked eating there, imagining that I'd run into someone that Frank and I knew. They'd approach me and say, "Aren't you Frank Wilder's wife?"

It was nice to feel your husband's success, even if it happened from afar, or if you were waiting for it to perhaps pass through the lobby, while you nursed your salad and watched from the inside the restaurant.

"Owen really needs to get out of the heat if he expects his allergies not to …"

But then Susan stopped talking.

I followed her gaze to the lobby, not sure what she was looking at.

"What is it?"

"Remember that woman I saw in front of Natalie's house?"

"Of course." I was instantly on alert, leaning forward, craning my neck toward the lobby.

"I swear I just saw her, and she was in that glass elevator right in the middle. That's the one that goes up to the penthouse, right?"

"Yes." Frank rented the penthouse every once in a while. As a business expense. He had hosted parties, closed a few deals, and even taken me up there three unforgettable times. "But who would Natalie know with access, other than me?"

Susan shrugged, helpful as always.

I called over the waitress and ordered another drink. Susan said, "I thought you didn't want any more."

"I changed my mind."

"You're curious about that woman, aren't you?"

"Of course," I said. "You see her at Natalie's house, then riding up to the penthouse a week or whatever later? Aren't you dying to know more?"

"I guess, but I'm not sure that I want to just sit here."

"Order a dessert. Or have another drink with me."

"I don't want a dessert. Steve and I are eating clean together. And you wanted me to drive, so I shouldn't have another drink."

"Then just sit there and enjoy my company," I snapped. "But I'm going to see how this plays out."

"We need to pick up the children, Lynette. Owen will flip out if I'm not there. And we don't know anything about that woman. What if she's staying in the penthouse and is in for the night? It's not like we're going to camp out in the Grill on a stakeout."

"No, but you just said: *we don't know anything about this woman.* And I want to. Come on, we don't have to leave for an hour and a half or so, we might as well sit here for a while longer. One more drink."

Susan finally agreed, as though she had any other choice, but one drink turned into two after the first hour was behind us. I wanted a third, both for the alcohol and the few extra minutes, but that was a push.

Fortunately, I didn't have to ask.

Just over an hour later, I finally saw the mysterious woman for myself.

She came out of the elevator and sauntered through the lobby, her hair a mess.

My wheels weren't just spinning, they were pirouetting all over the place.

Susan caught my expression. "What is it?" Then she followed my eyes. "Oh."

"One more?" The waitress appeared at our table.

I was already standing. I looked down at my wallet and turned to Susan. "Put it on the Amex. I'll be right back."

Then I was out of the Grill and stomping through the lobby, making my way over to the front desk.

There was a line of four people waiting to check in or ask some idiot question or something else, but I wasn't waiting. Instead I went to the far end of the counter where the person who appeared most in charge was thumbing through some sort of directory.

"My name is Lynette Wilder," I announced, hoping that might mean something. I'm not sure it did, but the man came right over. His name tag read, *Norman.*

"Yes, Mrs. Wilder, how can I help you."

"My husband, Frank Wilder, is a regular at this hotel."

He nodded. "Yes, Mrs. Wilder."

I took a risk, praying that I was wrong. "I'm a total ditz today, and can't remember his schedule. I think Frank is supposed to be here, but he's not answering his phone. I'm in a hurry and don't want to go all the way up to the penthouse if he's not, and I definitely don't want to intrude on someone else if he isn't there at all. Would you mind calling up for me?"

Norman looked uncomfortable. He had a hard time meeting my eyes. I could tell that he was searching for some excuse, and I wasn't going to let him.

"Look Norman, I'm going to need you to dial the penthouse and hand me the phone, unless you want a really big scene, starting in six seconds."

"Mrs. Wilder …"

"Five … four …"

"*Please* …"

"Three … two …"

He picked up the phone, dialed, handed it to me.

My husband answered on the second ring.

I didn't say anything, just handed the phone back to Norman, turned around, and ran out of the Broadway to see if I could find the woman who was sleeping with my husband.

Natalie's friend, who was sleeping with my husband.

Chapter Twenty-Three

Wednesday Evening …

OLIVIA

I PARKED my Mercedes and got out of the car, nervously looking over my shoulder.

I was apparently spotted the last time, and that was what had created my current predicament.

Natalie's street was empty, so I walked up her driveway, knocked on her front door, and waited for her to open it.

I shouldn't have been surprised that Ryan opened the door — he did live there after all — but I was. Enough that it was work to recover my breath.

"Olivia," he said, seeming surprised by his own smile. "It's great to see you."

He invited me in, then on the other side of the door, he embraced me, filling me with something I didn't expect to feel. A twinge of longing, or maybe more like a spasm, a Charley horse in my heart, reminding me of all that I could have had but had always told myself I didn't even want. Everything that might have been if Ryan hadn't cheated, or decided that I wasn't worth fighting for.

We pulled apart, then, inexplicably, we embraced again.

That one went on for longer, with my heart beating against his. I felt sure that those same feelings I was trying to stifle were also pouring from him. Was he sorry for what he did, and what he'd thrown away? Did he think about me during Thanksgiving, Christmas, and New Year — the season when I had no one and he had it all?

We broke apart again, but I couldn't meet his eyes. Ryan's stare was too intense, and the whole exchange felt surprisingly intimate, especially for someone who made their living getting penetrated by random men.

We parted just in time. Natalie walked into the foyer. I gave her my biggest, fakest smile, then widened my arms and, with a sugary sweet, *Natalie!* I pulled her into them.

She couldn't hide her disgust, at least not from me. Natalie hated having me anywhere near her house. But that's because she couldn't have any idea that I was here to help her, or honestly, both of us.

"What are you doing here?" she asked, in a different tone than the one she certainly meant.

"I thought we could go out for a drink."

Natalie gave me a look that Ryan couldn't see: *Fuck that and fuck you.*

But she said, "I'm sorry, sweetie. But I can't. It's a school night."

"It's okay with me," Ryan said. "I've got things around here. You two go out and have fun."

"We could go to that Ale Mary's place," I pressed. "It's a few minutes away."

Natalie was relentless. "I promised Alec that I'd help him with his language arts homework."

"I can do that," Ryan offered.

"That's okay," Natalie shook her head. "We've already started."

"Ryan can finish," I said, my voice insistent. "I really need to talk to you. *Tonight*."

"Sounds serious," Ryan said. "You better go."

Natalie smiled, to prove that it sounded like fun, even on a school night. "Okay, one drink! That sounds great."

Then she tried to murder me with her eyes.

Fifteen minutes later we were sitting at a table in Ale Mary's. I wouldn't tell her anything on the way over, despite her asking, because I wanted to be sitting, with eye contact for sure, and drinks, if the servers were fast enough.

"You can't just come into my house whenever you want. Remember? That's part of why I'm letting you steal a quarter of all my fucking money. *Literally*."

"This isn't about any of the shit between us, Natalie. Something happened today."

"With Victor?" I felt suddenly scared. "With Jade?"

Who's Jade?

"No. With your friend Lynette."

"Lynette?" That obviously scared her. "What happened with Lynette?"

"Frank was my regular, the one *you* were supposed to take. But since you called Victor and whined like a little bitch, the rhinoceros went back to me. As you know, he likes to meet at the Broadway, but apparently he isn't smart enough to book a room for his escorts in a place that his wife doesn't regularly frequent."

"Shit."

"Exactly. She accosted me outside the hotel, while I was waiting at the valet for my car."

"I'm sorry," Natalie said, seeming to mean it. "But you covered, right? What does this have to do with me?"

"She knows that we know each other."

"How does she know that?"

"She saw me coming out of your house or something."

"Double shit."

"Yeah," I agreed.

"Does she know … what I'm doing?" Natalie finally finished.

"I don't see how she could, yet. But at this point I don't think it would be all that hard to start putting things together. I know what I'd be doing if I were her, and yeah, I think your secret might be in trouble. Which is why I came over. Your secret is *my* secret, and more importantly, it's my twenty-five percent."

Everything changed on Natalie's face. "Are you kidding me? You're here because you're worried about your cut?"

"Of course I'm worried about my cut. I don't have a husband to help ensure my retirement, because you stole him from me."

"He wasn't your husband then."

"Keep telling yourself that, sweetie."

"I do. Just like I keep telling myself that it's not your fault that you've turned into a total fucking bitch."

"Watch it," I growled.

This wasn't going how I wanted it to, though I'm not really sure what I was hoping for.

"What am I supposed to do?" Natalie asked, sounding thoroughly defeated, enough to make me almost feel sorry.

"Just be aware. And be careful."

"Fine. Are we done here? You can keep drinking. I'll take a FASTr."

"I'm sorry," I said. "I didn't mean to ambush you like this."

"Like hell you didn't."

She was right, but I didn't acknowledge it. "Not to get personal, but is there anything else bothering you? We earn a lot more when we're at our emotional best."

"Wow. It's like we're becoming best friends all over again."

"Is there anything I can help with, or not?"

After a moment of hesitation, Natalie said, "I don't like what's going on with Victor and some of the clients he's booking."

The waitress interrupted and we ordered our drinks. Natalie ordered a strawberry daiquiri, I think to be obnoxious.

After she left I said, "Be more specific. What don't you like about Victor?"

"How he's treating us."

"Victor's an asshole," I shrugged. "What do you want?"

"There are different levels of being an asshole. Sure, he's an asshole to me, and he's probably an asshole to you, but I doubt it's the same for either of us as it is for Jade."

"Who's Jade? That's the second time you've mentioned her."

"You don't know Jade?"

"I don't really know any of the girls. I'm in and out. But good for you, wanting to be their mommy."

"He's sending girls on some rough parties, Olivia. Shady guys. It sounds like bad shit."

"You do know you're an entitled, spoiled brat, right? That's the sort of shit that happens in this business all the time. It's not always nice puppies sniffing around your pretty little pussy, Nat. Sometimes there are wolves."

She shook her head. "That's not what Victor promises. These girls aren't standing on street corners, they're getting booked for two grand an hour."

"And you don't think a client's entitled to what he wants for that amount of *cash*?"

"Would you take a client that made you uncomfortable?"

"Of course. I have plenty of times."

"Twice? And would you *now*?"

"No. And no, because I've earned it, Natalie. But like always, you just want to fly to the top without any of the work. Spend without earning. Start a family before you have a relationship."

"That isn't what this is about."

"It's what *everything* is about."

We stared at each other.

"I know that you're just being a bitch because that's how shit is between us now, but I also know that deep inside you care. So I'm going to keep talking, and you're going to listen."

The slut had a point, and so I said nothing.

"I don't know much because none of the girls want to talk about it. But I do know that the stuff isn't just rough, these guys are putting on a show and livestreaming it. That's bad enough, and I think there's more that no one's willing to say. I told Victor and he promised to look into it, but I'm not sure that he will, or that he really cares."

"Victor is all about the money. He'll look into it if he said he would, but that doesn't mean that it'll stop. I imagine he'll just get better at vetting the girls, making sure that he only sends the really damaged ones who are actually down for that sort of shit, or the ones who are too meek to squeak a word about it."

"He can't do that."

"He absolutely can."

"It isn't right."

I shrugged. "It's all relative. These girls are getting *a lot* of money. You've lost perspective because you're doing this to pay off your five-figure impulse shopping sprees."

"Stop being so mean to me!" Natalie blurted.

"I'm just talking business. We have the world's most intimate business, but oddly, we need to keep our emotions out of it. I know how Victor thinks. And in his mind, so long as the jobs are okay by the contract, the girls are obligated to fulfill them. They're doing a difficult job, sure, but they're being well compensated."

She shook her head. "It isn't congruent. If Victor wants to build a world-class ring of girls, then he can't be operating this way. Even when you take all of the emotion out, it's still bad business."

Natalie was absolutely right.

Our drinks arrived. Her had an umbrella that was twice as big as it needed to be.

"What about your clients?" I asked.

"They're fine. I had a few I wasn't happy with, but right now I like them all. When something is off, like fucking Frank, thanks for that, I tell Victor and he blocks the guy. And I appreciate that, but we're not talking about me."

Except that we were. And I wanted to know more. Because it was bullshit that Natalie was getting pick of the litter, which she very clearly was. I didn't like anything she was saying, not about the other girls, nor how it was going to affect me. It sounded bad. Maybe terrible. I hadn't suffered anything as awful as livestreaming, but I'd dealt with my share of less-than-desirable clients. Frank was the worst of my guys. He was disgusting, but he was also easy enough and I knew what to do to minimize the stomach-turning aspects of servicing him. It was only an hour and he always tipped, with none of that going to Victor. But he was the one I wanted to drop, and with a snap of her fingers, Natalie had sent him right back to me.

It was easy to see. Soon I would be standing in line for Natalie's sloppy seconds. Any of the men she refused to sleep with. Clearly my star was falling.

I told myself that it didn't matter — Natalie needed to be a star because twenty-five percent of her light would be shining on me — and tried to ignore the truth that she would be out of the game the second she could.

I'd heard it firsthand. Not from the other girls, but from my clients, wanting to talk about the MILF. If they hadn't been with Elle, they wanted to know about her. If they had, they wanted to share. Berto Reyes used to be my regular, then he tried the MILF, came back to me once, and I haven't seen him since. I'm sure he's one of Natalie's now.

So many things in this life she'd stolen from me.

I'd been off my game for a while now. It was time to reinvent myself. Climb back to the top and reclaim what was mine.

"To the game," I said, raising my glass.

"To the game," Natalie echoed, each of us meaning it differently.

We clinked, and drank.

Chapter Twenty-Four

Saturday Afternoon ...

NATALIE

I'D BEEN AVOIDING Lynette since long before she found out about Frank and Olivia.

Museum night? "No thanks! I promised the kids we'd go to Inside Scoop and watch *Stranger Things*!"

Game night with the girls? "Oh my God, I know it's totally different playing with you, but that's *all* the children want to do lately! If I see another board game, I swear I'm going to barf."

Book swap? "That's a great idea! Ryan just got home and I promised him we'd do something as a family, but I do have a box of books I can drop by, if that will help."

I'd let all her calls go to voicemail and replied by text, and I'd let Ryan pick up the kids so that I wouldn't run into her at school. But it was only a matter of time before she tracked me down, now that she knew about Olivia.

But I had completely forgotten to come up with a reason to cancel Family Day with the Wilders. And I think the prospect of living it up on Frank's yacht was the only reason Ryan had come home.

I wondered if I could fake a migraine, or something worse. Pregnancy. Cancer.

My marriage was a mess, Lynette was on the hunt, and — fucking hell — an entire day with Frank, the troll who had actually laughed while spraying me with his man jam and asking me if I wanted him to pull my hair.

I had no idea how I was going to keep my secret from coming out. Today was the day my family would finally realize I was a monster. Ryan would look innocent by comparison.

Frank won't say anything, I argued, *because he doesn't want Lynette to know.*

Lynette can interrogate me all she wants about Olivia. I'll swear she must've seen someone else, claim Olivia's been out of town.

Ryan can believe whatever the fuck he wants; I'm leaving him anyway.

I just have to protect the kids.

"What do you want to listen to?" Ryan asked the children as he started the engine.

We listened to Taylor Swift all the way to the docks, then parked and walked a few hundred yards to the Wilders' slip. Lynette was in peak form, wearing a hat that was wide enough to gather a seagull's crap within one-mile radius, carrying a brightly colored beverage with an impossibly bulbous bottom, and giving us a wave that was a little too over the top, even for her.

"Monroes!" she yelled. "Happy Family Day!"

Go to hell, Lynette.

I didn't see Drew as we boarded — hopefully he had fallen overboard and drowned — but Frank was already cheerfully drunk. He leered at me, right in front of my family and his wife. "Natalie ... Monroes."

He nodded and took a drink.

I imagined myself driving an ice pick right through his eye.

Drew ran out onto the deck yelling, "Everyone is here to play with me!"

And goddammit, I wanted to die.

As the captain pulled away from the dock, it took everything I had not to jump overboard.

But Frank offered Ryan a drink, and the two of them settled into a conversation, if you call Ryan guzzling expensive bourbon while Frank rambled a conversation.

Lynette was ridiculously friendly toward me. Almost like she was still sorry for her son calling me out as the hooker I was. She pressed a daiquiri on me and poured herself another.

I kept on trying to keep everyone together. I didn't want to be alone with Lynette, or anyone on the boat. Except for my children. The yacht would be great if it were just the three of us and the captain.

Everyone was playing well ... and playing along. So far.

Lena settled down on a lounge chair and pulled a coloring book and some markers from her tiny green backpack.

Alec and Drew headed for the front of the boat. To do what, I have no idea.

Lynette slugged her daiquiri and commented on how gorgeous the ocean was as their bajillion dollar yacht cut through the waves.

"Natalie," she said, friendly as ever, but something in her tone raised my hackles. Here it came. "Come downstairs. You have to see the new spa Frank had put in."

How could I say no? Even though deep down I knew, this was where she would put the screws to me.

Lynette was six steps off the stairs before she reeled around to face me with an accusing finger and murder in her eyes, slurring, "How could you do this to me?"

I had no idea what to say because I didn't know what she knew. Or what she suspected.

"Is this about Alec punching Drew? I talked to him about it, I swear."

"How could you be friends with a woman who slept with my husband? A *home wrecker.*"

Then she started to cry, almost silently.

Whew. Lynette didn't suspect me, at least not yet. She probably didn't know Olivia's name. It wasn't like she would ask Frank. This situation could be salvaged.

But I had to play it smart, and that meant following the number-one rule of telling an excellent lie: *starting with a reasonable truth.*

"I'm so sorry that you had to find out about that. At least this way." I shook my head in solidarity, then went to give her a hug. Lynette seemed surprised, and sank into it.

"I did know about Frank, but that's a really hard thing to tell someone. It's why I haven't been answering your calls or responding much to your texts. It's why I've refused all of your invitations. It was too hard, all the lying to you." I shook my head to let Lynette know just how sorry I was. "But I'm sorry, that wasn't fair to you. I've been talking to her, convincing her to end it. She's done with him. You have nothing to worry about, Lynette."

She pulled out of the hug and her face softened. "Thank you, Natalie."

Then: "What's her name?"

I shook my head. "I can't tell you that, Lynette. But I promise, it's over."

Her face changed, full of rage again. She fell a step back, waggling that accusing finger rising at my face. "I didn't think you'd tell me the truth. That's why I'm looking into it."

Even slurred, Lynette's words were clearly a threat.

But I had no chance to respond.

"Lunch is ready," he called from the top of the stairs, breaking up our little powwow.

Lynette gave me a dirty look before storming up the stairs, leaning heavily against the railing. I waited until she was all the way up before I followed. As I reached the top, Ryan asked, "What was all that about?"

I didn't know what he'd heard — probably nothing — but I also didn't care.

"Disagreement about the fundraiser," I answered.

"Well, knock it off, you're ruining Family Day."

I spent the rest of the afternoon down below, pretending to be seasick.

Chapter Twenty-Five

Monday Evening …

I WAS IN A BAD PLACE.

Click.

Another purchase, another hit of dopamine. I was feeling a little bit better one purchase at a time.

What was the cure for not knowing when the other shoe might drop? Buying a few new pairs. One for me, and since the children were both growing so fast, one for each of them.

I shouldn't have. But I told myself that it was only two hours of work to pay for them, and if it helped me get through the next few weeks while I dealt with Ryan's bullshit and Lynette's investigation and Olivia's extortion, it was worth it.

Click.

A 120 dollar pair of panties from Mirror Mirror. I'd wanted to get them when I was getting the dress, but felt embarrassed to ask for them. Silly since Bennett had spent twenty-five thousand to fuck me, but it was the truth. As the receipt hit my inbox, I told myself that the hardest-working snatch in the neighborhood deserved a little kiss of luxury.

I loved the buzz. The hit that spending gave me, whether I needed the things I was buying or not. I could always tell myself that I did, that I deserved them. But I didn't and I knew it.

The guilt made it even better.

Click.

Another black dress, slightly different than the other dozen in my closet.

More LuluLemon, though I had more than enough.

I was out of control, and it felt good

This was so stupid. *I* was so stupid. Why was I in my bedroom alone with my laptop, buying stuff that I already knew I'd regret, before I even clicked on it?

But the idea of walking out into the living room where Ryan was helping Alec with his homework while Lena watched TV — I couldn't make myself do it. He'd been giving me the silent treatment since our day of yachting with the Wilders. I didn't give a shit if he talked to me, but the kids clammed up too when we were both in the room, as if they weren't sure whether they were allowed to say anything until things went back to normal.

I found a gorgeous cashmere sweater at Fancy That! and bought three — pink, cream, and a periwinkle that I almost wanted to get two of. See? I still have some restraint.

I was buying to buy, because I could. And maybe because in a strange way, even depleting my account as it did, it was a reminder of my power to earn, and all of the hard work that I'd done. It proved that I wasn't dependent on Ryan.

Click. Click. Click.

"Mom!"

Alec yelled out from somewhere, maybe from his bedroom. What happened to Ryan?

I slammed my laptop shut, jumped up from my bed, and headed out of the room, grateful for the interruption.

His door was open. I walked in just as Alec was shoving his sister onto the floor.

Her ass hit the wood and she started to cry.

"Alec, stop! What's going on in here?"

"She won't leave!" He jabbed a finger at his sister. "I keep telling Lena to get out of my room, but she won't listen!"

"Okay, calm down. Why are you so upset? It isn't just because your sister is here."

"Yes it is!" Then he ran to his bed and collapsed onto it, rolling so that his back was to me as he was swallowed by a fit of sobs.

I turned to Lena. "You're not in trouble, but I need you to go play in your room while I talk to Alec. Can you do that?"

Lena nodded.

"Where's your father?"

"He's watching a movie downstairs."

Hope you're enjoying Netflix, asshole.

Lena closed the door behind her.

I went over to Alec's bed and sat. I touched his shoulder and he shrugged me away, but then he surrendered and let me hold him while he cried.

Once his tears had eased up enough that he could talk, I asked him again what was wrong. Turns out that some of the kids at school were still saying bad things about me. Alec wouldn't say what, but I had an idea and it filled my stomach with a syrupy acid and made me glad that Ryan was being an absentee father downstairs.

Alec was suffering, and it was all my fault.

I said things that probably didn't help much.

Those boys don't know what they're talking about.

You can just ignore them. Some people are just jealous.

Sticks and stones can break your bones, but words will never hurt you.

I couldn't believe that I had resorted to Sticks and Stones, especially when words could hurt more than anything else. And worse, I was a coward because I should have been saying something like, *Do you have any questions? Is there anything I can help you to understand?*

But I couldn't say that, because what if he asked me? Was I really ready to explain?

With all those platitudes, who was I trying to convince — my son or myself?

"You know your sister is only trying to help you, right? Because she loves you?"

"She's really annoying. She won't stop bothering me."

"That's because she knows you're upset."

"It's because she wants to annoy me."

"She isn't trying to be annoying, sweetie. She—"

"You're just saying that because you're her mom. If Lena was your sister, then she'd probably annoy you, too."

"Probably," I admitted, and that made him laugh. "But I'd also probably think that *you* were annoying."

I tickled him right in his ribs, and got him to laugh even harder.

"I want to see you two getting along better." I put a hand over my stomach, though it did nothing to quell the butterflies or the burn. "I think we need more time as a family."

It's what I needed to say, and what my son needed to hear.

That's what I was best at. Being their mom. Helping people. Listening and understanding.

All things in life that didn't pay nearly enough.

I called Lena back into the room and got them both laughing before they said goodnight to each other and I tucked them both in. I didn't say shit to Ryan, hoping he'd stay downstairs until after I fell asleep. It was my night off, and I didn't feel like servicing a client for free.

I had to be smarter and make a better plan. Find a better way of dealing with the stress than a shopping spree. I needed better, stronger allies at school, and to not feel so woefully alone.

I knew exactly where to start.

I opened the Constellation directory, found Theresa's number, and dialed.

Chapter Twenty-Six

Wednesday Evening …

JADE

I COULDN'T STOP LAUGHING. I'd never been so high in my life.

This was how I wanted to feel every day for the rest of forever.

I didn't have any bookings tonight. Neither did Brandi and Amber, so Brandi thought it was a good idea if we went out with her friend Mark, and his friends Jason and Robbie. Three of us, three of them. I wasn't so sure, but it sounded better than wasting away in my room drawing crap that didn't matter and that no one would ever see. So I put on my jeans and a light sweater, instead of the getup that I typically left in, and went out for a night to remember.

I asked if I would have to fuck anyone. It would have been fine either way, but I like to know ahead of time if possible. Brandi said probably not and that sounded good. Mark did want a blow job, but not from Brandi since they were friends and that would be weird, and Jason had disappeared with Amber after a spell, so I didn't mind, and then after I did Mark, he gave me more of my share of that little fiesta that we'd been passing around.

And now here I was, definitely the most fucked up of my friends.

"You're going to have to be quiet before we go inside," Amber warned me again. "Victor's going to be pissed if he sees you like this."

I thought of something so hilarious, that I couldn't stop laughing as I delivered the punchline. "Then Victor can drink it!"

The two of them looked at each other, probably wondering what they should do with me. Amber turned to Brandi. "Take her straight to her room, okay?"

Brandi nodded. "Okay."

We went inside, but didn't make it more than a few steps before we ran into Kristi.

"Hey Jade. Elle came by to give Victor his cut, but then she was hanging out for a while, asking about you."

"The MILF wants to know what size panties I wear," I announced to everyone. "Because she's hoping to tighten her pussy." Then I doubled over laughing.

"What's she talking about?" Kristi asked.

Amber shrugged.

Brandi said, "I haven't understood a word she's said in fifteen minutes."

"You better not let Victor see that shit," Kristi said, pointing at me, now clutching my stomach.

"I'll be fine," I gasped.

And really I meant it. I was high, but perfectly aware, even if it was hard to see that from the outside.

Brandi took me to my room, nervous the whole way that I was going to start yelling or laughing or something, anything that might get us in trouble. But I wasn't going to do that.

Not when my bed was only a minute away. I was planning to crash into that shit hard.

"You bet," I said, before giving Brandi a thumb's up then opening my door.

The MILF was sitting on my bed.

I was ready to pick a fight with her, excited for it even, but she immediately disarmed me.

Elle was staring at my drawings, studying them like she was at some damn museum.

She stood, and with awe in her voice that touched me like cold wind on a raw nerve, said, "These are stunning, Jade. There's a darkness to them for sure, but they really are incredible."

What could I say to that?

I wanted to lash out at her for disrespecting my privacy. She didn't have permission to be in here, and I didn't want her to be. But no one had ever given a shit about my drawings before. If anything, people had always told me they were a waste of time, then proved it by throwing 'em away, or even spitting on 'em like my mom and dad had both done.

I thought of a handful of things to say, but none of them really made much sense, once I turned them around in my head a time or two.

I tried to make words, tell her to go away, but I realized that I couldn't get my tongue to work.

Or maybe that was just in my imagination?

I thought about singing *Call Me Maybe* to find out.

Then I thought of the perfect joke:

How do you tenderize some hot MILF ass?

Throw it on the kitchen counter, then pound it for ten to fifteen minutes.

I wondered if Elle would think it was funny and decided to find out.

So I told her the joke, but she just stared at me. I think it might have sounded something like this:

"Thrwetunthektchncntrthenpnditfrfftnmnts."

"Christ," she said walking over.

She took me gently by the arm, closed the door, and led me over to the bed.

"What are you doing?" I asked.

That must have been clear enough because she said, "I'm putting you to bed, Jade. You need to sleep this off. Whatever it is."

"I don't need to sleep anything ..." I might have snored.

"You're going to be in trouble if Victor sees you like this. Maybe get kicked out of the house. You know the rules, no drugs of any kind. Ever."

"Just say no!" I laughed.

She moved me into the bed and settled the covers around me. "You've lost a lot of weight since the last time you yelled at me to get out of your room. Are you eating?"

Her question made me sorta wanna throw up. But then again, so did the spinning room and the giant bat that may or may not have been flying around in the corner.

"You're a hypocrite."

"I'm a what?"

"A hypocrite."

"I have no idea what you're saying. It sounds like you have a mouth full of marbles."

"You have a mouthful of marbles."

She had no idea how hilarious this was.

So I started laughing, to show her.

"You really need to take better care of yourself."

That pissed me off. What a hypocrite. I'd smelled weed on her before. And weed was definitely a drug. Hell, Victor smelled like it half the time himself. The world was full of hypocrites, and one of 'em was always in my room.

"You're not my mother."

"What about your mother?" The MILF looked concerned, like she really wanted to know. "Do you want me to call your mom?"

I sat up and swallowed. Narrowed my eyes as I focused, intent on getting my message across. Palms planted flat on the mattress I leaned forward, speaking slow so I could articulate every word.

"You don't belong here. You're old and sad, and I feel sorry for your children."

I didn't expect her to look so sad.

Maybe the drugs made me say that, since I normally wasn't that mean. Or maybe I just couldn't stand her looking down at me with all that pity in her eyes. Like a tractor beam of misplaced condolences, dragging me into its big empty belly.

She stood abruptly, and I was glad that hurt her feelings, except that I wasn't.

I wanted to laugh and cry and vomit, all of it at once and none of it at all.

I wanted to sleep or die, maybe one then the other.

I wanted her to go away.

"If Victor finds out, he'll confiscate your pay for the next three parties. Then you'll be giving yourself away. Never do that, Jade. You're better than this."

I wanted to tell the MILF thank you, or maybe that I hated her.

Instead I fell asleep.

Chapter Twenty-Seven

Thursday Morning ...

MELINDA

RYAN CAME RIGHT when I called, like a good boy.

This time we were meeting in my office, or the office I shared with Dominic. Our business was so intimate, taking those meetings at home felt more natural. But today I needed to work in the office, and so it made more sense for Ryan to meet me there. That was also the best place to enjoy lunch from our private chef, Warren.

Today he was making Shallot Tarte Tatin, a vegetarian, caramelized puff pastry tart with a lightly dressed salad. As usual, the meal was delicious. And the meeting, I expected, would yield just what I wanted.

"So can you tell me more about this job?" Ryan asked after swallowing his first bite. I'd insisted that we didn't talk any business until after our food had arrived.

"Of course." I took a sip of my wine. "What do you want to know?"

"Everything, please."

"We've found a potential candidate for someone to help us run Blush from the operational side."

"Okay …"

"The person we're looking at will be able to manage the girls, but hopefully, if I'm right about this, she should also be able to help us build profiles for our varying clients. If you accept our generous offer for a permanent position with us, then she would be working directly with you."

"What do you mean by profiles?"

"There's nothing amateur about Blush. Just because we're interested in the world's oldest profession doesn't mean that we have any intention of doing things in antiquated ways. Psychographics matter, as do personality profiles."

"Is there anything different you're wanting from this assessment?"

I shook my head. "Same as the others. The woman's name is Elle. Her track record with clients is impeccable, from everything I've heard."

"*From everything you've heard.* So you haven't worked with her yet?"

"No, and I won't. At least not until we hear back from you. This is too important. We can't afford mistakes. But she has a fantastic reputation."

Ryan cleared his throat before he asked, "This business is all about secrets, and I assume she works for a rival organization, so how is that you've heard about her 'fantastic reputation'?"

"One of my close friends is a regular client."

"So this is a reputation founded on the opinion of an *individual*, correct?"

This was just one of the many reasons I liked him. "Correct, but he is an avatar for this business. A connoisseur of courtesans. I would trust his opinion on this, same as I would trust Warren's opinion on food."

I placed a delicate forkful of Shallot Tarte Tatin into my mouth with a light little moan to prove my point.

"What makes her special? At a glance?"

"She's in her early thirties. Definitely older than most of the girls."

"So she's been at this for a while."

"No." I shook my head, smiling. "That's one of the things that stands out. She just started."

This seemed to surprise him, but I wasn't sure if he liked that or not. "Jess is twenty-seven, and that struck me as a tad late to get started in this field, for a few reasons. Do you not see that as a potential drawback?"

"Not at all. And besides, I see her as being out of the field, anyway. She's much more valuable to us on her feet than she is on her back."

"Have you met her yourself, in person?"

"I have."

"And …?"

"I was impressed." Another bite, followed by a sip, just enough to drag it out, make him want to hear more. "She's sophisticated. I'm not where she went to school, but she's been around wealth enough to blend in, even though that isn't who she is to her core. She's compassionate, smart, and sexy in all the right ways. Not like a Hadley Witt or a Jess Lindley, but more like an Allison Brie. She knows what she wants, but if I'm reading it right, the woman has little idea of what she is capable of. She underestimates her abilities. Something about her seems trapped. And I believe we can release Elle from whatever those bonds are, but we need you to help us understand what they are."

"Keep going, what else do you know?"

"It usually takes a while for these girls to get going. There's always a number of clients who only want to party with the newest girls, but those guys don't really build a stable of regulars for that exact reason. It takes a while to get established in this game. But Elle's roster has been full practically since she started. According to my friend, she's booked solid and refusing new clients."

"And how long has she been at this?"

"I'm not sure," I shrugged. "Maybe a month."

"Wow."

"Exactly. She doesn't want to be in the game permanently, which is good for us, and from what I understand she just sort of fell into it, rather this being a vocation she was actively seeking. I'm sure you would agree that these are all elements that perfectly fit our profile."

Ryan nodded, looking both close and far away, thinking hard. It was there in his eyes and the set of his jaw.

"Why did she start?" he finally asked.

"I'm not exactly sure, and neither is my friend. Only that it had something to do with her husband. That's why she's doing this now. She wants to leave him, but needs to earn enough to climb out of the matrimonial ditch."

I took another bite and let that settle, then I finished the thought.

"I see this woman as the missing piece, someone we might be able to build the bones of Blush around, but I need assurance that she's right for the job, and I want the specific breed of comfort that can only come from an appraisal made by Mr. Ryan Monroe."

He opened his mouth to speak, but I couldn't let him. Not yet, not until a *No* was impossible.

"Whatever you're worried about, don't be. You don't have to spend a time building a relationship with this woman. She is an escort, after all. Their art demands distance. So we'll book you for a party, and then you'll tell us what you think."

He was right on the edge. It wouldn't take much.

"Look Ryan, you know us well enough by now. We pay unreasonably well, trust you implicitly, and appreciate your work. You want to be doing business with us, and both of us know it. Whatever it is you're worried about, we'll fix it. That's what we do. Just give me a yes, and I'll put you in touch with Elle."

And the final shot: "I don't need you to sleep with her or anything, that's up to you, although I would highly suggest it. But we won't be needing her to do that for us unless she wants to, so the same should go for you. Having said all of that, there should be nothing standing in your way. Am I right, Ryan?"

Ryan nodded.

Chapter Twenty-Eight

Friday Morning ...

LYNETTE

I WISH I wasn't addicted to so many things.

I blame it on Frank. Ever since our first date he's always given me whatever I wanted. On our second date he said, "I want you to forget that the word *No* exists, okay, Lynette? Stick with me and you'll never have to hear that word again."

I believed him. It was easier then. He hadn't hurt me so much by forcing me to pretend that he wasn't sleeping around on me, a lie I told everyone in my life, especially myself.

Frank was overweight when we met, a few years before we had Drew, but he had gained almost a hundred pounds since then. It was gross, but he was always so good to me, and I was grateful for the life that we had. In some ways it made me feel safe. Maybe he wasn't sleeping around on me. I had seen Frank naked plenty; who would want to fuck that if they weren't married to it? No one. Not unless they were really in a relationship and he was buying her things, like he did for me. It was always theoretical, the idea that he'd cheat on me.

Until I saw that woman at the Broadway, and I knew it for a fact.

And something I never considered came sharply into focus.

My husband was probably paying for women to fuck him.

That woman was up there for an hour, and she looked like a very expensive whore. Exactly the kind of thing Frank would buy for himself, now that I was giving myself permission to admit it.

So yes, Frank was responsible for my many addictions, at least in part. I was lucky that I wasn't fixed on anything truly awful like pills. But I was plenty dependent on buying things and experiences, the more exclusive they made me feel the better — I *loved* having things that few others could — same as I was addicted to people acknowledging me, making me feel important. The only one of my addictions that had nothing whatsoever to do with Frank was caffeine. I'd been drinking coffee since Daddy bought me my first white chocolate mocha on my fourteenth birthday.

That was exactly what I needed now.

I entered Hill of Beans, shuffled into the back of the line, and nearly lost my mind.

Over in the corner, in a pair of small armchairs, turned slightly toward each other and away from the crowd, I saw Natalie Monroe having a coffee with Slut Mom.

I felt so slighted, standing there in line alone while the two of them looked so close. Like friends.

That's not what I expected after our time on the boat. Sure, I was maybe a little drunk, but I remember what Natalie said just fine.

You have nothing to worry about, Lynette. I'm going to help you with this.

It was all lies, because that woman wasn't in a relationship with my husband. She was a whore, and Natalie was her friend. Apparently she was Slut Mom's friend, too. And they would probably judge *me.*

What if one of them looked over and saw me?

What if they started wondering, or even worse, *whispering?*

I wanted to leave.

But even more, I wanted to stay and find out why a woman like Natalie Monroe would want to hang out with someone like Theresa. She wasn't in uniform for once, but that meant she wasn't zipping to or from work. This was casual, day-off time.

Maybe I'd answered the question for myself. I already knew that Natalie associated with a whore. Who cared if the blonde carried a Michael Kors purse while Slut Mom carried a bag from Target? They were both bottom of the barrel as far as I was concerned. If Natalie rubbed her spindly little elbows with one, why wouldn't she break bread with another?

Clearly, I was wrong. This wasn't out of character at all. This was exactly the kind of company kept by the likes of Natalie Monroe.

"Ma'am?" The cashier was smiling, waiting for my order.

"I'm so sorry," I said, glancing at the menu, flustered, my eyes falling over to their table before settling back on her. No need to look anyway. I knew what I wanted before I started the car. "A white chocolate mocha, please."

"Of course."

"Your name?"

"Lynette." I said it soft, just on the off chance that it might float across the room to land in their laps as something familiar, either the name or my voice. But then I remembered that they would have to yell it, so I said, "Actually my name is Susan."

Gross. Why did I think of her? And what if she looked anyway? Too late to change it.

"O … kay." The cashier gave me a crooked smile, then rolled her eyes at the barista when she thought I couldn't see.

I went over and waited for my drink, wishing I was invisible, and hoping that neither of them turned and saw me before my white chocolate mocha was ready.

"*Susan.*"

Said with an audible eye roll, to match the cashier's, but whatever.

I grabbed my drink and took a seat — not too near, but still within earshot.

My stomach fell, because even as I was waiting for my drink I was hoping that maybe this was something professional. Maybe Theresa had reached out to Natalie for some sort of help, like a lot of the moms did.

But no, this wasn't that. Or at least not anymore.

They had the sort of easygoing conversation that was passed between the best or at least the oldest of friends. It sounded effortless, nothing like the exchanges that we always had, where I had to work hard to keep the conversation going. They were bonding over coffee and a bagel. *Singular.*

"Enough about me," Natalie said. "Your turn."

"There isn't really much else to say, other than what I told you." Slut Mom shrugged. "But I sure as hell never imagined that I'd be thirty-five, divorced, and raising a kid alone."

"It doesn't help that you're stuck in Cherry Hill."

"Ah, it's not bad." Her back was still to me, but I could picture Slut Mom, smiling like a … slut. "There's a lot to like about Cherry Hill."

"Yes, of course. But it isn't the easiest place to start over, or fit in. Not everyone is especially welcoming. The entire town is made of plastic, including the people."

Slut Mom said nothing, probably agreeing with all the awful things Natalie just said about her neighborhood. Had she really been thinking this the whole time she'd been pretending to be friends with us?

"Just know that you can call me any time," Natalie went on. "If these bitches get to be too much, or even if you just want a night out. I know how stressful it is, pretending to me the mom who has her life together."

"I don't want to bother you."

"You won't be bothering me, Theresa. I'm always happy to help a friend. You have my number, use it."

Natalie touched Theresa's arm. The sweet mocha tasted sour in my mouth.

"You're just so different from the other moms. Thank you for that."

Natalie didn't respond. Probably giving Slut Mom a sympathetic and unfairly one-sided smile.

I had to say something. How could I just sit there, sipping my coffee and saying nothing?

Slut Mom continued. "I was optimistic coming here. Even though I'm on my own, Elliot agreed to pay for tuition. He went to Constellation when he was a kid, and really wanted for Emily to go there too. So I'm grateful, but yeah, I didn't really expect the moms to be such a …"

"Nest of snakes?" Natalie finished.

And that was it.

I was up and out of my chair, the thought of a white chocolate mocha now making me sick.

"So, I was never really your friend, was I, Natalie?"

Then I waited for her to turn around.

"Lynette?" Natalie was obviously surprised to see me, but more than that, she was uncomfortable. I could tell she rewinding the tape on this conversation and asking herself what I might have heard.

Good. Let her wonder.

"Mind if I sit?" I pointed at an empty chair.

Slut Mom looked wide-eyed and worried. But Natalie was cool.

"Of course," she said. "Did you want to get a coffee first?"

I didn't want either of them to know about the one on the table behind me. "That's okay. I'll wait until the line dies down."

Natalie looked at the line. "There's only one person in it."

"Then I'll use the app. Even one's too many when you could be sitting and waiting with friends instead, right?"

"Right," the girls agreed uncomfortably.

"So, what are we talking about?"

"The culture at Constellation," Natalie said.

"Ooh, sounds juicy," I said. "Are we talking about how everyone is plastic, like all the people in Cherry Hill? And how all the moms are bitches?"

"No," Natalie said, clearly unrepentant. "We already talked about that."

But Slut Mom said, "Sorry," while avoiding my eyes.

"Okay," I said. "Then let's talk about something else."

I smiled at Natalie, then turned toward her friend.

"Theresa, did you know that one of Natalie's good friends is sleeping with my husband?"

Theresa looked caught off guard, almost slapped. She looked to Natalie with questions in her eyes.

"It's true," Natalie said, neither denying the truth nor making excuses.

"I didn't either. Not until recently. Because she didn't bother to tell me."

"That's—"

"You can imagine how devastated I was by the betrayal. Not my husband sleeping around on me. That hurts, of course, but that stuff happens and after a while you maybe start to suspect. I'm talking about Natalie's betrayal. It's so important for us women to stick with each other. So it was devastating to learn that someone I thought was my friend didn't share that belief."

I looked into her eyes, drawing Slut Mom over to my side. "Women should be able to trust other women, right?"

Natalie opened her mouth, but Slut Mom spoke first.

"Do you think I can't hear the things you say about me? I'm not deaf, Lynette. Or stupid. Some of the moms are perfectly nice, and not condescending or spiteful at all, but Natalie is the *only* mom who has gone out of her way to be nice to me. So whatever this is between the two of you, I'd believe her first."

"You ready to go?" Natalie asked her.

She grabbed her coffee and said, "Yes."

But before she stood, Slut Mom turned back to me with shoulders that were a whole lot straighter than they had any right to be. "Let me give you a little friendly advice, Lynette: Stop blaming other women for your problems, and find your own backbone. Then maybe things will start happening for you instead of to you."

Then they were gone, and I was left empty.

Chapter Twenty-Nine

Friday Evening ...

NATALIE

I LOVED THERESA.

Lynette tried to make our morning miserable by intruding on our conversation, but all she ended up doing was bonding us further. It was a shame we had to cut it short, but I was back-to-back on my back after coffee and had to get going. Normally I hated two in a row, but these were both in the same hotel with a two-hour break between them. Victor made it easy with the two suites in the same place with that nice little window. He even sprang for a room where I could rest between parties.

One was a regular, and the other a new guy. Both were great.

Ryan didn't believe my story that I was out all afternoon juggling a million errands, but I didn't care. I didn't even try to make it believable by embellishing with details.

He didn't care enough to press me.

So here I was, making dinner, pretending that things were normal, doing math in my head like I had started to do whenever I was trying to quiet my mind, figuring out how many more times I would have to say *yes, sir* in some way before I would never have to say it again. The children were playing in the living room, together and well from what I could hear. Ryan was reading on the sofa, watching them without having to interact.

The doorbell rang.

I stopped sautéing my mushrooms.

"I got it!" I yelled, turning off the burner and rushing toward the door.

Unannounced visitors made my heart leap in my chest. But there was no argument from the living room, or scrambling toward the front door like I expected, despite their proximity. I guess having a lazy family occasionally paid off.

I opened the door.

Because, *holy shit*, Jade was standing on my front porch, looking like someone had just scared all the color right out of her face.

What was I supposed to do?

Ryan was home and so were the children.

A few feet behind me in the living room.

I stepped out onto the porch and quietly closed the door behind me, hoping that no one would come out to check on me. I had no idea how I would explain how I knew Jade — she was too old for Constellation and too young to be a mom.

"What is it?"

"I'm so sorry … about the way I treated you. The last time, when you were trying to help me."

"You remember that?"

She looked embarrassed. "A little. Enough."

"Don't worry about it."

"And all the times," she added. "I haven't been very nice to you."

"You didn't come to my house to apologize, so what is it? Why are you here?" Even though I really wanted to ask, *And how did you get my address?* I finished with, "And how can I help you?"

"I was on my way to a party," Jade said, firming her jaw. "As usual, Victor just gave me the time and a place."

She stopped, hesitant to say more. But my family was right on the other side of the door, and I needed her to keep going. "What is it, Jade? *Please tell me,* so that I can help you."

"I don't know exactly," she shook her head. "I just got this really terrible feeling. And then I had a full-blown panic attack. I couldn't breathe and I had to pull over. I wanted to throw up. It took me fifteen minutes before I could get back in the car."

"Are you running late?" I asked, because that was one of the *no-nos.*

"No. I always leave myself plenty of time because you never know. But I don't know if I can do it."

"Do what, Jade? What's the job?"

"I don't know." Still shaking her head. "But I've been listening to some of the other girls talk, and I have a feeling."

The girl was terrified, and tugging on every one of my heartstrings. It was easy to see how hard it was for her to ask for help. Showing up here told me that Jade didn't have anyone else in the world she could turn to.

I couldn't open my door, but that didn't mean there wasn't anything I *could* do.

"I'm going to help you," I said.

She started to cry. "I'm so sorry I was so mean to you!"

"It's okay, but you're going to have to talk more quietly, okay?"

Jade looked at me with wide, glassy eyes then nodded.

"Do you know how to get back onto Leviathan?"

She nodded again.

"Great. I want you to get in your car, drive to Leviathan, then make a right. Four blocks down you're going to swing another right when you see what looks like a big pink umbrella, about the size of a restaurant. That's the Parasol. They have the best pie around. Get yourself a slice and a cup of coffee. You're not working that job tonight."

"I didn't say no ahead of time. Victor will kill me."

I felt ripped apart at the middle, because seriously, this was the second last thing in the world that I wanted to do.

"I'll take the job. Just give me the information."

"Won't Victor find out?"

"Victor knew what he was doing when he booked these guys. If he's mad that I took your place, I'll deal with it then."

"How can I make this up to you?"

"Go to the Parasol, order the chocolate silk, and forget about tonight."

"Thank you." I could tell that she wanted to hug me, but that was probably against her religion or something.

"I need to get back inside, to get ready. Text me the info and I'm on it, okay?"

When I went back inside, Ryan was waiting. "Who was at the door?"

"You want the short story or the long one?"

He eyed me suspiciously. "Surprise me."

"Susan got into a fight with Steve, and he stormed out. She needs someone to talk to for a while. Girl stuff, but not the fun kind. I'm not sure when I'll be home, so you shouldn't wait up. Dinner's ready to dish out."

"Is Susan the uptight one?"

"That's her."

"I thought you hated her."

"Her marriage is falling apart. She needs to talk to someone who knows what that's like."

Ryan didn't like that at all. But he didn't argue, either.

Was he as tired of lying as I was?

I WAS ABOUT to do the most dangerous thing I'd ever done. I'd offered to take Jade's place with a false bravado that was now faltering under the weight of my swelling fear and growing apprehension.

There was a reason I hadn't been booked with these guys. I was about to enter a situation that would surely be out of bounds. I wasn't the malleable young thing these men would want, and it wasn't going to go the way they expected.

I don't know why I'd believed that Victor would take care of this.

I was done with him. I didn't know how I would go about becoming independent, or if it would be possible to find another agency, run by someone who actually gave a shit about its girls. Then there was Olivia — would she be fine with taking her cut from my new clientele?

Or if I left Victor and she could no longer keep tabs on me, would all my secrets come scurrying out of her Michael Kors?

Beyond Victor, a part of me worried that whoever had booked this party wasn't going to be happy with me. Sure, everyone was loving the MILF, and I was booked solid, so maybe they would see this as the upgrade I wanted them to.

Otherwise, I wasn't sure what I'd do.

Same for if they asked me something that I didn't want or wasn't willing to do.

For better or worse, I wasn't just another one of the girls.

I got to the assigned room and knocked on the door. A giant answered. The top of his head was above the doorway, and he had massive shoulders and a jaw like the front of a truck. He looked like his name might be Boulder or something.

"I'm here for the party."

Without a word he let me in.

I was immediately unsettled. The hotel room had four guys, including Boulder, a blanket on the floor, a laptop, and a tripod with a camera.

The shortest one of the trio inside pointed at me. "Who the hell is she?"

"I'm Elle. Here for the party."

"No you're not," said an ugly Ed Norton, younger and ganglier than the original. He turned to his buddy, a man who somehow had the body of a forty-year-old man and the face of a pre-pubescent child. "This isn't what we ordered."

Then Shorty repeated, "You're not what we ordered."

"Jade couldn't make it. She's really sick."

I felt sick myself, seeing the laptop and camera. I wasn't getting paid to be on video. I wasn't getting paid to make a sex tape. The thought of anything intimate I was going to do getting streamed made me want to vomit.

"We requested someone young," Eddie said.

"I'm not—"

"Younger than you," Shorty clarified.

Chubby said nothing, and I got the feeling that was the norm.

We requested someone young.

Of course you did, you fucking monster. Young enough, and they'll do whatever sick thing you want.

I wondered what they had in mind.

How far things would go before I said no.

And if I was going to refuse, and not see this thing through, why not just turn around and leave right now?

Except that I couldn't do that because then Victor's rage would fall on Jade. Unless I persuaded the clients to cancel the party.

The men started arguing among themselves, except for Boulder, who was still standing by the door, trying not to touch the ceiling with his head.

I was glad I stopped Jade from coming, but I didn't want to be here.

And they didn't want me here.

I should go.

"We're live in fifteen minutes, so is this a go or what?"

Or what.

"Why don't you tell me exactly what you're looking for. I know a lot of the girls, and Victor listens to me. I'll find someone perfect for what you need, then everyone will be happy."

Not really. There wasn't a chance in Hell I would send a girl here. There was a chance I was going to rip Victor a new asshole, though. If he couldn't see that this kind of shit wasn't just wrong, but that it was going to ruin his business, then I was out of there; I couldn't be a part of it.

"We don't have time for that," Shorty said. "We go with what we got."

He just said fifteen minutes, so there was still time to

wiggle my way out of this. A win-win wasn't out of the question.

"Ace," Shorty nodded at Eddie, who then went to the laptop. "Jerrod." The second nod was for Chubby. As expected, he found a home behind the camera.

I looked back toward the door where Boulder stood like a statue, then at the empty blanket on the floor. The camera. The laptop. The trio of men in position, and Shorty the bulldog leering at me.

"I should call for somebody else. I'm not right for this job."

Shorty stated the obvious. "You're already here."

Boldly I said, "But I don't want to be."

"Well then, I'm sorry that it's too late." He looked at Boulder, then at me. "You want to get on the blanket, or do we have to persuade you?"

Maybe I would see my way out from the blanket. Since I had no other choice, I went to find out.

"Requests are coming in," Ace announced. "Twelve minutes until we're live."

Shorty gave me a serpent's smile. "Great."

I misunderstood what fifteen minutes had meant, and ended up trapped in that blanket, feeling like I was about to make the biggest mistake of my life.

Were they really going to physically stop me if I tried to leave?

I wanted to think no, but every hair on my body stood on end. There were four of them and only one of me. Any of them could end me. Most people might have been most scared of Boulder, but Shorty had meaner eyes and a lot more to prove. I was much more scared of him.

Without preamble, Shorty came over and ripped off my trench coat, leaving me on the blanket in lingerie. I'd had clients rip that coat off of my body before, and I'd enjoyed it every time, because I liked the game. But this was different, and I loathed it to my core.

He laughed. "Want something to drink? You should probably stay hydrated."

Then Boulder was behind me, holding my arms with one hand and tilting my head back with the other.

"We didn't get a young girl, but we'll make good with second best." He made an ugly noise with his throat, then walked out of my line of sight — I couldn't move my head with Boulder holding it in place — and back into view, this time holding a bottle.

I tried not to whimper or cry out, but the first one slipped out as a prelude to the second.

The liquid spilled down my throat. I thought it was going to be alcohol, but it wasn't. Expecting liquid fire, I got some sort of sour syrup instead.

I tried to gag but they forced me to swallow.

I needed to cry and they let me, surely enjoyed it, better for the show to see my mascara running for its life.

The liquid was already down my throat and doing its work.

I wondered if *drug her* was the first request, or if this was only foreplay.

I wished I could scream, but my throat was a forest in ashes, and my tongue, the petrified timber in its wake.

I was warm and then woozy, my body heavy as lead.

It almost felt good, and I thought I might be smiling. I wanted to reach up and feel for myself, since something like that shouldn't be possible. I imagined my smile, ghastly like the Joker. I tried to touch it but couldn't, and that made me laugh.

The world was going in and out around me. Then it got sassy and started to spin up and down.

I heard voices, but not what they said.

Plenty of laughing, yet nary a joke.

Breathing and grunting. What looked like a line.

Shorty came at me first.

I tried to fight whatever it was that they gave me, but that was like battling the night. He was sweaty, and his breath was sour. I know he finished fast, and that there were more in line behind him. I drifted in and out enough to know that he returned for at least another round.

But I don't remember more than that, and I count it as a gift.

I HAD no idea how much later it was when I finally opened my eyes for longer than a second.

Though I didn't really have much of an idea about anything at all.

I weighed about a thousand pounds, and most of those were in my head. I didn't know why it was so leaden, or why it felt like I was sinking into the floor.

Then I felt the blanket under me, and wondered where I was. I opened my eyes. The room wasn't familiar, at least not beyond my fraying memory.

Had I been here before?

It was dark and empty. Graveyard still.

My eyes hurt when I kept them open, so I squeezed them tight and tried to remember where I was, going back to the earliest thing I could—

Jade.

That one hit me hard. I heard the doorbell, remembered answering, only to find Jade on the other side of the door, about to get into a terrible situation.

One that I took for myself.

Then I remembered the men. Not what they did to me, but that it was done without my consent.

I had been violated. Defiled.

The truth hit me like a bullet.

I opened my eyes and looked down at my naked body, but it was too dark to see if I had any bruises. Though of course I did, the way they were manhandling me. I felt it before I lost consciousness, and could only imagine what they did to me once I was dead to the world.

I tried to stand, suffered through all four attempts, then made my way to the envelope, sitting on a table by the door, surely stuffed with enough cash to try and convince me that this hadn't been rape.

Sure enough, I found two grand in hundreds, plus an extra ten Benjamins worth of hush money for me.

My stomach swam and I could barely stay on my feet, so I crawled over to the bed, cursing the monsters for using that floor and the blanket instead, and climbed on top of the covers.

This was the worst thing that had ever happened to me, other than the shower of lies from Ryan that had started this all, and yet for some reason I still felt grateful that it wasn't Jade, lying on that bed instead of me.

I still didn't know what time it was, whether it had been hours or days, or if my family was waiting on me. But the room was dark, so it was probably sometime in the middle of the night.

Whenever it was, I had to get home. But it wasn't like I could drive.

I was still too fucked up to go anywhere on my own. If they wouldn't let me behind the wheel after losing my wisdom teeth, then driving now would be a disaster waiting to happen.

Like my entire fucking life.

I wondered if it was possible to feel any more alone.

So I rolled off of my bed and crawled to my phone, intent on calling the only person in the world that I could.

It took around five minutes before I could locate my cell and focus enough to dial, but the few seconds it took her to answer felt even longer than that.

"What is it, Natalie?" Olivia asked.

I tried to answer, but must have done a terrible job because there was suddenly concern in her voice.

"Where are you?"

I tried to tell her. Many times. Eventually I think she got it.

"I'm coming to get you." Then she hung up.

The saddest part is that I wasn't sure I believed her.

I drifted off, but it didn't feel like all that long before I opened my eyes to hear someone pounding on the door.

She was still pounding when I got there.

I opened the door and she stared back at me with actual concern.

"Fuck the contract," I said. "I'm done. Out of this, permanently."

Chapter Thirty

Friday Evening ...

OLIVIA

I WAS DRIVING to Victor's, in Natalie's Volvo. Natalie was passed out in the passenger seat beside me.

He would make this right. He *had* to.

I couldn't imagine that he would turn a blind eye to this sort of bullshit, but from the little I could get from Natalie before she started drooling all over her imported leather, that's exactly what had happened.

I didn't want to believe it. Sure, Victor was kind of a jackass, but I'd always seen him be reasonably smart when it came to running his business, and only an idiot would operate like this. I would talk to him, he would listen, and things would get better.

I had no idea what I would do if they didn't.

For now, focus was my friend. Getting to Victor and thinking about what I was going to say once I got there.

I would take a FASTr back to the hotel for my car later. Right now, it was Natalie first.

It had been terrifying, finding her like that. She was so strong, that's why the last few weeks had been so much fun. She had hurt me and I was happy to hurt her back. Natalie's strength made it a victory, but now it felt like bullying.

What she told me was slurred, but that didn't slow my understanding. At least not much. Apparently, Natalie didn't even know what had happened to her, after they trapped her in a room, poured liquid drugs down her throat, and took requests from an audience while livestreaming their gang rape.

I punched the steering wheel. I'd feel that tomorrow, but shit, was I pissed.

I hoped Victor was outside when I pulled up. The way I was feeling, I'd run him over.

This wasn't just about the girls, or even about Natalie. If this could happen to his prized little MILF, then it could happen to me. I had seen and even lived through some pretty terrible shit, but nothing like that. I agreed to high-end escorting, not to being a canvas for a depraved audience acting out their most violent fantasies.

It was sick. I wanted to throw up.

Then I did, and had to swallow it.

Natalie rolled her head to the side like it was a struggle, and started blinking. She made a noise, a moaning whimper.

"You okay?"

She made the moaning whimper again. Then, a moment later, "Fine. Thanks."

"You sure you don't want to go to the hospital?"

"I'm sure."

"Even as a precaution?"

"No," she said, still slurring but sounding stronger. "It

was a job. I got paid to be there. I agreed to do whatever by showing up. That's what whores do."

Natalie buried her face. I wasn't sure if she was crying into her arms, because it would be just like my old friend to keep all her screaming inside.

I winced at her calling herself a whore. That's not who she was at all.

It's certainly not who I was. I never saw myself in that light. I was a provider of services, and excellent at my job. Men appreciated me, and I appreciated them. I didn't get paid more for my time than anyone I knew, but only because I knew a lot of people who could afford to pay me. But I did get paid more for my time than at least ninety-nine out of any random hundred people that I'd meet on the street. Though there had been a few rough spots, for the most part the work had always been fun, on my terms, and lucrative.

I did what I loved, and loved what I did, making more money, having more freedom, and living more life than I ever could have imagined with a desk job. I'd been to Barcelona, Paris, and New York, in the last year alone. I was in *Australia* six months before that. I'd never been and always wanted to go. So I went, all expenses paid, plus five grand a day for the pleasure. Some of the best sex and sights of my life. And the conversation was even better.

But none of the perks were worth this.

I looked at Natalie, feeling something an awful lot like sorry stewing inside me. "You're not a whore."

She didn't answer. I wondered if Natalie had fallen asleep, or if she was maybe still silently crying.

"Natalie … Nat?"

I wished she would respond. I felt so awful, for all of it. I'd been so much more comfortable deep in the ice. I had to freeze myself to approach her, then stay frosted to keep the plan in place. But Natalie had been my best friend for a long time, and then for an even longer time after that she was the girl who used to be my best friend. That hurt more than anything else, except for the fact that she also stole the only man I'd ever loved. The person I'd only stopped seeing in every other John until a couple of years ago.

But that ice was thawing, and I was shivering with a new and certain chill that I didn't expect to be feeling on my skin, or anywhere inside me. The responsibility of helping my former friend, and the guilt of getting her into this mess.

She had a family at home. What was I thinking?

Exactly that: She had a family at home, and it should have been mine.

I couldn't think about that now.

I pulled into Victor's. "We're here."

Natalie groaned.

"Come on, Nat. We need to go in there and kick Victor's ass. He needs to see what they did to you."

Another groan.

I got out of the Volvo, walked around to Natalie's side, opened the door, and gently pulled her out and onto her feet. "Are you ready?"

"No."

But she sounded more sober than she was when she answered the door, and her eyes had lost some of their glaze.

"Come on, sweetie."

I held my arm out for her and she took it. Then together we went inside.

I was ready to rip into Victor; I hadn't expected that he'd be tearing into me.

He saw us the second we opened the door and marched right over like he'd been waiting all night.

"What the fuck is this, Olivia?" Victor growled at me and pointed at Natalie. His words were relatively quiet, but he was seething. I'm not sure I'd ever seen him more furious. "And where's Jade?"

"*This* is you being a shit businessman, Victor, sending your girls out on parties that they should never, ever be sent on. I don't know about Jade, or anyone else. Natalie called me after she was *assaulted* by the clients you booked, and I went to pick her up."

The word worked as intended. Victor bristled. But didn't respond, at least not to my implied accusation.

"Jade," he said, barely holding his temper, "is the girl who was supposed to show up, the girl they requested. I had to stay on the phone for ten minutes while they yelled at me for an unauthorized substitution."

I was livid. Was he kidding? The asshole had to be punking me.

"What the fuck, Victor? You can't be serious."

"Serious about what?" He was still fuming, obviously not getting it, pissing me off more by the second.

"Serious about your priorities."

"My priority has always been the business."

"Then stop being an idiot!" I screamed. "This is some of the worst 'business' I've ever seen! You're worried about getting yelled at, when your girls are getting drugged and livestreamed? You can't be serious! You want to know where Jade is, but you've barely glanced at Natalie."

She made a sound of acknowledgement beside me.

"She told you about this and you promised to look into it. But you didn't. Instead you sent Jade, and whoever before her, and Natalie, being who she is, apparently wasn't going to let her take that party. So tell me Victor, why should she care more about your business than you?"

"You don't have any idea what you're talking about."

In that moment I realized that Victor was right. I didn't, and that was a problem.

I was seeing the real Victor for the first time. Our relationship had always been good. Business-like, with respect between us. We were trusted colleagues, not exactly close, but close enough. But I suddenly saw that there had to be so much more going on behind the scenes than I ever imagined; so much that I couldn't control; so much that had put my old friend in danger, and would eventually do the same thing to me.

I couldn't afford to be a fool any longer.

I turned to Natalie, now standing upright without swaying, but still a bit out of it.

"I need you to go to the car."

Natalie shook her head. "I want to stay."

"Please, sweetie. I'll be out there in a second. I just need to finish in here with Victor."

I wasn't even sure what that meant, but there was an inferno burning inside me and I wanted to burn this fucker with my flames.

"Let's both just leave and never come back," she said, sounding far off and defeated.

No surprise, Victor said, "Leave all you want, but you will be coming back. That's what your contract is for."

I took her hands, then asked Natalie to do something I didn't deserve. Looking into her eyes I said, "Please, I need you to trust me."

Then Natalie was gone, waiting for me in the car while I dealt with Victor.

The living room was otherwise empty, no other girls daring to stay for the skirmish.

We eyed each other like gunslingers, both of us waiting for the other to speak, neither willing to show the weakness of going first. I thought of Natalie alone in the car, needing me, and probably longing to get home to her bed where she could sleep the rest of this nightmare off, and broke the deadlock.

"She's done, Victor."

"Like hell she is."

"I mean it. Natalie isn't ever taking another party for you." I shook my head. "Not ever again."

Smiling like a predator he said, "Natalie has a contract."

I closed the distance between us, until my eyes were inches from his and I could smell the stale nicotine and tobacco on both his breath and his clothes.

"You and I both know that those contracts aren't enforceable, Victor. That part of your business is illegal. I don't give a shit what words you use in the contract. We both know it, and there's nothing you can do."

"You're in this just as much as I am, Olivia. You really want to lose your little cash cow? Ten percent, every day, and the requests never stop coming. Remember, this was *your* idea."

"Well, I wish I never had it. She's done."

"Wishes ain't washing the dishes, Olivia. We had an agreement. If Natalie is done being Elle, then you're done here, too. You got it?"

"I sure do."

Then I turned around, marched out the door, and promised us both that I'd never be back.

Chapter Thirty-One

Friday Afternoon, One Week Later ...

NATALIE

I PICKED up my phone and studied the screen, let it buzz in my hand.

It didn't say *Private Caller,* but the number was unfamiliar. I wondered if it was Victor. Probably. It's not like he could get me on the burner anymore, not after I had crunched into so many pieces beneath my Volvo's back tire.

Despite Olivia securing my exit a week ago, I didn't feel safe, expecting a call like this at any moment. Or even worse, for Victor to drop by my inner sanctum unannounced.

I'd never told him where I lived, but of course he could find out.

I was pretty sure he was mad, considering that Olivia had quit and Jade had disappeared.

The first one was a surprise to me, but the second terrified me. Olivia hadn't been able to find out if she'd left of her own volition, or if something had happened to her.

The call buzzed through its fourth alert, but still I didn't answer.

Maybe they'd leave a voicemail.

The caller didn't. Instead there were a few silent seconds, and then the phone began to buzz again.

I hated to answer, especially with my heart beating fast enough to fill my voice full of stutters no matter who was waiting on the other end of the line. But two calls in a row without a voicemail surely meant something urgent, and with Alec and Lena not yet home, not answering felt downright irresponsible.

But I sure didn't expect to hear *him* on the other side of the line.

"Elle," Bennett said, even though he was calling on Natalie's number.

My heart slowed, at least a little, but it was making up for a more leisurely beat by sending prickles all over my skin. Thank God the children were gone with friends for the night and Ryan was working. I was alone in the house for the first time all week. I'd been looking forward to the solitude, but now I was eager to see where this conversation might go.

"How did you get my number?" I asked.

"Victor let it slip that you were friends with Olivia the first time he suggested that I book you. So I called her after I heard that you were no longer working."

"She gave you my number?"

"It wasn't easy," he laughed. "She wouldn't give me your name, and it did seem like she took the request rather personally, even though it sounded like she was *trying* to be nice."

"That sounds like Olivia." There was a quiet awkward beat, so I spoke into the silence. "I'm not sure what this is about Bennett, but I can't see you anymore. I'm retired."

Saying that out loud felt good, like my freedom was inching back in a different way, but the thought of never seeing Bennett again was not unlike a stab.

"I heard." He sounded concerned, and the beat before he continued felt pregnant and long. "But I have a job that you might be interested in, anyway."

I made a sound, but he cut me off.

"Before you say no, this job will pay you twenty thousand dollars."

Everything stopped.

My heart stopped pumping blood and my stomach stopped digesting its food.

The world might have stopped turning.

Twenty thousand dollars.

It wasn't enough, but it was *enough.*

Quitting Victor's had been the right thing to do, and I was grateful to Olivia for getting me out, but I was still trapped in my marriage to cheating Ryan.

But now it sounded like I might have a way out.

"What would I have to do?"

"Nothing you haven't done before."

That didn't sound quite right.

"You're going to pay me twenty grand to sleep with you when you've already had me for free? I appreciate the offer, but that sounds a bit generous, Bennett. And while that is consistent with your nature, I feel like there's a piece of this I'm missing … something I would be agreeing to beyond the norm."

Bennett laughed. "This job isn't for me, it's for a friend of mine. You remember Melinda?"

Of course I remembered Melinda, and I did like her. A

lot. I envied her, totally in awe of how put-together she was.

But I'd never had a female client. Even though two of my parties had been with couples, I hadn't interacted with the other women much, since that wasn't really the point with either client and all of us knew it.

I was willing, but also concerned, because what made me great at being a friendly neighborhood geisha was the ability to tap into my genuine desire. I wasn't interested in women like that, and was worried that my lack of passion might show.

"I'm not sure I know how to be with a woman," I admitted. "And Melinda seems like the kind of person who knows exactly what she wants."

"No, Elle. She doesn't want to hire you for a one-on-one; she wants to hire you on someone's behalf."

"No," I said, almost on instinct. "I need a direct line to the client."

"I understand." And it sounded like he did. "But you can trust Melinda. She would never, *ever* put you in harm's way. That's the whole point. It's what she's trying to build …"

It sounded like he might want to say more, but he didn't.

"Is there anything more you can tell me?"

"Yes. After you agree to the job."

"Twenty thousand dollars," I said, more for myself than Bennett. "How long do I have to be gone?"

"It's one job, Natalie. But the Shellys like to 10x their offers. If you're used to getting two grand, then they're going to give you twenty."

I couldn't stop crunching the numbers. What I still owed, and what I needed to escape.

Every equation pointed to *Yes.*

"Okay," I finally agreed.

"Great," he said, sounding pleased. "Melinda wanted to make this easy for you. Be at the Broadway penthouse, seven sharp."

"Wait. What? This is *tonight?*"

I had agreed only seconds ago, and I was already regretting it.

"Believe me," Bennett said, and oh sweet Lord did I want to. "You don't want to let this opportunity go."

"But it's last minute," I argued, because I needed to have a say in something.

"Most chances of a lifetime are."

I trusted Bennett, and Melinda, as much as that was possible in the scant time that I'd had with her. I didn't get the feeling that either of them would want to see me in harm's way.

There was just one more thing.

"It isn't with Frank Wilder, is it? You can pay off my house and I wouldn't fuck him."

"No. It isn't Frank Wilder."

I needed backup. Someone to intervene if anything seemed off. Olivia would have to do it.

She would make me give her my cut because even though she saved me twice in one night, we hadn't spoken since. We weren't in the business of being friends. She didn't even call to ask if I was cool with her giving Bennett my number.

"Fine. I'll do it.'

"Excellent. Like I—"

"But you need to call Olivia and tell her to meet me in the lobby."

"I'll do that right now."

"Thank you, Bennett."

"Of course."

"Can I ask you one more thing before we hang up?"

I was dying to know, though it killed me to ask.

"Anything."

"Why haven't you booked me again?"

"I heard you retired." He sounded sweet, almost wistful.

So I said, "There's always room in my schedule for my favorite client."

Chapter Thirty-Two

Friday Evening ...

LYNETTE

I'D BEEN FOLLOWING Natalie all week, in what had turned out to be five of the most boring days of my life.

I'd fantasized about doing something like that before, but never seriously. Just the sort of silly things you think about while trying to fall asleep. But after that scene at the coffee shop, I couldn't sit around anymore. I had to do something, figure this out. Get behind the wheel instead of sitting in the back seat and waiting to see where we were going to go.

I was looking forward to seeing what Cherry Hill's hottest mom did every day. What kept her calendar so full of color that there wasn't ever any whitespace left for me — even though Slut Mom had apparently earned herself a block, and more than one, judging by how chummy the two of them were.

It was also great to spend a week away from Frank. He'd been working from home a lot more, and now that I knew what he was doing for a fact, he had never been more repulsive. A big, fat, cheating, slovenly ogre of a man. It was painful to realize how much I hated him.

But it looked like I might have been wrong about Natalie. By all accounts, her life couldn't have been any more mundane. All week, she had dropped her kids at school, then either went immediately home or done something tedious.

On Monday she went to Provisions, leaving with only one small bag, before driving to Ralph's and coming out with a fully loaded cart. Tuesday, straight home and she never left. Same for Wednesday, but she went out and met Theresa at two. That was annoying. She went to yoga on Thursday and Friday. Weird that she didn't go the other three days, then did two in a row. Maybe she was starting the habit back up.

But she didn't go to the salon. No massages, or shopping sprees.

I wondered what she did all day at home.

It was the opposite of what I'd expected. I'd imagined that I'd be driving around, keeping two cars back to stay unnoticed. I even bought a pair of binoculars. A good pair, too. Zeiss Stabilization. I didn't know anything about binoculars, so I went to Forage, did a search for "best binoculars," and paid eight thousand dollars based on their promise that if there was something to see, I would definitely see it.

Unfortunately, there had been *nothing* to see.

No excitement. No mystery. Not anything.

I thought *maybe* something might happen on Friday night, but was ready to give up when I'd spent my usual hours in total boredom. I had a sitter for Drew, but this was getting silly. At five-thirty, I told myself that I'd give it until six. Then at six, I told myself, *ten more minutes.*

And thank God that I did.

At exactly ten after six, the garage door opened, and Natalie's silver Volvo backed out into the street.

No surprise as she turned right onto Leviathan, passing the Parasol and the rest of the hopping shops in that overpriced but beautifully landscaped strip mall. But after five minutes, Cherry Hill was behind us, and if Natalie was picking up either Alec or Lena at a friend's house, then we had already passed them.

Maybe she was picking them up at a birthday party.

Her Volvo merged onto the freeway and that seemed a little less likely.

The theory took another hit when she was off the freeway and barreling down Avalon.

Then it was dead when she pulled in front of the Broadway and handed the valet her keys.

Natalie got out of the car, and I suddenly couldn't breathe.

She was stunning. I always thought she was beautiful, and maybe the warm lights hanging over the valet stand were helping, but her hair had never looked so luminous, her skin so flawless, her arms so lean and defined, sloping into gorgeous shoulders, all of it framed like flowers in the vase of a lacy black dress. She walked toward the lobby in heels like a goddess.

This was at least interesting. And probably something better.

I parked in the general lot, so we wouldn't both be stuck waiting for the valet, then hurried back to the entrance, entering the lobby just in time to see Natalie bypassing the bank of elevators, heading to the private one that shot a select few directly to the penthouse.

The glass doors closed.

I watched Natalie press a button, then reach into her purse and emerge with a lipstick.

She raised it to her lips and I *knew*.

"Fancy running into you here."

I turned toward the voice and nearly choked. It was the blonde whore who was fucking my husband. Casually sipping a martini. Looking at me as though *I* was the one who was doing something wrong.

But if this woman was a whore, then so was Natalie. Frank wasn't in the penthouse tonight, but someone was up there waiting for her. And I'd bet any one of our cars that she was heading up there to sleep with him for money.

It was disgusting. Natalie was disgusting. This whole thing was disgusting.

This woman in front of me was responsible for it all. *She* was the one who was screwing my husband. *She* was the one who had corrupted my friend. And *she* was the one who would be the container for all the rage I was feeling and had no other place to pour it.

"I know what you two are up to!"

"Do you now?" Olivia just smiled, sipping her martini.

"Oh, you think this is fun?"

Olivia shrugged.

"You just wait until the school finds out about Natalie's extracurricular activities. Do you think I won't tell them?"

"I don't know, Lynette? Will you?" She finished her martini then let her hand and the glass fall to her side. "Do you really want everyone to know that your husband has been paying me to fuck him? Does that seem smart to you?"

We stared at each other. She looked like she might hate me as much as I hated her, but I didn't really see how that could be possible. She wouldn't look smug much longer because if that was the worst that she had, letting the world know that Frank paid women for sex, she didn't have nearly enough.

Let people find out. It would be humiliating, but more for Frank than for me.

I would reclaim what had been taken from me.

"You just wait," I told her, refusing to blink. "And you can tell Natalie that she's going to wish she never met me."

Then I turned around and left, certain that Olivia was still standing dumbfounded behind me.

NATALIE

I DROPPED the lipstick back into my purse, tapping my feet, not knowing whether I wanted the doors to ding open or stay closed forever. Maybe the elevator would get stuck, and I'd have to spend the night on the floor of this glass box. I'd be like an exhibit: *Behold the Gilded Hooker!*

Twenty thousand dollars was a lot of money, and I still didn't know what I would have to do to earn it, or who I'd be doing it with. My faith was in Bennett, and Melinda by association.

Ding!

I stepped out into the hallway and was at the penthouse door before the elevator closed behind me.

I checked myself in the mirror before knocking, then surprised myself with a smile.

I was glowing. This last month had changed me. Shaped me into someone capable of being so much better than I was. What I did with that new energy was up to me, and even though I had to wonder if I was making the right decision, I had to admit that I liked what I saw.

Ryan had really blown it, because he was a great guy

who could have had the girl in that mirror, if he hadn't been stupid enough to throw it away. All those years together, and he'd never seen me like this.

Now he never would.

I raised my hand to knock on the door, but it swung open and there he was, mouth open in a wide O, big enough for little Lena to fit her fist into.

My husband was the client?

For a second I thought that maybe he'd set me up, but he looked more set up than me. His mouth finally closed, but then it just fell right back open like a hinge was busted. He swallowed and snorted, then swallowed again.

"Natalie …" But that word was hard, and the next few even harder. "What are you … how …"

Apparently, this was up to me.

I swallowed my panic, pushed past Ryan into the penthouse, and shut the door behind me, trying to put pieces in my mind together, knowing that I didn't have enough to assemble whatever this was.

I scanned the room for clues. Saw nothing. The place looked just like it had every other time I'd been here.

"I thought you were working," I said.

He looked flummoxed. His brow was beaded, even though Ryan rarely ever sweated.

"Ryan? You told me that you were working tonight. So tell me, what is it that Conquest is having you do on a Friday night, in the Broadway?" With a sudden fury rolling through me, I added, "*In the penthouse?*"

"I know it looks odd," he said, raising his hands, palms out as if to ward off intruders. "But I am working."

I looked around the penthouse, then out the window at the glittering city below. "Sure looks like it, Ryan. I'll ask you again, what are you doing here?"

"I'm here to talk to someone. Assess them. Sorry it's in

a penthouse. I didn't decide on the place. How did you—?"

"You quit working for Conquest last year." I didn't take my eyes off of him. "Imagine my surprise when Nora gave me the news."

His face went white and his skin seemed to wither as his shoulders hunched forward.

"Nat … please. We should talk."

He thought I had tracked him down, followed either his car or his scent to this hotel. He had no idea that I was the woman that he had been waiting for.

I was angry, humiliated, and everything else.

I took a deep breath, drawing him in for the few seconds I still had before our world turned upside down. This was the night our marriage ended.

I gave it to him straight.

"I came here to fuck a stranger for twenty thousand dollars."

Ryan looked unsteady – not just surprised, but like he was going to fall right over onto his ass. Clearly that's not where he expected the conversation to go. I gave him seconds to respond, counting down in my mind. *Three … two … one:*

"I've been doing it ever since Olivia showed me all those pictures of you with other women. I didn't do it because you weren't enough, Ryan. I did it because I needed to save up enough to escape."

"You're lying." His voice cracked after *lying.* "Stop it."

"Stop what?" I was antagonizing him and liking it. I'd waited a long time for this conversation. "What is it that I'm supposed to stop, Ryan? Did you stop cheating on me? Did you pay back all the debt you took out in my name? Where's all your money coming from, huh? How can you possibly afford to fuck someone like me?"

I laughed at the irony, and his expression. Then I kept going.

"Did you think I was going to wait for you to get tired of screwing around behind my back? That you could buy me a nice house and that would make it all okay?"

He firmed his feet and straightened his shoulders. Finally found something to say.

"I've given you a good life." Indignant now. "A *great* life."

"And that makes this all okay?" The absurdity had me laughing, then laughing harder, until I was doubled over and practically crying.

He waited for me to stop laughing.

I finally finished, caught my breath, and uncorked the bottle.

"Fuck you, Ryan! For all of it. For cheating on me, for seeing Olivia in Cameo then pretending that you hadn't seen her in years. Just so you know, she's a whore like me!"

He flinched again, I kept on going.

"But *you* did this to us. You left me without anywhere to go. I cheated on you because I had to. But you *cheated* on me because you wanted to."

A punch to the gut as I swallowed an image of Bennett, there in the Cameo restroom. Okay, I wasn't completely innocent, but I never would've met Bennett if Ryan hadn't already turned me into a whore.

"You've made a career out of assessing people psychologically? What do you think I felt when I discovered that you've been cheating on me with at least half a dozen women — and worse, to find out that *we* owe a quarter of a million dollars that you never told me about?"

"Why didn't you—"

"Why didn't I ask you about it? You mean, like I asked

you about your job over and over again, without ever once finding out that you'd quit it nearly a year ago?"

"I didn't want you to worry."

"You didn't want me to tell me one truth because you were afraid I'd find out the rest."

"That's not fair, Natalie. You can't—"

"That's what I thought at first. *I can't. I can't leave Ryan because we're broke. I can't support my kids because a stay-at-home mom isn't qualified to do anything that pays enough to live on. I can't let my kids suffer in poverty because I couldn't make my marriage work.*"

I was ranting and I couldn't stop.

"Olivia offered me the power to save myself, save the kids. I took it."

"No." He'd had enough. Ryan shook his head, then sounding resolute he said, "Everything I've done has been has been for you and the children, whether you believe it or not."

He stood there looking at me, his eyes full of hurt, as if I was the one who had wronged him.

I slowly undressed, kicking off my shoes, then peeling the lacy black dress from my body, before removing a string of pearls from my neck. I was in my lingerie. Pink, black, and as I'd discovered — though Ryan still had no idea — exactly what I liked.

"It doesn't matter now," I said. "Not anymore. But we've learned two things here tonight. One, that you pay women to fuck you. And two, that I fuck men for money."

I stripped out of my lingerie and shimmied out of my panties.

"So are you going to fuck me and pay me, or what?"

"THAT'S NOT why I'm here," Ryan said.

You can understand why I didn't believe him, can't you?

"You're paying for it, so I'll do whatever you want. What do you want?"

I crawled onto the bed on all fours, mashing my elbows into the mattress, lifting my ass toward him so he could see everything. Then I glanced over my shoulder to throw him my sexiest eyes.

"Ready when you are."

Ryan stared at me in disbelief. What was he waiting for? Permission? He'd gotten that when I'd accepted the job.

"Or maybe something more straightforward, but with a twist." I ran my fingers between my legs, then showed him how wet I already was. "You can have whatever you want. I'm sure you heard about my reputation. I'm sure that's why you were willing to pay for me. And I'm sure that you're about to have the best fuck of your life. Because the rumors were true, Ryan. I am that good. But you know one more thing I'm sure of?"

He didn't deserve the chance to answer, even if the cat wasn't chewing on his tongue.

"I'm sure that you're never going to have me again. So enjoy me tonight while you can."

I liked the way he looked at me right then, realizing that every word out of my mouth was true and that he didn't have to parse fiction from fact. He was struggling to process it all, that much was obvious, but later. Now, his animal self was taking control.

Ryan started with his tie, stripping it from his neck while he held my stare, finally breaking away from my eyes only to rake his gaze down toward my pussy.

I was surprised to find that I already missed his eyes on mine. They were a mirror, where for a second I could see myself as Ryan saw me. The confidence, the independence, and the craven hunger of his wanting to claim me.

His shirt came off faster, he worked on his socks and shoes while he unfastened the buttons, then his pants even faster than that. Underwear next, then his socks like a good boy.

He walked toward the bed and pulled me up to a kneeling position. Not too rough and no fumbling at all. Just about goddamned perfect. Then he kneeled behind me, our bodies meshing together in easy familiarity.

"Now," he said, the confidence now rich in his voice, almost matching my own. "Like this."

He entered me from upright and behind.

Our bodies moved easily together, like they always had, but without the usual inhibitions.

"I only did it because I needed the money," he grunted mid-thrust.

I push back against him, wanting him deeper.

"We had mountains of debt with Ambrose — he helped me out when you got pregnant. Gave us whatever we needed, but we needed a lot."

It took a few moments for him to get that all out between gasps and grunts as he picked up the pace.

"We couldn't have done it without him, but it got to a point where he owned me. I had to make more money fast."

Well that sounded really fucking familiar.

"Why didn't you just tell me?" I reached down to cup his balls with my free hand.

"And have you think you were stuck with a total loser? Hell no."

He fucked me harder, grabbed a handful of tit and squeezed it. Why had it never been like this before?

"Everything snowballed. School. The baby. The next

baby. The house. And the shopping. Oh my God, the shopping. Sometimes it seemed like the only thing that made you happy."

I could've taken that as an accusation and felt guilty, but I didn't. It was a relief to finally hear a truth I could believe: that he hadn't been trying to burden me with debt before abandoning me, he'd just dug himself a hole he couldn't get out of.

No, we dug that hole together, and he'd been trying to keep me from finding out how deep it was because he wanted me to be happy.

Ryan groaned and finished, seconds after I did. It felt like goodbye.

It was a cataclysmic revelation, to finally understand that Ryan and I weren't all that different. We'd both been trapped in the same hell together, and yet each of us suffered alone. Tormented by loneliness, guilt, and frustration that the other person couldn't or wouldn't give us what we wanted.

We'd been friends, but we didn't love each other. We never had. And I'd gotten pregnant with Alec before we'd had time to figure that out. Our marriage was based on the excitement of a forbidden tryst, a defective condom, and the belief that if we tried hard enough, we could make it all work.

And we didn't have to pretend anymore.

We stared at each other side-by-side on the bed, looking deeply into each other's eyes. Ryan looked at me in a way that I'd never seen before, and I wondered what he was thinking, not yet daring to ask and break this beautiful stillness between us. It was already fragile enough.

I realized in that moment that I could've loved him, if we'd started out with total honesty, but it was too late for that now.

He didn't love me because he wouldn't have done what he did to someone he loved. We were two people trying so hard to do the right thing that we ended up doing something that was so very, very wrong.

"I'm sorry," he finally said, stroking my hair tenderly. "I wanted to be good enough for you. But I could tell that I wasn't. When Melinda wanted me to sleep with other women, as part of the assessment, I said yes because I wanted to feel good enough for someone."

None of that mattered, not anymore.

"You never told me how you ended up here," I said.

"I told you, I'm working." But now he was smiling.

I was still confused.

"Melinda Shelly sent you, right?" he asked.

I nodded, but that didn't mean I wasn't in shock.

"I've been freelancing for Shellter Productions. They've offered me a job. This was an assignment for me, and an interview for you."

Chapter Thirty-Three

Saturday Morning ...

"KIDS," I said, looking at Alec and Lena. "There's something your father and I need to tell you.

The four of us were gathered in the living room, assembled around the coffee table. I'd made the fuck out of the guacamole, with two versions, jalapeños to make the boys holler — Ryan would love it and Alec would love to pretend to — and mild for Lena. Not that chips and guac would take the pain out of what we were going to say, but I hoped it would soften the blow.

The children looked up at me expectantly. This was going to be harder than I thought.

Alec looked especially hopeful, certain that his parents were about to reassure him, tell him that all the things he had been worrying about lately wouldn't be a problem.

I was about to break his heart, and that was the worst part of all this. Unlike Lena, he'd probably already seen the writing on the wall and had been stubbornly refusing to read it. The light in his eyes would sputter out, and I'd have to live with the knowledge that I was responsible.

But for now, I clung to those final few seconds of feeling like a family with my two beautiful, amazing children. Everything I'd gone through, they were worth it. They made me feel grateful for my time with Ryan. No matter what had already happened between us, or what our mutual future still had in store, I would always respect him as the father of our children.

I looked at Ryan and gave him a reassuring smile.

He gave me one right back.

We're in this together, it said.

And for the first time in forever, I believed him.

He was also brave enough to take the first bullet, and I loved him a little bit for that, too.

"Your mother and I will be taking some time apart …" he started.

Lena was still too young to fully understand the gravity of this moment, but her big brother was not. His face withered inside itself, his lip starting to tremble, fists clenched and knees shaking, his entire body working to keep him from crying. Alec knew *exactly* what his father was trying to say.

"But everything is going to be okay. This is a transition, and we're going to grow as a family through it."

Alec shook his head. "How are we supposed to grow as a family if you two are taking time apart?"

He was one wrong word from crying. Ryan looked at me. Batter up.

"No matter what," I said, taking the ball. "We're still a family. The four of us will always be a family. Your father and I both love you two very much."

The dam broke and Alec began to cry.

"Jeffery's parents separated, and now they're divorced.

Same for Avery's. Why don't you just say you're getting a divorce?"

Lena went to comfort her brother. That warmed my heart, just as much as it hurt me when Alec pushed his sister away.

Her little face puckered, so I gathered her up into a hug.

"Everything will be okay," I said.

"Your mother's right," Ryan added.

"This is your fault!" Alec yelled at Ryan. "It's because you're gone all the time!"

Lena clung to me, clearly scared by Alec's outburst.

"The important thing is that we love you," I said. "We're tired of fighting with each other, we just want to be there for you two."

Alec was crying too hard for Lena to hold back. She finally lost it, too.

"There will be changes," Ryan said. "If you're living right, you can't avoid them. But we're going to make sure that this will be the good kind of change." He waited a beat, wanting their full attention, then finished. "I'll be getting a place in the city, and you'll get to come visit me."

The children cried just as expected, and we took turns rocking them back and forth, petting their heads, just like we planned.

I knew we were going to be okay when Alec asked if we could order pizza for dinner, and watch a movie after.

As Ryan helped the kids choose toppings, I got started on setting the table. It wouldn't be our last family night, but it was one that the kids would remember for the rest of their lives, and I wanted to make sure that when they looked back, they didn't just remember the bad news, they also remembered we'd cared about how they were hurting.

And it wasn't like being separated meant Ryan and I

would avoid each other. The opposite, in fact. Now that we weren't burdened by the need to pretend we were happily married, working together would be so much easier. We had a plan for that, too.

Ryan had a meeting with Melinda on Monday, and I planned to crash it.

Chapter Thirty-Four

Sunday Morning ...

OLIVIA

OLIVIA, *sit straight, and close your legs like a good girl.*

I kept hearing my mother in my head, reminding me of all the ways I was supposed to be good that I'd been ignoring now for more than half of my life. Mom popped up in my mind when I was about a block away from the Church of the Trinity, then refused to leave as I parked, as I walked inside, and now as I stood in the back, watching the parishioners and waiting for my chance to balance the karmic scales.

I was wearing a modest skirt, light pink and flowing, kissing the skin just past my knees. Plus, matching heels, a white button-up with only the top one undone, and a chunky gold necklace to tie everything together. I hadn't worn anything this chaste since my First Communion. Walking into the church, I was half surprised I didn't fall through a trap door and straight into Hell the second I set foot inside.

I liked being in back, where I could listen and observe, without the burden of everyone looking at me. Watching the Wilders, who had no clue that I was here.

Father McCurdy was likable, charming even. I didn't buy into the religion, but I believed in the relief it gave people.

"We need three things to make them happy," he said. "Something to do, something to love, and something to look forward to. And yet, to be *truly* happy, to feel *deeply* satisfied, we need more than that ... we must ensure that we are doing the *right thing*, loving the *right thing*, and looking forward to the *right* thing."

"Jesus gives us everything we need to feel true happiness and experience joy and unspeakable glory, but we must listen to him, and to ourselves. Ask yourself, *What makes me most happy?*"

He looked out across the pews and began to question us.

"Are you happy when you go hunting or fishing? How about when you see a friend or loved one, or go to church on a beautiful Sunday morning and experience an excellent service?"

He waited for the ripple of laughter to fade before he continued.

"Are you happy when you have fun with your children?" He waited a beat and then narrowed his eyes. "How about when you are high, or fornicating with someone you aren't married to?"

The Father was finally speaking my tongue.

Was I *truly* happy?

No, I had to admit that I wasn't. Maybe there was

something to those three things. I had plenty of things to do and to look forward to, but not all that much to love.

Time for Communion, so I fell into line. What came next would be the right thing to do, and I was going to love doing it.

Frank and Lynette were seated up front, singing from their hymnals.

They turned and saw me, Lynette a second before her beast of a man. Both looked well beyond shocked, but Lynette's overriding emotion appeared to be anger, while Frank's was clearly some cousin of fear.

I wanted to die laughing, but first I had to accept the blood and body of Christ.

I held out my tongue for Father McCurdy, looking up into his eyes and waiting for him to press the wafer atop it and bless me.

Body of Christ.

Amen.

Then I turned around and let them see me again, chewing the eucharist with a smile.

The gap had widened between them. Frank was avoiding my eyes at all costs, surely hoping that this situation would just go away. But Lynette knew that it wouldn't. She met my eyes with a murderous glare, gestured toward the atrium, and started marching outside.

She waited for me there, hands on her hips, fists clenched, and shoulders hunched, her body already leaning slightly toward me, unsteady but aggressive. Looking like she wanted to fight.

"What the hell are you doing here?" she hissed.

I looked at Lynette, pretending to be aghast. "Watch your language, please. God is watching."

"Oh fuck you, you whore!"

I laughed out loud, remembering something that Natalie said.

She tries so hard not to swear because it's what the 'lower classes do,' so it's always funny when she loses it.

Yes, this was pretty hilarious.

I didn't respond, waiting to see if she'd entertain me by losing it. But finally she said, "What do you want? Why are you here?"

"Frank is one of my regulars. And you know what?"

I waited, made her say *what*, only continuing after she did.

"I always hated fucking that guy." I shook my head in disgust, and what would have been pity, if Lynette Wilder wasn't such a bitch. "I mean, my God he's disgusting. A Heffalump, with a Woozle of embarrassing size." I looked up to the heavens and muttered, "Definitely not your best work."

Then I looked back down at Lynette, enjoying her trembling bottom lip before going on.

"But, he has a very big mouth, your husband. He loves to talk. *A lot.* And I listen to him. Not because I have to, but because it helps to have something else to concentrate on when the nausea creeps in – which happens whenever his cock approaches my mouth. Maybe later you can tell me how you manage to choke it down, but for right now I'd rather discuss a few facts."

I took a second to study her, wondering if Lynette might actually hit me. I put the odds at an even fifty-fifty.

"Did you know that your husband has been paying off judges?"

That look on her face. No, she didn't know, but she also wasn't surprised.

"That's exactly the kind of thing that would ruin a

fancy, high-powered lawyer like him, don't you agree Lynette?"

I waited. She nodded. *Barely.*

"I can't imagine the Bar would be very happy to find out. And it would trigger the sort of financially draining lawsuits that would destroy his practice, and probably every other part of his life. Few families can get through something like that. It takes a special kind of bond, and Lynette, honey, I can tell you from the amount of times I've had your husband's sweaty little sack in my hand, *that's the kind of bond you simply do not have.*"

Lynette's lip curled with disdain as she said, "You have no proof."

Then I smiled, to chill her.

"You have a good life right now, wouldn't you agree, Lynette? Of course, you would. Fancy house, fancy cars, fancy boat. And a lot of insurance."

I could see it on her face. Lynette already knew where this was going to go.

"Things are a little different for me," I continued. "Because I don't have the fancy house or car. I'm also not married, or trying to raise a son. So my needs aren't quite the same. But insurance is security, and a girl like me needs to protect herself. Would you like to see how I did that, Lynette?"

She shook her head and then nodded.

So with a smile I showed her my phone. Screenshots of texts between Frank and a judge, and then a few more texts with a second judge after that.

"I took these after one of our sessions. After I fucked your husband into a temporary coma."

Lynette was starting to panic, just like I wanted. "What do you want?"

Her voice had cracked in half, which sounded just about perfect to me.

"You don't have to worry," I assured her. "I'm not a snitch, not ever. Like I said, this is insurance, not vengeance. It's about protecting my friend. You know what this is really about, don't you, Lynette?"

It took her a while to finally nod, and in a whisper she breathed, "*Natalie.*"

"That's right, Natalie. You're not going to mention a thing about our mutual friend now, are you?"

Lynette shook her head.

"You're going to leave her alone, and let her live her life in peace, aren't you?"

Her head shake turned into a nod, but Lynette was staring me down, furious. *Fuming.*

I might have misjudged her, and maybe this whole situation.

Looking into her eyes, it looked very much like Lynette was going to kill me.

But she lost her nerve and then her chance, as the atrium began to fill with churchgoers pouring out of mass.

I gave her the sweetest smile I had and said, "Good. I'm glad we agree."

Then I left Lynette standing slack-jawed behind me as I walked out of Church of the Trinity, making the sign of the cross as I stepped over the threshold.

Father McCurdy was right — it did make me happy to do the right thing.

Chapter Thirty-Five

Monday Afternoon ...

MELINDA

I COULDN'T STOP LAUGHING.

Ryan had brought company to our meeting. And I still couldn't believe the story they'd told me.

I looked between my two guests, shaking my head with a smile that I couldn't wipe off of my face. "So, you're *married?*"

It wasn't the first time I had asked, but again they confirmed. But this time Elle — no, *Natalie* — spoke instead of Ryan.

"Twelve years."

"You're both taking it so ... well?"

Most married couples in this situation would be trying to murder each other by now, but they seem almost happy.

I couldn't wait to tell Dominic.

"We're separating," Natalie said.

"Amicably," Ryan added.

"So I assume that you were unable to finish the assessment, after the two of you made your discovery."

But Ryan surprised me. "Oh, no. I finished it."

He picked up his satchel from the ground and pulled out a thin folder from inside, identical to the one he'd handed me for Lindley. He passed it across the table.

These two were more than surprising. They were an unexpected revelation, staggering in their potential.

Ryan looked admiringly at his wife. There seemed to be plenty of love and respect in his gaze, even if passion had gone AWOL. "The entire document is worthy of study, but in general, I would say that you have a star candidate in Elle, and that she has the full suite of skills that I imagine you're wanting for Blush."

This morning was so unexpected, and for so many reasons. I wished Dominic were here instead of stuck at the office, dealing with a little situation that one of our actors had gotten himself into.

The birds outside seemed especially loud as I studied the folder.

The assessment was excellent, not just Ryan's work as expected, but the details surrounding Natalie herself. The details were beyond promising, and when it came to this type of evaluation, I trusted Ryan's judgment more than anyone in the world. No wonder I had liked Elle — or Natalie as it turned out — so immediately.

I closed the folder, set it on the table, then looked at the couple that wasn't a couple, patiently waiting to hear what I might say.

"Impressive work," I told Ryan, "though that doesn't surprise me in the least."

"Thank you." He said with a smile and nod.

"Have you reached a decision about my offer, acting as Shellter's HR assessor?"

He looked at Natalie, then back at me, and with an ever-widening smile he said, "I'd be honored to work for Shellter Productions."

Ryan would be as much a partner for Shellter as he was an employee, and if the next few minutes went like I both hoped and expected, the same would be true for Natalie.

"So that leaves you," I said, looking at Natalie.

"And what would you like to do with me?"

"Dominic and I would love for you to manage our Blush line."

"So Ryan said. But what does that mean? I think I *might* understand what it is, but not how it's different from Victor's organization, or Rosebud."

I could feel my nose wrinkling. Blush was little like Rosebud, and even less like that outfit managed by Victor.

"What do you think it is?" I asked, turning the question on her.

Natalie considered, then took a sip of her water and said, "I think you want to create the most exclusive suite of escorts in the world, a small circle of girls worth whatever you want to charge, mostly comprised of models, actresses, and stunning academics."

"You're close." God, she was great. "But there's nothing *small* about this."

"Then tell me what's big about it. Then tell me everything else."

Desire danced in her eyes. Dominic was going to love her.

"Rosebud was an elite escort service, made up of some truly wonderful girls. That business had the right idea, but they got greedy — blackmail, political favors, and worse. But that was management's issue, not the Rosebud girls themselves. Not all of them, anyway. Eleven have made our cut, and are now enrolled in a sort of finishing school, where they will be taught everything from the art of conversation by some of the best writers in the world, to the art of sex by erotic performers with skill sets that neatly reside in the thinnest slice of that single percent. Classes with masters of whatever arts our girls are interested in learning, because from dancing to cooking, each one is different."

"Like geisha," Natalie said.

"Exactly." I couldn't tell her the rest until she'd agreed to join us.

"So you want me to be a Madame?"

"That isn't the word I would use." I looked at Ryan, studying us both. "As your husband will tell you, our vision is sweeping. We have indulged him with a deeper peek, but you both will know everything once you're fully on board."

"You want me to accept without knowing the full picture?"

"If you accept, money won't be an issue for you anymore. In a year, you'll look back and laugh about how worried you were about your current debts. You'll earn a percentage off the top, you know how that works. We don't do anything half-assed, and you will have the full resources of Shellter behind you."

"What would I have to do?"

"Of course we'll get more detailed after all of the paperwork is signed, but you would be looking out for the girls, and helping to shape what Blush becomes."

"Tell her the other part," Ryan said.

I smiled. "And you'll be helping to create our coitatypes."

"Coitatypes?"

"Sexual profiles, unlike anything the world has ever

seen. Of course we'll be protective of our client data, and all research will be encrypted, but because our girls will be the best in both the bedroom and the opera hall, they will also be the carriers of behavior data that will help us to change the world."

Natalie stared at me. She didn't understand. But how could she? Ryan barely did, and he knew so much more.

"Victor is history," I said, changing the subject. That was plenty for now. "We've shut him down, with the help of our inside woman. You owe him nothing, and his place will be raided later today."

Concern came like a shadow to Natalie's face. She leaned forward and opened her mouth, but I spoke first.

"Don't worry. We took care of the girls." When we talked them, many sang Natalie's praises. They talked about her like she was a mother bear who watched out for them.

She was perfect for this job.

Natalie visibly relaxed, settling back into her chair.

"Of course, you'll need to help us decide who we should bring over," I added.

"Who was your girl inside?" Natalie asked.

"Kristi."

She nodded, like that would've been her guess. "I'll accept under two conditions."

Ryan was on the edge of his seat.

So was I. "Go on …"

"I no longer take clients. I'm out of that business."

"Absolutely," I agreed.

"And I'd like final say on the girls, and some sort of apprenticeship program, so that they can use this experience as a stepping stone. If someone wants to be a lifelong escort, then bully for them. But if it's not for them, they should legitimately be able to put their training outside the bedroom on a resume."

"What do you think our finishing school is for?"

Natalie leaned back in her chair and grinned. "I'm in."

Some time later …

JADE

A FEW DAYS after Elle saved me from going to that ill-fated party that had caused her to quit, I moved into the second floor of an old building called the Brick. It was the sorta place where people were always coming and going. My time to come happened the same morning as it was someone else's turn to go.

I wanted to hide there forever. Never come out.

Nobody knew where I was. I'd gone into hiding that night, after eating my way through a quarter of a pie at the Parasol all by myself. The MILF had been right, Victor did know what he was doing when he booked those guys, and he hadn't done a thing about it. Something bad was gonna happen to me and I could feel it.

I heard something bad did happen after that, though no one I talked to would give me the details, even if they knew 'em. I didn't know what to do, so I took the money I'd already made and went apartment hunting.

The place was a dump, but it was good enough while I figured a few things out. I'd done all right for my first couple of months as a grownup, but everything had been easy come, easy go, and I was afraid that it would get hard before I came up with a plan.

I paid my first and last in cash, then spent a couple of

weeks doing nothing but drawing, pouring all of my feelings in ink. Until Kristi called and told me the news: Victor had been shut down, but all the girls were fine because someone had tipped them off about the raid. She asked for my real number, and after a moment's hesitation, I gave it to her.

After I got off the phone with her, I counted the money I had left and realized that I would need a plan pretty soon, if I couldn't find another service like Victor's to bring me clients.

So I tracked down a friend from high school who'd been in the computer club and got her advice. Then I went to Best Buy and bought the equipment I needed to set myself up as a cam girl.

I liked it so much better. My clients couldn't touch me through the screen, and they couldn't make me do something I didn't want to do. Instead of older rich guys, I was attracting shy, nerdy types who liked me to talk while I got them off.

My favorite clients so far were a couple, Charlie and Alissa. She'd been paralyzed in a car accident. I sorta cried the first time Charlie was telling me the story, then I cried harder when Alissa cut in to say how bad she felt, that she'd ruined their sex life. But she hadn't done anything wrong. That's why they call it an accident.

But even though she couldn't really have sex with Charlie, both of them could enjoy watching me together. Alissa would tell me her fantasies — mostly about being with another woman while Charlie watched — and I would do my best to act them out with her while he got off.

Charlie and Alissa had each other, but most of my clients had one thing in common: They were incredibly lonely. I did my best to make them feel a little less alone.

My next client wasn't just nerdy, he was a full-on dork.

The kind I like. A graphic designer who promised to help me out with a few of my initial branding concepts, bartering a session for a session.

I was setting up my camera and putting on the Princess Leia bikini he'd requested when someone knocked on my door.

My first thought was Victor — I'd been looking over my shoulder at first, worried that he would drag me back and punish me for going to Elle. My paranoia had faded by the time I'd moved in here, but now I thought about Kristi, conveniently calling to tell me I didn't have to worry about Victor anymore.

What if that was a trick, to find out where I was so she could turn me over to him?

I peeked through the peephole. It was the MILF.

And now I felt bad even thinking of her that way.

We hadn't talked since that night, even though I'd been wondering what had happened. I was relieved to see that she looked good. I opened the door.

Elle walked in and looked around, shaking her head. "First things first, we need to get you out of here."

"What are you doing here?" I asked.

I wanted to feel mad, marching in here like she was my mother or something. Except my own mom would never have cared.

The MILF was inspecting the place, probably judging me. I know, it's not like my apartment is as nice as her place, but give me a break, I had to find a way to make the money last while I built up my own clientele.

But she'd saved me from something awful, so instead of telling her to get out, I repeated my question. "Why are you here?"

Elle looked at my camera, then back at me.

"It's what it looks like," I admitted. "And a lot more fun than you probably think."

She looked at me like she was trying to catch me in a lie to myself.

"Really," I insisted. "And oddly enough, I got my idea from the guys who wanted to … you know."

The corner of her mouth twitched.

For like a half second there, I'd forgotten that what they didn't do to me, they'd gone ahead and done to Elle instead.

She was now circling my desk, studying the pile of stylized drawings I'd been working on.

"And these?" She pointed to some of my favorites, the logos I'd been working on for my independent site. I didn't want to be a part of one of those cam networks. I wanted to do my own thing. Charge a premium, for fewer relationships.

But for some reason, I felt embarrassed to admit that to her.

Sheepishly I said, "I've gotta attract a following somehow."

"Your art is wonderful, Jade. And you're smart."

"I barely graduated high school."

"So what? You're resourceful, independent, willing to work hard. And you have a good mind for business. Most of all, you're talented. Wickedly talented."

I looked up from the table, glad that she was staring at the drawings instead of at me.

All of these compliments were making me itchy. I sorta wanted to leave, or maybe crawl under the bed and wait for her to. I'd spent a lot of time living like that before I ran away. It's funny how rare it was that someone got down on their knees to look for you.

"Did you come all the way here to tell me that?"

"I came here to offer you a job, Jade. An apprenticeship."

I'd heard about apprenticeships before. "You mean you want me to work for free?"

"No, sweetie," she smiled. "I would never ask you to do that."

"Then what do you want me to do?"

She told me about a company called Shellter Productions. I'd never heard of them, but I'd heard of Logan White, who was one of the biggest stars in the world. They were the ones who supposedly gave him his start. She said they were starting a company called Blush, and for a minute I thought she wanted me to go back to doing parties.

But no. She thought I might be interested in working for Shellter's marketing department, for a graphic designer guy named Stefano Catalano. I hadn't heard of him either, but then Elle did a Forage search; he was some sort of branding guru or something.

A job that paid well and didn't require me to take my clothes off. It sounded too good to be true.

"This isn't a cover for working parties, is it?"

"You could work as an escort, if you wanted to. Bring in extra money on the side. Or you could just be Catalano's apprentice, and earn your way into a full-time position by proving yourself."

That also sounded too good to be true.

"How do I know that once I'm an apprentice, Shellter won't make me work parties on the side? How do I know they're not just like Victor?"

"Because I'll be running Blush. My way."

For the first time in my life someone was giving me a real choice — a choice where both options were good and I was free to pick the one I actually wanted.

The MILF wasn't pretending to care about me, the way my parents had. She really did care.

Tears stung my eyes, and I blinked them back.

"I want the apprenticeship," I said. "And I want to be able to keep doing cam work on the side."

She hugged me and whispered, "Welcome to the family."

Then I did cry, for real.

Some Time Later …

OLIVIA

I WAS on my way to a job … at least, that's what I thought.

Nat had been stingy with the details. I wasn't sure if it was payback for all the hell I'd dragged her through, or some legitimately classified shit. Probably a little of both.

Probably, I deserved it.

She had told me that it was also a test — for Blush. Natalie had apparently decided to fill the void that Victor's arrest created in the market by starting her own service. She promised similar pay and better clientele, if I passed. (Her exact words: "You'll never fuck another Frank Wilder, ever again.")

Of course I said yes. What else was I going to do, fill out an application at Hill of Beans?

So now I stood in front of a new client's door.

I knocked and waited. This part was always thrilling, and slightly scary. Those moments when everything was possible, and anything could go wrong.

The door swung open.

I fell a step backward, and nearly to the floor.

I couldn't believe it. Almost rubbed my eyes like a cartoon character.

Ryan's mouth was moving, but he wasn't making any sounds either.

We stared at each other, both of us chewing on silence. Then he opened his mouth and I knew what he would say as he said it. I hurried up so we could say it together.

Natalie!

And then we laughed, even though neither one of us understood it just yet.

The suite was magnificent, no surprise there. The shock was standing a few feet away from the first man to ever fall asleep inside me, the first to ever kiss me in the rain or promise forever, the first — and last — to ever break my heart.

I'd never stopped loving Ryan, despite the fact that he'd cheated on me.

"I didn't know that you …" He didn't finish, eating me up with his eyes. I was wearing something that clearly said, *I'm ready for you to undress me.*

"Natalie didn't tell you I got her started?"

"I mean, I knew that, but I didn't know about … this." Ryan laughed, his arms casually crossed, shaking his head in disbelief or better. "It's been a long time, Liv."

He was still as handsome as ever. Trim waistline and square jaw. Dark eyes that had always managed to bore through me. His jacket fell neatly enough on his shoulders to pass for a shadow. Even his tie was knotted to perfection.

"That wasn't my choice." Tears pooled in my eyes.

"I'm so sorry for what I put you through. I was an idiot." Ryan shook his head. "I didn't see what I had in front of me and I blew it."

"I thought you loved Natalie?" That had been the

worst part, the thought that he could stop loving me so easily.

"Natalie and I were always friends. And I love our children. But I married her because she was pregnant. Even though ..."

"Even though what?"

"Even though I was still in love with you."

I tried not to feel it, the thing that was slithering under my skin and taking control of my body.

The emotion that had been an echo, ripping through my soul with diminishing intensity for the last dozen years.

I was screaming in my mind: *Stop it, Olivia! You're not allowed to fall in love with him again. That's the last thing you want to do!*

"And I definitely don't regret any of it," he continued, "if it means I'm here with you right now."

"So then, what is this? I don't understand. You're my ... client?" I laughed uncomfortably, hating the part of me that wanted him to say *no*. But he didn't, so I added, "That's a little weird, even for me."

"I'm thinking that it could be a new beginning, if you can forgive me?"

Could I?

I flashed him a wicked grin as I grabbed his tie and led him toward the bedroom.

"Let's find out."

Chapter Thirty-Six

Three Months Later ...

NATALIE

I WAS in my office at Blush, if that's what you could call it.

It was a lot more like a lush suite, and except for the front area, which did have a tidy desk and two chairs, the space didn't remotely resemble a place of business.

First off, Blush was run from a mansion rather than an office building. Because this particular operation wouldn't be popular with the neighbors and because privacy would be one of the chief ingredients in our five-star dish, we had acres of empty land to surround us. Our girls would hold their affairs outside the home, of course, but the estate had an embarrassing number of rooms in its twenty thousand or so square feet. The rooms were themed, from posh to preposterous.

My office wasn't in the main house. It was in one of the

several small structures off to the side, overlooking the pool. I loved it.

Working with the other women had been my favorite part so far. We had twenty-nine to start, with varying interests and availability. We were developing profiles. Each girl would spend three months with us before taking their first client.

Blush wasn't just a luxury brothel nestled in the hills. It was a game changer, even if it took twenty years. The Shellys were patient, and to hear them tell it, they had all the time in the world. A large part of their mission was to change America's hypocritical attitude about sex.

More than forty million regularly visit sites and more than thirty-five percent of all Internet downloads are related to porn — but we refuse to legitimize the industry and pass laws that would improve the lives of porn stars.

Millions more pay for sex on a regular basis — but instead of decriminalizing prostitution and regulating it for the protection of both sex workers and their clients, we allow human traffickers and other predators to make sex work the most dangerous profession in the world.

Yet we're steeped in sexual imagery, using it to sell everything from clothes to cars.

And we eat up television shows whose directors seem determined to cram as many naked bodies as possible into each episode, mothers of dragons and tween assassins notwithstanding.

We're raised to be ashamed of our natural desires, taught to hide them from the world. Then society uses that shame to control us.

We're lying to ourselves as a culture, and that can be fixed.

Decriminalization is a good start, but it's not enough.

The Shellys wanted to build an entertainment empire with a sex-positive spin, and Blush was a part of that.

As I logged off my laptop, I thought again about the women's studies class Olivia and I had taken in college, how we'd been just like everyone else, looking down on the women of the past we'd been studying who'd resorted to a sexual economy because their society prohibited them from participating in the larger one.

How we'd assured ourselves that we would've made a different choice, if we'd been in the same situation.

Ironic, isn't it?

Just like it's ironic that telling Ryan the truth about hiring myself out bled out all the hatred we'd been feeling for one another.

Because we'd been lying to ourselves about our marriage, about who we were and what we wanted from each other.

We'd lived according to that old saying: *Ask me no questions, I'll tell you no lies.*

But the truth had set us free.

And I intend to stay free for the rest of my life.

What To Read Next

Superstar chef Amanda Byrd had it all -- a loving husband, two beautiful kids and a critically-acclaimed restaurant -- until her epic meltdowns caused her marriage to implode. After a humiliating year of therapy and eating crow, her husband agrees to take her back, *if* she can keep her inner diva in check. But Amanda's guilty secret…

A Quick Favor ...

If you enjoyed this book, please take a moment to write a review on your favorite bookselling platform so other readers can enjoy it too. It would mean a lot to me.

Thank you,
Nolon King

About the Author

Nolon King writes fast-paced psychological thrillers set in the glitzy world of entertainment's power players with a bold, insightful voice. He's not afraid to explore the darker side of human nature through stories featuring families torn apart by secrets and lies.

Nolon loves to write about big questions and moral quandaries. How far would you go to cover up an honest mistake? Would you destroy your career to protect your family? How much of your soul would you sell to get the life of your dreams? Would you cheat on your husband to keep your children safe? Would you give in to a stalker's demands to save your marriage?

Also By Nolon King

Cold Vengeance

Cold Vengeance

Cold Reckoning

Hidden Justice

Hidden Justice

Hidden Honor

Hidden Shame

Hidden Virtue

No Justice

No Justice

No Escape

No Hope

No Return

No Stopping

No Fear

Once Upon A Crime

Once Upon A Crime

Twice Upon A Lie

Three Times a Murder

Dead For Good

Dead For Good

Left For Dead

Dead Of Night

Wake The Dead

Dead For Life

Stand Alone Novels

Pretty Killer

12

Blown

Miserable Lies

The Target

Secrets We Keep

Close To Home

Heat To Obsession

A Simple Kill

Tell Me No Lies

Red Carpet Black

Fade To Black

Victim

www.ingramcontent.com/pod-product-compliance
Lightning Source LLC
Chambersburg PA
CBHW010534100726
47903CB00011B/2999